If Only He Knew

KELSEY HODGE

*To Des
Remember love always wins
love
Kelsey ♡*

Copyright © 2023 by Kelsey Hodge

All rights reserved.

No portion of this book may be reproduced in any form without written permission from the publisher or author, except as permitted by U.S. copyright law.

Contents

Dedication	V
1. Chapter 1—Addy	1
2. Chapter 2—Beau	10
3. Chapter 3—Addy	18
4. Chapter 4—Beau	26
5. Chapter 5—Addy	35
6. Chapter 6—Beau	43
7. Chapter 7—Addy	51
8. Chapter 8—Beau	60
9. Chapter 9—Addy	69
10. Chapter 10—Beau	78
11. Chapter 11—Addy	87
12. Chapter 12—Beau	96
13. Chapter 13—Addy	105
14. Chapter 14—Beau	114

15.	Chapter 15—Addy	122
16.	Chapter 16—Beau	131
17.	Chapter 17—Addy	139
18.	Chapter 18—Beau	148
19.	Chapter 19—Addy	157
20.	Chapter 20—Beau	166
21.	Chapter 21—Addy	175
22.	Chapter 22—Beau	184
23.	Chapter 23—Addy	192
24.	Chapter 24—Beau	201
25.	Chapter 25—Addy	210
26.	Chapter 26—Beau	218
27.	Chapter 27—Addy	227
28.	Chapter 28—Beau	236
29.	Chapter 29—Addy	244
30.	Chapter 30—Beau	252
31.	Chapter 31—Addy	260
32.	Chapter 32—Beau	269
33.	Chapter 33—Addy	277
34.	Epilogue—Beau	285
Acknowledgments		288
About Author		289
Also By Kelsey Hodge		290

This is for the real Beau and Addy.
Thank you for being very special people and inspiring these characters

Chapter 1 — Addy

Leaning against the fender of my car, I look over to the man currently bent over underneath the hood of another car, tinkering with something I have no idea about, yet for some reason, he seems to know everything about. Honestly, there really isn't much point in me having a car. Most of the places I would want to go to in my hometown are within walking distance, but I got one if only for the excuse to bring it here and watch it being worked on.

Beau is the best mechanic in the town. Okay, so he's the only mechanic in town, but he's still the best. Of course, I might be a little biased, as he is also my best friend and has been for as long as I can remember. Growing up in a small town, everyone knows everyone, but it was in high school that the friendship was sealed, and we haven't been that far from each other since. Oh, and there's one other thing.... I've been in love with Beau since high school, too, but he doesn't know this. There is *no way* you can go up to your best friend and say, "Hey, just thought I'd let you know I love you." Well, not without ruining the friendship, and that's not something I am willing to risk.

When I had come out to him as gay at sixteen, I thought he was going to run a mile. Who in the hell wants to be the straight guy with a gay best friend? But he just smiled and said it meant there were just more girls for him, and it was never really mentioned after that. It was just accepted, and honestly, it had been great. If we went out anywhere, he would be scoping out guys and asking me if they were hot, and I would do the same for him with the girls we saw. It was fun in some strange way.

It became our secret. There was no way I was ready to come out to the school — remember, small town — but it worked, except for the part of my falling in love with him. Beau was the cool kid in school, the one everyone wanted. The girls wanted to date him, and well, the guys wanted to *be* him. It was so cliché, but Beau didn't seem to notice. I was sure that some of his friends would have teased him for being friends with me since I was what was called a nerd in high school. I did well in classes, teachers liked me, and in any other school, it would have meant no social life, but being Beau's friend changed that. I was invited to parties and to hang out. Okay, most of the time I didn't go, but it was still cool to be with the 'in' crowd. This also meant I wasn't picked on because who was going to mess with Beau's best friend, which made school fun.

It's been like this for years, me admiring him from afar and torturing myself with opportunities. Staring at the curve of his ass as he's bent over. A noise from the garage brings me back to the now, and looking over, Beau has moved from under the hood to stretch out his back before bending back over and tinkering with the engine again. I thought he hadn't noticed me until I watch his ass wiggle. *Busted.*

"You know I've heard you from the moment you arrived," Beau says to the engine in front of him.

"Is that me or the engine you're talking to?" I reply, but I'm smiling all the same.

"Hope you're enjoying the view," he says, wiggling his ass again.

Laughter spills from me. Even though Beau has no idea on how I feel about him, he knows he has a nice ass and he also likes to tell me — or show me with a wiggle — as often as he can, thinking it's a joke, but every time I get so hot under the collar, always going red. Beau thinks I'm embarrassed because he's my best friend and really don't think of him in that way, which is why he gets such a kick out of it.

"What, your grease covered ass? Yeah, it is a great view," I fumble out, trying to hide the want from my voice.

"There's no grease on my ass," Beau protests, jumping up and trying to look behind him, which makes me laugh hard. Beau is smart, but sometimes he'll do something like this and he reminds me of the cartoon character that races around in circles trying to see their backsides even though they can't. Beau stops looking and walks over to a broken mirror in the corner and spots the big blob of grease, because yeah, I also hadn't been lying.

"Shit!" And now Bcau is reaching for some paper towels to wipe it away, cursing under his breath.

"It's only a small bit. Do we really need all the language?" Beau just shoots me a look like I might have grown another head before chuckling at me, cause yeah, I can swear worse than a sailor if the occasion calls for it.

"Yeah, cause I have no idea how long it's been there or if it was there when I sat in the cars." Beau looks genuinely concerned.

"Beau, you know you always put seat covers on when you get into cars. You'll be fine," I point out, trying to get him to see sense. In the years here, he has never forgotten to protect his customers' cars, he is a professional to a fault. Which is why he's probably the best and why everyone comes back to him. Not that many break down in town, but that probably also boils down to Beau's work.

"You going to the cemetery?" Beau asks, changing the subject and bringing me back to earth with a crash.

"Yeah, but later on. Will you come with me?" I question even though I know there's no need to as Beau has made sure to come with me every year since the burial.

"You know you don't have to ask. When are you thinking of going?" Beau asks, giving me a quick look before heading back over to the car he'd been working on.

"Few hours."

"You doing okay?" And every year Beau asks this, too.

"Yeah, just still miss him."

Beaus stops tinkering with the car and looks up at me. "He would have been so proud of you and what you've achieved in life," Beau states, giving me a smile.

Beau never mentions his name; he knows it's still painful to hear it. But then is one ever ready to lose one's dad? I wasn't. Beau and I had only been in college a couple years when I got the call that Dad was sick, and like most twenty-year-olds, didn't think much of it, instead asking my family to keep me updated. But he got worse. I rushed home, and of course, Beau was not going to let me travel alone, and we found my dad to be a lot sicker than we thought. And yet, even at this stage, I thought he was going to get better, and for a while, he did. Dad even left the hospital and went back home; I went back to college but started calling him daily, needing to get updates. Everything went back to normal again—until it wasn't.

My cell ringing in the middle of the night I will never forget, and when I saw the word 'HOME' scrolling across the screen, my heart had immediately sunk. I knew the moment I answered that call, everything was going to change, and I had been right. Dad had taken a turn again, was back in the hospital. He'd been given only a few hours, and I needed to get home.

Honestly, everything that happened after I hung up the phone had been a blur. I vaguely remember calling Beau and telling him, and then he was at my door, bag slung over his shoulder. It was at that point I think I knew Beau was more than just some crush, that my love was bone deep. He had dropped everything, came over, and took charge.

After I told him, he packed a bag for me and called the college president—even though it was the middle of the night—and told him the situation. Beau reassured me he had been understanding and would let my professors know. Next thing I knew, I was being walked to his car and we were driving home.

We had gotten lucky that the college we attended was only a few hours from our small town, far enough away to be independent but close enough to be home quickly. Beau had dropped me off at the hospital, knowing he wouldn't be able to come in with me, and said he would be at his parents and to call him. Looking back, I knew if it hadn't been for Beau, there was no way I would have got to the hospital in time—but I had. Dad ended up lasting a few days, but then one day, he drifted off to sleep and never woke up. The first person I called was Beau.

Over the next few days, Beau had been there supporting me in every way a friend can, and knowing how he had been there for me made us closer, if that were at all possible. Beau was the shoulder to lean on when I needed someone the most, and now, ten years later, he's still there, even knowing the date without any prompting from me.

"Addy?" Beau's voice brings me out of my musings, a worried look on his face.

"Sorry, lost in thought," I say, answering him honestly.

"Understandable." And Beau doesn't say anything more before turning back to the car and giving me a few minutes. "Let me just finish this up, and we can go. Shouldn't be more than an hour. Do you want to wait there checking out my ass or come back later?"

"Wasn't checking out your ass," I mumble back to him, and all he does is laugh. "Can I wait here?"

"Yeah, of course. But just don't distract me," Beau replies while still looking at the engine.

"Again, is that me or the engine that is distracting you?" I love winding him up as much as he does to me.

"You," Beau says, still looking at the engine, but there is a humor in his voice. "Go sit in the office but don't touch anything. I'm sure you can find something on your phone to keep you occupied."

"I don't snoop," I say, trying to defend myself.

One hour later, Beau is still working on the car, his brow scrunched up, and it looks like he's glaring at the engine. *I guess it's not playing ball. Looks like we're going to be here longer,* but really it isn't too bad. That just means when we get to the cemetery, it will be just us.

"From the look you're giving the car, it's not playing ball?" I ask the back of Beau's head but am met with silence other than the sound of his mumblings.

"Beau?" I try again, and still nothing, so I say it a little louder. *"Beau!"*

Jumping at the sound, he turns to face me, "What?" He snaps, his piercing blue eyes staring at me. The look on his face makes me laugh, and there is a streak of dirt on his face from where he has wiped his fingers over it. His hair looks to be dirt and grease free by some miracle, which considering the blond color, is good. But then, even though he has shortish hair, he always wears a hair band to keep it out of the way.

"Just asked if the car was not playing ball," I say, smiling at him.

"No, she is being a bitch." Beau stands there glaring at the car as if it can hear him.

"Why are all cars she?" I ask, trying to take his mind off the problems. Sometimes, if you can distract him, get him to not over think the problem, the answer will come to him.

"No idea, but everyone knows cars are girls. It's probably because they can be both beautiful and a royal pain in the ass." Again he turns to the car and talks to it.

"Okay."

"Look, just give me thirty minutes..." But Beau doesn't finish the sentence; instead, his eyes widen slightly as an idea hits him. Walking over to his toolbox, he opens a few drawers, finally finding the tool, and then walks back to the car. This time, instead of bending over under the hood, he pulls out this metal frame thing with wheels and a panel in the middle. He lifts the car on a lift so there is enough room for him, straddles the middle panel, and lies down, pushing himself under the car where I hear him shout, "Yes." Looks like he's found the problem.

Twenty minutes later, he's pushing himself back from under the car and walking around to the driver's side, opening the door, and turning on the ignition. The car comes to life, and it actually seems to purr. Leaning in, Beau presses the gas pedal with his hand, revving the engine.

"Sounds good," I say, having to shout over the noise of the engine.

"Yeah..." He opens his mouth most likely to explain what he'd done but then closes it as he knows it would just go over my head. "Yeah, it's sorted."

Beau turns off the engine and lowers the car to the ground. "Give me five and we can get going."

Nodding my head, I watch as he strips out of his overalls, walks over to a sink in the corner, and thoroughly washes his hands with some strange looking soap. He explained once that it helped to remove all the grease and dirt, but I think it has become more an ingrained habit over the years and then washes his face and all traces of grease and dirt are gone.

"Ready?" Beau asks, coming back up to me.

"Yeah."

Beau locks up the garage making sure the lock is secure—not that there is much crime in this town, it's too close knit for that— and we both walk over to my car.

After starting the car, I wait for Beau to get in before reversing out of the space and making my way to the cemetery. We stay silent in the car, somber. It's not a long car ride and soon enough, we're pulling into the parking lot. Once I've parked, I stay seated for a second and just stare in front of me. It's like this every year, taking the time to compose myself, and as with every other year, Beau just sits with me, not pushing, just waiting.

Finally, I get out of the car and walk to the back of the cemetery, my legs knowing the way to go without my even looking. They finally stop in front of the gray granite headstone, and I look at the words.

"Hi, Dad," I whisper while brushing some leaves off. Looks like today is going to be a quick visit. If the leaves were untouched, it means we're the first there. "Can you believe it's been another year? Another year without you. But everything is good Dad... just wish you were here to see it."

Beau is standing behind me; without even turning around, I know he's there letting me have this time with Dad. Normally I would sit and talk and catch Dad up on all that's happening with me like he can hear me, but not today.

Standing up, I turn and give Beau a look. "Quick visit today." He'll understand what it means. Looking back at the headstone, I wish Dad a goodbye and tell him I'll be back to see him soon.

Beau takes a step forward and pays his respects to Dad and then we turn and walk back down to the car, again in silence. His words from earlier rattle around my head: *He would have been proud of you,* and it makes me wonder, would he? Yes, I've done everything I wanted; graduated college and gotten my independence, but there is no significant other in my life. Maybe it's because this year marks ten years since Dad's passing, but maybe I just need to stop fantasizing about someone who I can never have and start looking out there for someone who's going to love me back. But as I look over to Beau and catch him looking at me with concern and affection, I know that's going to be a lot easier said than done.

Chapter 2 — Beau

Staring over at Addy, I try to think about what's going through his mind but can't. How do you process losing your dad, and at such a young age? I don't think I'll ever forget the sound of his voice when he called me that night. It was dead, void of any emotion, and it spurred me into action. There was no way I could let him drive, so I had quickly packed a bag, called all the people at the college I could think of, and dashed over there. If I had thought his voice had been dead, looking at him was another thing all together. It was a mixture of worry, concern, and dread. I had pulled him into my arms and held him close, but I don't think he remembers that.

Every mile of that drive home had been painful, neither of us knowing what we were going to find when we got there, but somehow we'd arrived in time, and Addy had the chance to say goodbye. That date has been ingrained in me ever since, and every year I make sure to get him to the cemetery and pay my respects, too.

Usually I'd let him go up to the headstone alone, give him five minutes, and then follow behind, never interrupting but just being a presence close by for him as a best friend should be. And every year it was the same; it would end in silence with Addy deep in thought, going over all the things his dad would have missed in his life. But this year he seems to be more pensive than normal. Every bone in my body wants to ask him what's going on, what I can do to help him, but I also know that this is something he must sort out himself.

Ten years ago when we had returned to college, I thought Addy wasn't going to be able to cope, that he would drop out and maybe travel the world, but he did the exact opposite: he threw himself into his courses, studying harder than I'd ever seen him do before. He stopped partying completely, too, and didn't come to any more of my games. For a while I worried he was going to burn himself out, and more than once I had wanted to talk to him and ask him to slow down, but the selfish side of me couldn't. I enjoyed having my best friend still in school and close by, being that someone I could vent to if things were going wrong in my life.

A few months after Addy's dad had passed, he finally began to slow down. He was probably ahead in most of his classes, and I was pleased to see him attending my games again. There was some light back in his eyes, and even if I didn't want to admit it, my focus went back to my games.

Football had been my life for as long as I could remember, and playing the game had always been my dream. When I graduated high school, my only thought was of colleges where I could play with the hope of finally getting drafted by the NFL. I couldn't believe the luck when a college a few hours from home offered me a full scholarship. I was so excited, but when I told Addy, he explained he had applied there, too, and both of us were going to be attending the same college. Addy had made it out that it had been a complete coincidence, but over the years, I had started to doubt that. Not that I ever said anything, of course.

The coach had noticed that I hadn't been on my game after I returned from Addy's dad's funeral, and of course I had tried to explain to him how worried I'd been for Addy, but I don't think he understood. No one at college could understand our relationship. Yes, we were best friends, but it was more than that. Being an only child, I used to try and explain it like we were brothers—the bond was that close—but even that hadn't felt right. Everyone just kept telling me to give him space, let him grieve in his own way, and I tried, but I didn't like leaving him alone too often. The good thing to come out of it all was my grades improved, too. But considering the amount of time I spent studying next to Addy to keep an eye on him, that wasn't surprising.

Then, about a year after Addy's dad's death, my world changed in ways I could never have imagined. We had a big game and everyone was excited about it. There was a buzz within the team, and it showed with our playing. We were on fire and were in the lead just before half time. We were just trying to watch the clock count down when the ball was thrown to me, and I jumped into the air to catch it. The moment I landed, I knew something was wrong. Pain shot up my leg and I collapsed on the field. The medical team ran over to me, but I could feel how tight my trousers were around my knee and knew it must be swelling up.

Addy had run down onto the field, as well, after spotting I hadn't got up as normal, and was asking everyone questions, demanding to know what was going on. The medics called for a stretcher and took me off the field. Though the pain was excruciating, I still wasn't prepared to accept it as anything serious. Ice and painkillers were all that was needed as far as I was concerned, but from the hushed voices around me, this *was* way more serious than just a simple sprain.

When I was told that they had called an ambulance for me, I knew it was a bad sign. Once I arrived at the hospital, they carried out some scans, and the doctors confirmed I had torn my Anterior Cruciate Ligament, or ACL. The moment I heard those words, I knew I was never going to play again.

Don't ask how, but I did. That didn't mean I wasn't going to fight. The doctors explained I needed surgery and then some rehab but didn't foresee me playing again in the future, and yet I still couldn't quite accept it.

Addy, of course, had been there every step of the way, listening to what the doctors had said and keeping my parents up to date until they could get there. He never once believed me when I had told him I was never going to be playing again. No, he just kept saying that I was scared, and he wouldn't let that happen.

The surgery was done as soon as the doctors cleared it. They had to wait for the swelling to go down, and the doctors said it had been a success, but I needed to rest and follow the guidelines. And that's what I did. If there were times when I wanted to give up, Addy would appear, tell me to buck up, and push me forward. Six months, that's what the doctors said, but six months came and went, then nine months, and even the physical therapist was becoming concerned. Twelve months after the accident, I was told I would never be able to play again. My knee had healed, but the strength and endurance weren't there anymore. My coaches and teammates had been devastated, and they all became worried when I just accepted it. They couldn't understand how calm I was. It was all a façade, and Addy knew this and was just there listening to me as I talked about what I was going to do with my future.

Football was all I had ever dreamed of. I didn't think I could do anything else, and now suddenly I was faced with trying to decide what I was going to do about my future. It was Addy who put the idea into my head about maybe training to become a mechanic. Cars had always been a second love but was something on the sidelines. I wasn't sure how I felt about working with cars all day, but it was better than staring into the nothing wondering what I should do, so I looked into it. I found the qualifications I needed, and by some weird twist of fate, the college had the vocational courses

I needed and agreed to transfer me over. They even agreed to honor my scholarship, but I really think that was more out of pity and wasn't about to argue with them.

From the moment I had completed my first day, I knew mechanics was going to be perfect for me, and it left me excited for my future. The rest of my college years passed in a flash, I gained the certification needed, and I managed to find a garage a few counties over that agreed to give me the employer training I needed and was eventually granted my Master Technician. The garage had offered me a full-time position after my training had ended because they had been so impressed with me, and for a while it had been amazing. The other guys who had been there before me had been nice enough, but something was missing. I wanted more than to just be an employee.

And there, through it all, had been Addy. He had graduated college with a business degree, but for a while became a little lost himself. I had encouraged him to find something he was passionate about like he did for me, but as always, he just ended up helping me find my dream. A building came up for sale in our hometown, and it was perfect for a garage. The town didn't have one, so people travelled for miles when they needed work done, and they all knew me. I was the boy who could have been an NFL star; that was a big deal even if it had never happened. Addy had helped me get all the paperwork together to get the loan needed to buy and renovate the place, and Jackson Autos was born.

Unconsciously rubbing my knee, I'm brought out of my daydreaming by the slight ache. Most of the time, my knee doesn't cause me any problems, but every now and then it will act up, especially if I've been on my feet a lot like today. But that damn car had me stumped for a while, and I had spent most of the day bent over, a lot of weight being placed on my knee.

"Knee playing up?" Addy's voice fills the car, making me jump.

"Nah, just aching a little." I could have lied, but Addy has this annoying ability to see right through me.

"How long were you standing on it today?" And there's no missing the disapproval in his voice.

If it weren't for the fact it would royally piss him off, I'd be laughing at him. It had been nine years since that day, and he's still looking out for me, still pushing me to look after myself. Addy had come to every physio appointment I had, and he would actually take notes on his phone even though he pretended to be playing a game. He would be listening to what I was being told and then would make sure I was doing all the exercises as instructed. Addy even started coming to the gym with me to keep an eye on me, but I think that might have been an excuse to look at all the half-naked college guys.

But here we are, Addy still looking out for me. "Not my fault," I reply, trying to defend myself.

"So someone forced you to stand on the leg longer than necessary." Addy states back at me and I know, I am not going to hear the end of this, and I can see the random bag of frozen peas we keep in the freezer going on my knee in my future.

"I needed to fix the car," I counter, hoping that me being conscientious about my customers will take some of the heat off.

"Considering said car is currently locked up in the garage and the customer hasn't collected it this evening, that means two things." Holding up one finger, he starts. "One, we could have left for the cemetery earlier, or two,"—Addy adds a second finger—"you could have rested your knee."

"But..." I can't think of what to say because he is right, of course.

"But nothing. You know I'm right."

Looking over to him, I see there is a smug look on his face. Then a thought hit me. "Actually, no. I needed to get the car to sit overnight to make sure it starts in the morning. The customer had been complaining that the problems had been happening after the car hadn't been moved."

I turn my head and bite my lip to stop from smiling at him. He might know when I'm lying about my knee, but when I talk about cars, it goes straight over his head. So whenever I talk about them, even when it's total bullshit like I just said, he believes me.

However, just when I think he's going to drop the subject, he says, "So that means it's okay to cause yourself mischief." *He really isn't going to drop this.*

"It will be okay," I say.

"I know it will because I still have my notes from your physio appointments," Addy states with a smug look on his face.

"Wait, what? You still have the notes you made. How? Or more importantly, *why*?" I'm surprised that this is the first time I'm hearing about this.

"Well, I was worried that when I was changing phones I might lose them, so one day I typed them all up, saved them in several places, and printed out a copy that I may have laminated, too." The laugh escapes me before I have a chance to stop it.

"But again, why?" I'm finding this conversation very strange. Why the hell would he do something like that?

"Because I know you. Know what you're like. I wanted to make sure I had all the information ready in case you pushed yourself too much."

Damn, I can't laugh at that because it's kinda sweet. And he's right; he does know what I'm like. But this explains the peas.

"At least that explains the peas," I finally say, and Addy burst out laughing cause he knows I'm right. We both hate peas, and I always wondered why there was a packet of them in the freezer.

"Well, icing it helps, even I remember that," Addy replies, apparently trying to explain away the peas.

"You know there are things called gel packs we could put in the freezer instead of peas?" I say, thinking we could finally throw the damn things out.

"And lose the enjoyment of watching you nurse your knee with something you hate."

My head snaps over to look at him, and even though he's trying to keep a straight face, I can see the laughter in his eyes. "But you hate them too," I say, trying to reason with him.

"Yes, but I don't need to use them to nurse my knee when I am being an idiot."

Opening my mouth, I quickly slam it shut because he has me there, and I watch as the smile spreads across his face and a relaxed silence comes between us until I decide to open my big mouth again.

"Do you think you were the first to visit your dad today?" Suddenly wanting to kick myself, I watch as Addy tenses up and grips the steering wheel tighter and then watch as he nods yes but doesn't say anything more.

Chapter 3 — Addy

When I arrived at the cemetery, I'd seen the leaves on the grave and knew that Beau was going to ask about my family, but it still came as a shock when he finally did. All day I had put off going until the last possible moment to lower the risk of seeing them, and yet it had been for nothing. They hadn't been there yet, which meant I wasn't going to spend much time there and risk running into anyone.

Gripping the steering wheel tighter, I fight against the anger rising in me. They did it on purpose. I know they did; they wanted to spoil my time with Dad. Make me feel bad in the hopes of changing who I am.

"Do you know why they left going to the cemetery for so late?" Beau asks.

"No," I squeak out.

"Doesn't make sense."

I doubt that Beau is actually asking me but more likely talking out loud, but I answer him all the same. "Not if they tried to see me," I say, talking to the windshield.

"They wouldn't," Beau states, always looking for the good in people but not really understanding that when it comes to my family, there is no good. Well, no good that's ever directed at me.

"You know they would." I turn to look at Beau.

Beau goes silent as he mulls over what I said, probably thinking about how my family would come to the gravesite just to give me grief — and on the anniversary of my dad's death — but they seem to be getting worse as the years pass.

Ten years ago, my family had been completely different; we had been happy. But of course, I had been lying to them for years. You see, the thing with my family is they are super religious, the type who have crucifixes around the house, prayers around the dinner table, and constant meetings at the church every Sunday without fail. So being gay was a big no. Telling Beau had been a relief, and he'd been aware of what my family was like and encouraged me to stay quiet until a time came when I was comfortable or maybe they changed their views.

Everything changed when Dad died. He left this world never knowing the true me and that stayed with me for a long time, gnawed at my soul, and I came to the decision that I was going to come out to my family. Beau had told me not to do it, and I'd really tried to ignore the thought, throwing myself into my college work, doing everything I could to keep my mind occupied, but nothing helped. Beau was worried about me, I could see it every time he looked at me, and there was nothing I could do to get the look off his face. After a few months, I made peace with my decision and slowed down, which finally made Beau relax until, of course, I told him what I was going to do.

Beau thought they were going to disown me, kick me out, or do something much worse, and honestly, I had thought the same, but I couldn't lie anymore. I needed them to know. Do I think their reaction would have been different if Dad had been about? No. Would they have been more understanding? Again, no. But something in me told me that Dad would have been proud that I faced them and told them the truth, and it was this thinking that kept me going. So, when summer break arrived, Beau and I came home. At the time, Beau was still having treatment for his knee, but even though walking could sometimes be a struggle, he'd offered to come over to my parents and be the pillar of support as I told them, but this was something that I had to do on my own.

Yet it had still taken me *weeks* to tell them, Beau asking me daily when it was going to happen. But in the end, I told them the night before coming back to college. At least this way I could run and hide depending on what they said.

We had just finished the evening meal, and my mom and brother Chase were talking about something to do with the church, but I couldn't tell you what because, as with most times church came up, I zoned out, and I just blurted out that I needed to tell them something important. My mom had gotten excited, jumping to the conclusion that I had met someone and I was about to tell them all about it, but Chase, on the other hand, just gave me a look. After some deep, cleansing breaths, I just came out and told them I was gay.

The color drained from my mom's face, but she didn't say anything, just sat there staring at me. Chase's face was a different story. He thought I missed the flash of joy that went across his face, but I saw it and the quick, smug smirk that followed. Anyone looking in would have thought Chase had been proud of me for coming out, but I knew differently. My brother and I had never got on. I think he was jealous of the relationship I had with Mom and Dad. He knew that the moment I had said those words, he was going to become the favorite, and he was loving every second of it.

We had sat at the table for a long time, none of us talking. In the end, Mom just got up from her chair, walked into the kitchen, and washed the dishes. I got up and joined her, standing beside her, Chase coming to stand on my other side, all of us saying nothing as we continued to do the same thing we had done every night. But the air was thick with words, silent words, words I wasn't sure how to process. When all the dishes were done, I turned to my mom, but she just turned away from me. She couldn't even look me in the eye.

Deciding to give them both space, I had gone up to my room and packed to go back to school, texting Beau to let him know I had finally done it. He, of course, started firing back questions, asking how it went. But what could I say? At that moment, there was nothing *to* say. All I told him was that Mom and Chase hadn't spoken a word to me since I told them, but Beau had made me smile when he came back and said he bet Chase had been pleased. Beau wasn't a huge fan of my brother, either.

The following morning, I had woken up earlier than normal, making my way downstairs, and had been surprised to see Mom making breakfast and Chase nowhere in sight. I had wished her good morning and again, nothing. I had asked if I could help and she at least shook her head no at me, but there were still no words. She placed a plate of breakfast in front of me and sat down, a cup of coffee in front of her. Before diving into my food, I waited for the prayer to be said, but it never arrived. She just pushed the plate at me. It was the first time in my life that we had never done a prayer before a meal, and it was unnerving. She sipped her coffee and I ate, the silence becoming deafening. I had steeled myself for the hysterics, the whole *God will never forgive you so repent for your ways*. I even expected a "We can get a cure for you," but the silence was something else entirely.

Once my plate was empty, I got up and cleaned it, drying it and putting it away before heading back upstairs to get my things. When I had returned,

Mom was still sitting at the table, still sipping her coffee, still staring straight ahead. Placing my bags by the front door, I walked back over to Mom and said goodbye, promised to keep in touch, then leaned down to kiss her forehead and felt her tense in the chair, yet she didn't move.

Quietly I turned and left the house. I thought I was going to feel relief that my secret was out there, but I didn't. Mom's reaction was scary, unnerving, almost frightening. It was the whole *what is happening* that scared me the most. What was she planning? At the time all I could think was at least she couldn't touch the scholarship. The college wouldn't care if I were gay or straight. I had got that funding on my academic record and that was all that mattered, but that didn't mean my family couldn't make my life hell at other times. I just wanted to know what they were planning to do. Chase, I just knew, was already hatching a plan.

"You've gone quiet. Everything okay?" Beau's question breaks into my melancholy moment.

"Was thinking about when I came out."

"Yeah? What made you think about that?" Beau sounds surprised where my thinking had gone.

"Just today."

"Today is a tough day," Beau says while looking over and trying to give me a reassuring smile.

The problem is Beau doesn't understand. He thinks that the feelings have just been brought up because of the significance of the date, but it's more than that. I've never fully told Beau what the family has been like. Instead of relieving myself of a burden, I created another one. Instead of lying to my family about who I was, I started lying — well not telling the full story — to Beau. Why, one might ask? That's a good question. You see it all over the LGBTQ community: if your family isn't on your side, walk away because there are people out there that will love you for you and that's all you need. They try to instill that it's the family's loss.

Yet here I am, my family never accepting *or* disowning me. It was a no-man's-land with me standing in the middle.

When I had returned to college all those years ago, I did as I promised and kept in touch with my mom. Texted her when we arrived back and kept her up to date on my classes, but she never once replied. I knew she had read them, and once or twice I had seen the three moving dots, telling me someone was typing, but no message ever came through. The only message I got a reply to was when I asked if I was welcome home at Christmas, but that had been a simple word *Yes*. If I had been hoping for a warmer welcome, it didn't happen. I was still met with silence, and I could tell Chase had cozied right up to Mom and see the affection in her eyes as she looked at him. Just like Chase had always wanted.

It was also the first time I got a glimpse into how my family was going to be toward me. They all got dressed for church Christmas morning, including myself, but when I came downstairs to attend with them, I was told not to. That I wasn't welcome in the church at the moment. It was also the Christmas they gave me a bible. Which in the grand scheme of things wasn't too bad. It was a nice leather-bound book that looked expensive, and I had to admit that a little bit of hope had ignited in me until I opened it. As I looked through the pages, I started to spot sections which had been highlighted, sections dealing with homosexuality being a sin, and just like that, my hope had been snuffed out. It was subtle, but it was a message all the same.

"You've gone quiet again," Beau says, invading my thoughts again.

"Sorry."

"What were you thinking about this time?" Beau asks, hoping to get me to talk.

"That first Christmas I came home," I reply, being honest with him.

"You know, I still can't believe that they gave you a bible," Beau spits out, trying to disguise his annoyance and failing even after all this time, "or that you took it."

"You know I thought it was going to help." I wonder why I'm defending my own actions that happened so long ago.

"Yeah, I know. But your family is just nuts." Beau's not pulling any punches and letting me know exactly how he feels.

Beau had been furious when I told him what they had given me and was even more angry when I told him that I had thanked them for it and told them I would read it. He had called me a few choice names and told me he was never going to talk to my family again, and honestly, to this day, I believe that still to be the case. I know my family refuses to take their cars or trucks for Beau to look at, preferring to go across the county even if it costs them more.

"They're not nuts," I counter, defending my family... because they're still *family, right?*

"I can't believe you're defending them." Beau is trying to act surprised, but he isn't, not really.

"Blood is thicker than water," I retort, wishing we could stop talking about this.

"In any other circumstance, yes, but not with yours." He pauses here and looks over to me. "They're madder than a box of frogs."

I can't help laughing at his analogy, "Madder than a box of frogs?"

"Well, I couldn't think of anything else. But you aren't going to get me to change my mind. They are nuts."

"Beau, they are just religious," I reply, stating the obvious.

Beau just makes a huffing sound but doesn't say anything more, just pulls out his phone and starts tapping on the screen. It has always confused me, why Beau's hatred toward my family grew so quickly. We had talked about what the reaction could have been, and I thought we had gone over everything, so this shouldn't have come as a surprise, and yet to him, it did. I've tried to ask him *why* he hates them, but he just tells me he can't believe how they are, and honestly I would dread to think how he would act if he discovered what they had come up with recently.

His cell beeping in his hand tells me he has a text, which explains all the tapping.

"Mom texted me while you were with your Dad asking if you wanted to come over." Beau looks up from the cell and glances over to me "I didn't reply because I wanted to see how you were, but I just told her we'd come over. I think you need a change of scenery."

And I know the reason Beau said that we would come over is because he isn't happy with where my thoughts have gone, and he doesn't want to spend the rest of the evening listening to me defend them. Honestly the thought of spending the evening with Beau and his family sounds like the best idea, something to make me smile on a day that has made me do anything but that.

Chapter 4 — Beau

From the moment I'd spotted we were the first to arrive at the cemetery, I'd wanted to leave. If Addy's family turned up while we had been there, I'm not sure I would have been able to hold my tongue, and today was not the day to cause more issues with Addy and his family. Today was supposed to be a day of reflection for the man they lost, but I can't deny that Addy keeping the visit short had been a relief, and we were back in the car before anyone had arrived.

But I hadn't expected Addy to go silent on me and think about his family and the time he came out, and then that first Christmas. I hated that he was thinking about that Christmas. Hell, if I could have my way, I would make him walk away completely, but that wasn't my place. He caught on quickly how much I hated his family, and he'd tried to get me to talk. Of course, I just told him it was because I didn't like how they were treating him, but it was more than that. The real reason was because I was in love with him and hated seeing the pain they caused him. Addy had no idea of course. He just thought I was being the overprotective best friend.

It's strange to worry about what your gay best friend is going to think when learning his so-called straight best friend is, in fact, gay, but I have been. For years I've known I was gay, realized it about the same time Addy did. I'd been so proud of him when he told me before anyone else, and I'd almost done the same. But I hadn't, too cowardly to say, "Yeah, me too." Images of the football team had flashed through my mind. They wouldn't have understood my coming out as gay. It was bad enough that they thought Addy was, and the insults traded about him in the locker room were heart-breaking enough, but to then possibly find myself on the other end of it.... No, I knew I wouldn't be able to cope with that.

College was going to be different, I told myself. The guys were going to be different, more mature, but yeah, I was wrong there, too. Then Addy's dad had died and everything changed. I knew I cared for him; he was my best friend. But being there for him, making sure he was okay... it changed me. I fell in love with Addy. My plan was to tell him, let him know he had someone close by who loved him, but again something stopped me. Would he understand why I'd been quiet all this time? Would he call me a liar and leave? Would the team think it strange that I was so cut up over a friend? So, I had locked my emotions away for another time and carried on the straight persona.

Then the accident had happened, and for a second, I'd thought he might have felt something more for me. But reality soon hit home that this wasn't the case. If he loved me like I did him, he would have listened to me when I told him not to tell his family, but he didn't. Instead, he'd told them and had spent the last ten years dealing with their bullshit. So yeah, I hated Addy's family.

"Hey, you're the one who's quiet now," Addy says, looking over to me.

"Yeah, it's turning out to be a strange day," I reply, hoping my emotions aren't showing all over my face.

"Was nice of your mom to invite me over," Addy says, and there is no mistaking the affection in his voice for my mom.

"She remembers what day it is." Being a small town, everyone remembers losing someone.

"Suppose," he says with a shrug, not quite believing me.

"Addy, this is Madison Springs. You know everyone knows everyone." Which generates a smile for me.

"Just still surprises me. Most of the town didn't really talk to my family much." Addy gives me a quick look before turning back to look at the road ahead.

"That's because most of your family are nuts." He hates me saying it, but I have no intention of stopping.

"Beau," he says, trying to reprimand me.

"Addy," I reply, giving him the same tone back, but we both end up smiling.

But he is smiling because deep down, he knows I'm right. For a small town in the middle of America, you would think that everyone here would be like Addy's family, but for some reason, that's not the case. No one cares who you are or aren't sleeping with, who you love, etc. In fact, I think some of the gossips in town love it. It meant I loved growing up here, and admittingly, when I got my master mechanic, I could have gone anywhere, actually moved somewhere where they didn't know me as the almost footballer player, come out, and been me. But I couldn't leave this town. I know I wasn't cut for the big cities or being a member of some big franchise garage where I would end up just being a number more than a person. So instead, I stayed here, close to my family and Addy, and it had turned out perfect, other than still being in the closet, but that was my choice.

"Mom is cooking too," I tell Addy because I know he will love hearing this, and I was right.

"Really?" he replies, his eyes lighting up.

"Yep. Think she was hoping you'd come over."

"Why, what is she cooking?" Addy asks, giving me a quick look.

I wonder if I should keep stringing him along to help make him forget about everything or put him out of his misery. But of course, it's at that moment he looks over to me, his green eyes shining and a smile spreads across his face, and I know I'll tell him just to keep the look on his face. "She mentioned something about steak, mashed potatoes, and greens with maybe some gravy."

"Did she mention pie?" But he's already licking his lips,

"There may or may not have been talk of an apple pie and ice cream."

"Oh god." A moan slips from his mouth, which goes straight through me, and I have to take several breaths to clear the sound from my brain before I get too excited. "My favorite," Addy mumbles.

My mom, of course, knows it's his favorite, which is why she probably spent most of the day cooking it. There was no way my mom would buy a pie from the store when it was easy enough to make yourself. I knew everything would be ready by the time we got there, and the house would smell amazing.

Five minutes later we're pulling up outside my parents' house, and I spot Mom peeking out of the window, apparently looking out for us, even though the moment we walk through the front door she'll pretend to have been in the kitchen the whole time.

Getting out of the car, we walk up to the front door. I only knock once before opening the door and walking in. "Hey Mom, only us," I call out and wait.

"In the kitchen," she says in a raised voice, and I smile to myself that I'd been right.

We both walk into the kitchen, and before I can even say hello, Mom is untying her apron, throwing it off to the side, and striding over to us, pulling Addy first into a hug.

"Arden, how are you doing?" Mom asks, looking him up and down like he's injured or something.

"I'm okay, Mrs. Jackson, but I think Beau could use some ice."

Mom snaps her head over to me and gives me the look, the one that tells me Mom isn't happy. Addy takes a step behind Mom, looks over to me, and smiles before poking out his tongue. The git did that on purpose so my mom would stop fussing over him and start fussing over me instead.

"Ice? Why do you need ice?" her tone relaying her annoyance.

"Addy's just being a shi—" I start but manage to stop myself from saying shit. It might not be a swear word, but Mom won't like it all the same "Worry wart. Just ignore him."

Mom turns to Addy who quickly wipes the smile off his face and just stands there waiting for whatever instruction Mom is going to give. "Arden, as my son is playing stupid," Mom starts, shooting me another disapproving look, "would you mind telling me why he needs ice?"

Addy shoots me a look, and I can see the glint in his eyes. He's going to sing like a canary, and I'm never going to hear the end of it, probably all night.

"Beau pushed himself too much at the shop today and now his knee is aching." And the moment Mom's back is to him again, the smile is back on his face.

"Beau Jackson!" *My full name, shit. I'm going to kill Addy*, I think as I watch Mom walk over to the freezer to pull out a bag of peas that's being held closed by a rubber band. Then she opens a drawer and pulls out a clean dishtowel, wrapping it around the peas before handing it to me.

"Take this and go rest your knee, while I sort dinner. Your dad should be home any minute," she says in a tone that brooks no argument as she points in the direction of the living room.

"I can help, Mrs. Jackson," Addy pipes up, giving her a sweet smile.

"Thank you, Addy, that is very kind of you." And again, when Mom isn't looking, Addy smiles and pokes his tongue out at me.

Walking out of the kitchen, I make my way into the living room, settle myself into a chair and pull a footstool over. Resting my leg on the stool, I place the cold peas on my knee and even though I wouldn't admit it to either Mom or Addy, the cold does feel good on my leg. Resting my head against the back of the seat, I close my eyes, my knee already feeling better.

The sound of my mom giggling drifts in from the kitchen and warms my heart. Mum and Dad have always liked Addy and had been pleased when we became friends, but they had also grown closer to him. When I told them what Addy's mom had done after he had come out, I think they decided to take him under their wing. They invited him to every family gathering, every Christmas or Easter celebration. They always asked him how college was going, and I think they were almost as proud of him as they were of me.

The sound of the front door has me opening my eyes and watching as Dad walks in.

"Hey, Dad," I say, and he jumps upon hearing my voice.

"What the," turning to look at me as he takes off his coat, then jacket, and hangs them on the stand next to the front door.

"How many other people say hey, Dad?" I ask, laughing at his reaction.

"None, thank God. One was enough," Dad says, laughing back at me.

"Charming,"

"Why are you sitting there?" Looking around the room, he obviously hasn't seen the ice on my knee.

"Mom and Addy are in the kitchen. Addy told on me," I reply, pointing to my knee.

"Pushed yourself?" Dad asks, but he isn't annoyed like Mom was, as he comes over and sits down in the chair next to me.

"Just a car that was being a pain," I say while moving the ice. "But the ice is helping. Just don't tell Addy. I won't hear the end of it."

"How is Arden doing?" Dad whispers, looking over toward the sound of talking coming from the kitchen.

"Think he's okay, but he thinks his family deliberately didn't go to the grave earlier in the hopes of catching him there."

Dad makes a strange clicking sound as I mention Addy's family. The disgust I feel might also be mirrored by my dad; he just hides it better than I can.

"God. Poor Arden."

"Yeah, but I think Mom cooking him his favorite meal has cheered him up." Dad looks over to me, and the delight is evident on his face. That's when I remember that Addy's favorite meal also happens to be my dad's, too.

"Steak and pie?" Dad asks.

"Yep. Addy's in the kitchen helping mom as we speak."

"Addy," Dad laughs. "Still find it amazing you still call him that."

"Yeah, well, I find it strange that you call him Arden. He has been Addy for years. In fact, you are the only people in town that call him by his full name. He wouldn't mind you calling him Addy, you know."

"We know, but that's not his name."

Back in high school I had started calling Addy, Addy, mainly because I couldn't be asked to say his full name, not when everyone else was shortening theirs. We tried calling him Ard for a while, but that didn't feel right, either. Then one night as a joke, I called him Addy, and it stuck and had followed him every day since.

Mom walks into the room at this point, a dishtowel thrown over her shoulder.

"I didn't hear you come in, love. You been home long?" Mom asks, giving my dad a kiss.

"Not long. Was going to come straight into the kitchen, but your son decided it was fun to scare the life out of me." Dad nods his head in my direction.

"Hey, it's not my fault you didn't see me," I say in an attempt to defend myself.

Mom just laughs at the pair of us. "Well, dinner will be ready in a couple minutes." Which is Mom's signal to move into the dining room.

"Mom, can you take this? Think it's melting a bit," I ask, handing over the peas.

"Fine, but you're having it back once we've finished with the food."

I open my mouth to argue with her when my dad looks over to me and gives the slightest shake of his head in *a don't even think about it* gesture.

"Fine," I grouse, admitting defeat.

As Mom turns and walks back into the kitchen, I give my knee a quick massage around the sides before carefully bending it back and forth and getting to my feet. Walking into the dining room, I see there are three big bowls with lids going down the middle of the table. One will contain the mashed potatoes, one the green beans, and the final will be the gravy, all ready for us to help ourselves.

Mom walks in holding a tray that has four glasses of iced tea, again homemade and will be sweetened to perfection, and right behind her is Addy, holding a platter with four large steaks.

"Hey, Mr. Jackson," Addy says, going up to him first while Mom sets down her tray and hands out the drinks before sitting down.

"Arden, nice to see you." Dad picks up the steak on the top of the pile.

Addy turns to my mom, who takes hers, and then he walks around to me where I take mine and put it on my plate before grabbing the final steak and placing it on the plate beside mine for Addy. Once the platter has been safely placed at the end of the table, Addy comes and sits next to me, and we all start helping ourselves.

We are just about to tuck in when Dad picks up his glass. "I'd like to make a toast." We all pick up our teas and look over to Dad. "To Mr. Walker. Sadly missed but never forgotten."

You would have thought it would have made everything awkward, but it has the opposite effect. Addy relaxes next to me and holds his glass up as he says, "To Dad," and we all clink glasses and take a sip before my dad is talking to Addy about anything and everything, and in that one moment, I don't think I could've loved my family more.

Chapter 5 — Addy

Beau's family has always made me feel welcome. In fact, I think Beau's dad took on the responsibility of being the father figure in my life. Many people might have complained, said they already had one Dad and didn't need another, but I actually didn't mind. It was nice to know there was someone I could go and talk to if I needed it. I think he might have listened if I had gone to him about my feelings over Beau, but instead, I kept it quiet. There are some secrets that are best kept quiet — that was something I excelled at — and this was mine.

Going to see Beau's family last night had been exactly what I needed, and Beau knew this. We had spent the night just talking about anything and everything. First we'd talked about Beau's garage, which had been doing really well, and considering the small-town nature of Madison Springs, that was, well, surprising. But what was lovely to hear was when Beau went on to explain there are more customers coming from out of town. Pride for him had filled me to know that word was spreading about how good he was. But then his parents had gone on to ask how my little venture was going.

Having Beau's parents take an interest in me personally was one thing, but to have them interested in my business was something altogether comforting, even if it did still surprise me. But I loved talking about my business. When I had graduated from high school, I knew I wanted to do a business degree; I had no idea what I was going to do with it, but I knew this was the course I wanted to take. Once I discovered that one of the best places to complete the course was the same school Beau was going to attend, I really couldn't believe my luck. Then my scholarship happened, and everything fell into place.

The only blip had been when Beau was told he wouldn't be able to play football again, and I thought for the first time ever, we would be spending time apart. It might have been possible for me to move colleges if he had to, but I knew I wouldn't. So, I just accepted we would only get to see each other on holidays until the time came when I moved back. You see, I never wanted to leave Madison Springs. With the degree, I could have gone anywhere, but this was my home. Some of my friends at campus thought I was nuts wanting to move back to a small town when there was a whole world out there to explore. They were right, but that world could be explored via holidays. It didn't mean I had to go out there and live in it, and not every place was as pro-LGBTQ as Madison Springs was, with the exception of my family and their church, of course.

In the end, there had been some separation with Beau when he'd had to train in another county, but not as much as going to different colleges. But it was during this time I finally figured out what I wanted to do. Coffee. As with almost every other student in the world, coffee had become a life-long friend, being there when I needed to cram for an exam, being there when I was severely hung over, or just there when I needed that boost in the morning. Of course, while studying, I could never afford the real good stuff, most of the time just buying instant, but on the rare occasions I could get something more fancy, I discovered my palate could pick up all the unique flavors. Those days where I could buy a new bean from somewhere far afield became the days which excited me the most.

One day I was sitting in my mom's living room while no one else was in the house and just relaxed there sipping the black liquid, allowing the bitterness to hit the back of my throat. It was when I detected the subtle tastes of chocolate and citrus that the thought hit me. *Coffee Shop*. Madison Springs didn't have one, and I was sure there would be no objection. But I also knew that it would take time to take off. Madison Springs might be forward thinking, but it was still a small town and change wasn't always welcomed.

When a shop became available with living quarters above it, I'd jumped on it. Having already spoken to the mayor of the town and some of the residents, who all thought it was an interesting idea and was all the go ahead I needed, I bought the shop and moved out of my parents' place. All within a matter of weeks.

The living area had been bare, literally just the walls and floors, but I really didn't care. The place was mine, even though for the first few weeks I just slept on the floor in a sleeping bag. My mom had refused to let me take my bed. I could probably have guessed why and really didn't think much of it. Anywhere was better than staying there with the constant looks and judgement.

To this day I remember standing in the middle of the shop and thinking about what I could do. There needed to be a twist… something to keep drawing people through the door while the coffee side hopefully took off. As I'd been standing there, one of the older ladies in town had walked past the window, stopped, turned to look at me, and waved before walking on. It was then that I spotted the knitting needles sticking out of her bag and the idea had hit. I immediately started running after the elderly lady, and other than making her jump out of her skin, then laugh at me, it had been a useful conversation. I found out that she had to go to the next county over to get her yarn and knitting needles or meet up with some of the other ladies of the knitting club . She also mentioned how she sometimes had to order online and didn't like doing that.

When I asked her how she felt about my getting some items in for them and if she would be interested in me maybe offering a meeting place or classes in the evening, I was worried the excitement that came over her would trigger a heart attack. But once the idea was there, it took hold. So, while I was waiting to get the coffee machines in and finding the best beans, I'd set up a small section of shelving in one corner that had a selection of yarn and knitting needles, also adding some paper craft items. Nothing major, just glue, stamps, cards, etc.

But then the most surprising thing that happened was when the ladies started coming to me and asking if I could order things in for them. Most of them were still hesitant about getting stuff online, so I did it for them. They would come with a particular product they wanted, like a specialist yarn, and I would order it. At first, some of the ladies' families had been a little worried that I might start ripping them off until they learned that I only charged them whatever the cost was, in fact, often paying any delivery charges out of my own pocket. They'd then called me nuts, but there was, in fact, a method to my madness — keeping them coming to the shop.

My plan had been to just have the craft section till the cafe took off, but even today, while my biggest seller is the coffee I produce, my small shelving unit in the corner is still there and the classes are still taking place. Why? Simply because I love the old ladies that come into the place.

They often came in, bought some wool, and pretended to look at other items before getting a coffee. They would then sit, and if it was quiet, I would sit with them and talk. It became someplace they could come to if they felt lonely; I knew this and went along with the pretense of them getting something I knew they didn't need.

The classes were also supposed to be temporary, but again, I still hold them a few nights a week. Normally they're run by one of the ladies. The classes have actually been a lot of fun, especially when I think back to the time when they tried to teach me to knit, which lasted about two classes before I gave up. Coffee I was good at; knitting was *never* going to happen. So instead, I just sit with them, make sure they have coffee, or on special occasions I'll get them some wine to share. The classes quickly become the highlight of the ladies' week, and even though it eats into my free time, there is no way I was going to stop them.

Beau had called me stupid when he'd learned that the coffee was now outselling the crafts section and yet I was still selling it, pointing this out to me on more than one occasion. Keeping them wasn't part of the plan. When I'd tried to explain, he just laughed at me and called me a softie. Even though I tried to think of a comeback, I couldn't because he was right.

The other thing I like about spending time with the old ladies is the fact they knew I was gay and didn't care. Every time I spend time with them is like spending time with my own grandparents, except these are grandparents who are understanding and very curious, though sometimes a little too much. They're always asking questions, especially when they want to know about my love life or lack thereof, but those are questions I avoid at all costs.

There is also the odd occasion when one of the ladies will ask if they can introduce me to one of their grandchildren. Now, one would think it's because they're trying to fix me up, but most of the time they just want to know if their grandchild is gay or not. What was funny was when they brought the female relative around, because apparently they think being gay automatically meant I would know if they were a lesbian or not.

Shaking my head to bring myself back to the present, I look around the shop, thankful there aren't any customers standing in front of me asking for an order. Instead, Mrs. Nichols in the corner is staring at me, a bemused look on her face. Picking up the coffee pot behind me, I walk over to her.

"Refill Mrs. Nichols?" I ask, showing the coffee pot.

"Thank you, Addy," she says, lifting up her coffee cup. She knows that I'm not going to charge her for the second cup; this is the coffee brewed just for the ladies that come in. It's not the best beans but still a hundred percent better than instant, and I filter it fresh every morning. There is the posh machine with a steamer for customers that want something more modern and complicated. "How are you doing today?"

"I'm okay, Mrs. Nichols," I reply, then turn to walk away.

"You looked lost in thought there for a second. Not sure if you would have noticed if another customer had come in." The concern for me is evident in her voice.

"Yeah, I've been being reflective on the past a lot the last few days," I say with a shrug, trying to explain my behavior.

"Well, of course. It's ten years, right?" she asks, tilting her head to me.

And right there is the other reason why I love living here in Madison Springs; you never have to remind people. They're always there with a smile.

"Yeah, ten years yesterday, to be exact," I answer, smiling down at her.

"Your dad was a good man. He had his flaws but was a good man." She pauses for a second, then mutters, "Unlike the rest of your family."

I turn to hide the laugh on my face. Mrs. Nichols had thought she'd been whispering, but it was just as loud as the rest of our conversation. But it's nice to know my family is disliked by others. Of course, my family thinks that *everyone* likes them and is on their side when it comes to me and often find it strange to know how many of the townsfolk come to my little shop.

Composing myself, I turn back to Mrs. Nichols. "Yeah, he was a good man."

Thinking this conversation finally over, I walk back to the counter, placing the coffee pot back on the warmer, and stare out over the shop.

"Addy?" I turn to face Mrs. Nichols again, "Your dad would be so proud of what you've done for the town."

I watch as she turns back to look out the windows, replying with, "Thank you, Mrs. Nichols," but I'm not sure that she hears me.

A few minutes later, the bell above the shop door jingles, letting me know someone has come into my shop. Looking up, I see Beau standing at the front with a smile on his face. A streak of grease is smeared on his face.

"Good afternoon, Mrs. Nichols. How are you today?" he greets, nodding his head at her.

Afternoon? Where the hell has the time gone? It only feels like five minutes since I opened the door to come in this morning. Mrs. Nichols looks up at Beau and blushes for a minute, which makes me smile.

"I am fine, thank you, Beau. Just waiting for Gladys to join me."

Well that explains why she hasn't left yet, though it was unusual for her to have another cup of coffee. Probably came in early to check on me.

Turning away from Beau and Mrs. Nichols, I start making up Beau's coffee. He's had the same order for years, so there's no point in asking him if he wants anything different. With the noise of the machine going, I can't hear the conversation, but I know Beau will stand there talking to her for as long as she needs.

Placing the finished coffee on the counter, I wait for Beau to come over to me.

"Can I have—" Cutting Beau off, I point to the coffee already waiting for him. "What if I wanted something else?"

"Beau, the day you order something else will be the day I buy a lotto ticket or a share in bacon," I say while trying not to laugh.

"Bacon?" Beau's looking very confused by my comment.

"Yeah, well, I presume the cost of bacon will go up because of all the flying pigs there will be." I'm not able to stop the laugh at this point, which causes Mrs. Nichols to look over to us with a smile on her face.

"Hilarious," Beau grumbles, but I can see he's trying to hide a smile, too. "Was on my lunch and thought I'd pop over and check on you."

"Yeah, he's been unusually quiet today," Mrs. Nichols shouts over.

So there is one thing I hate about Madison Springs... people jumping into conversations. But I don't say anything, just smile at her while I think it all in my mind.

"But it's nice to see Beau put a smile on your face." She gives me a wink that has me wondering what all that is about, but before I can ask, the door jingles again and Gladys walks in with some of her friends.

"Looks like you're gonna be busy. I'll catch you later," Beau says walking away from the counter and to the front door, tipping an imaginary hat to the ladies and completely missing them all swoon. Desperate, nosy ladies. Small towns really are the best.

Chapter 6 — Beau

Looking at Mrs. Nichols again, I try to hide the smirk at the pink that taints her cheeks from my friendly gesture and walk out of the shop. Addy thinks I don't notice the reaction I get from some of the ladies in this town, but I do and it's one of the reasons I love it here.

My plan was to always come back to Madison Springs regardless of where my football career had taken me. I'd had it all be mapped out: play for the best teams so I could travel the country but eventually come home and hope Addy was still here or that I could talk him into moving back. Of course, this plan also included telling Addy how I felt, him feeling the same, and then us settling down together, all of which hadn't happened.

In college, when the guys had talked about the future and what they wanted to do once their days were over, they had thought I was mad to want to come back to a small town where everyone knows you, especially if you had the chance to live in some of the biggest cities in the US. They used to ask me, "Surely you don't want to be one of those people who say, 'I was born here, lived all my life here, and plan to see out my days here.'" At first, I had to admit that it made me think and ask myself if I really wanted that. The answer had been yes, and this morning had proven me right. Just walking from the garage to the coffee shop had made my day.

More than one person had stopped to say good afternoon, ask after me, and ask how the garage was doing, but there had also been more than one asking if they could bring their car or truck over for me to look at it, then, of course, they asked after the health of my parents. Those who were on the other side of the road would wave and smile. Everyone knew everyone.

But it still helped that I was seen as the star of the town, the *almost* NFL player. They didn't care that I busted up my knee; they didn't care I never made it to the big leagues. All they cared about was that there was someone in the town who could have made it. I even think they planned a parade for me once, but thankfully my parents managed to talk them out of it.

This didn't mean that when I left for college I hadn't been excited; I certainly had been. Being away from the parents and all the freedom that came with it. Addy had felt the same, and it had worried me for longer than I care to admit that one day I would return to Madison Springs and he wouldn't. Addy had always seemed to want something more, and I had thought this meant being away from his family and this town. When he'd first mentioned he was coming back here after he graduated, I'd been surprised, and maybe at the time I should have encouraged him to find his own path. Yet instead I had found myself saying it was a good idea. Just knowing he would be there, close to me, was a reassurance.

But soon the guilt had set in. He had to live with his family and didn't seem to know what to do with his life. Had he stayed in the town because of me? Had I clipped his wings to prevent him from flying? Then he started the coffee shop and blossomed in front of me, relieving some of the guilt I'd been feeling, and of course I knew first-hand how much the ladies enjoyed his shop.

The best surprise was when Addy had moved into the living quarters above the shop and asked if I wanted to take the second bedroom. We would be living together. So many emotions had gone through me in that moment. What did it mean? Would the town think it strange? But it meant nothing; it was just two friends living together. Was I really worried what the town thought? As far as the town and everyone in it was concerned, I was straight. Don't think it ever occurred to them I could be anything else. Being gay in sports had been something never heard of, not that it wasn't happening now. People just thought it was nice that two friends got on well enough to be able to live together.

In my head, I had thought this was going to be easy like any other time Addy had stayed over at mine or my parents — in recent years, I'd refused to stay at his parents. But I had been very, very wrong. The first time he walked out of the shower with a towel wrapped around his waist, I almost fainted on the spot. It had been a while since I'd seen him semi-naked, and he had toned up. There was definitely a six pack because I counted it. His pecs were well defined with perky, pink nipples demanding to be tweaked, and the water droplets that trickled down from his chest, over his abs, and followed the happy trail that began at his navel and disappeared into the towel didn't help the whole vision in front of me.

If Addy had caught me staring or my odd behavior, he'd never said anything. But after that moment, whenever Addy said he was going to the shower, I quickly retreated to my bedroom, not wanting to risk catching him in that state of undress again. And for the most part, it worked.

I loved living here. It was close enough to the garage that I really didn't need to use my car, but when it was necessary, I was always able to leave it at the garage afterward, securely locked up and therefore avoiding parking it on the street .

Yet, as there always is with life, there was a fly in the ointment that came in the form of Addy's family. Because of the local gossip tree, I was able to keep track of what was being said. They couldn't get their heads around the fact that I was okay living with Addy. That I was a straight man living with a homosexual. On more than one occasion, I was told they had tried to use this information to get the town to turn on Addy, which had backfired in their face. By this point, the townspeople loved the coffee shop Addy had opened.

After a while, the gossip died down, and I thought they'd accepted it. But then out of the blue, Chase turned up the garage, suddenly asking me to look at his car. Initially I'd wanted to tell him to fuck off, but my business head had kicked in. He was a customer. Looking at the car, whoever they had been taking it to, had been doing a shit job. It needed all sorts of things done to it. My initial hope had been he would take it back to the previous mechanic, but he agreed for me to get a quote. So, I did. I also increased the prices well over what I would normally charge. If they wanted me to look at it, then they were going to have to pay extra. When they agreed to the price, I began to smell a rat. They were suddenly being genuinely nice to me.

I had decided not to tell Addy that his brother had come to the garage; he would have told me to send him on his way regardless of what was wrong with the vehicle, but I decided to see what was going to happen first. Admittedly, there was nothing. Chase just dropped the car off, let me do the work, picked it back up again once I was finished, and they paid the bill in full. It had made me think that maybe I'd been wrong, maybe Chase was turning over a new leaf, and hope had grown in me. Hope that Addy would get a healthy relationship with at least one family member, but I'd been right in my original misgivings.

On Chase's third visit to the shop, strange questions started to be asked. I, of course, had ignored them. Most of the time I pretended I hadn't heard the questions, but they were still being asked. I knew it was something I needed to discuss with Addy but couldn't figure out how to start the conversation.

As my garage comes into view, I spot a car waiting outside the closed doors, and my heart sinks. Chase is there waiting. Why the hell is he there? He didn't have anything booked in. Plastering a smile on my face, which anyone would know is fake, I greet him.

"Hey, what can I do for you?" I ask, trying to keep my tone as friendly as I can muster, all the while fighting the urge to punch him in the face.

"Hey, Beau." He's trying for the friendly tone, too, but I'm not sure he's able to hide the falseness like I can. "This morning I had to brake suddenly, and they just didn't feel right."

There is absolutely nothing wrong with the brakes. I know this because the brake discs and pads had been one of the first things I'd changed when he initially brought the car in to me. In fact, the old ones had been so bad that I should have made him leave the car; they were bordering on dangerous. But no, the evil side of me had let him go, and unfortunately he'd come back a few days later.

"Yeah, of course. Did they make any noise?" I ask, making out that he was right to be concerned.

"Nah, just they snapped on really quick." Turning my head, I bite my lip to stop from laughing and saying, "That's a sign they're working."

"Bring it in the garage and I'll have a look. Just give me a second." Opening up the huge garage doors, I walk in and place my coffee on the work bench off to one side of the bay. Chase is already back in his car with the engine running, so I wave him forward while pointing toward the lift.

He drives in and once the vehicle is in place, hops out, standing out of the way as I raise the car.

Grabbing a flashlight, I look at the wheels, shining my light over every section. As I thought, it all looks fine. As I make my way over to the other side, I hear a voice.

"You still living with Addy?" And the questions start again.... God, I *wish* I could turn on the engine to shut him up.

"Yeah," I reply, not willing to give him more than a one-word answer.

"Doesn't he creep you out?" *Where the hell is he going with this?*

"Nope," I answer, still not willing to engage him fully in this conversation.

"But he's—" and then Chase stops and goes quiet. I wish I could take a look at what he's doing, but the word "gay" comes in a whisper, and now I really want to watch him.

"Is he?" I blurt out, pretending to be shocked but really just wanting this conversation to be over.

"Yeah," he states, but he sounds surprised. He must not have picked up on the sarcasm in my tone. "Don't you worry he'll stare at you?"

Oh God, yes. I *want* him to stare at me. Hell, I want him to do a hell of a lot more. "Why the hell would he be staring at me?" I mentally kick myself for engaging further in this conversation.

"Well, you know..." And from hearing the slightest edge to his voice, this seems to be making him uncomfortable, and that works me more.

Making my way to the rear of the vehicle, I take longer looking over the back brakes, and at this angle, it's going to be harder for him to see me, which means I might actually be able to enjoy this conversation more.

"No, I don't know. Why would he be staring?" There's a sound of shuffling feet at my question as he paces back and forth. He really doesn't like the fact I'm not giving him clear answers.

He makes a huffing sound before he stops moving. "Cause you're a man," he replies, spitting out the words.

This time, I can't help but burst out laughing. He's being totally ridiculous, and now I can't wait to go home and talk to Addy about this.

"This isn't funny, Beau," he snaps at me. "He shouldn't look at you in that way. It's sinful."

Opening my mouth, I almost say, "Addy can stare at me all he wants," but I manage to stop myself since there's no point outing my feelings to Chase. Not that it would make much difference. "Addy's my best friend. There is no reason not to live together."

"But it's wrong!" he says forcefully, and I swear he wants to stamp his foot in frustration that I'm not agreeing with him.

"No, it's not," I bite back, trying to add something to my voice to make Chase aware that I'm never going to agree with him.

He finally goes silent, and I check the last wheel before walking out from under the car to find Chase staring at me.

"All the brakes look fine. Just take your time," I say flatly, praying this is going to be the end of it, but he still just stands there looking at me.

"It's wrong what he is. In the eyes of God," he spits at me, all the friendly tone from earlier vanishing from his voice. "He should stop tainting this town."

Oh God, this again. It's not the first time I've heard him say "taint this town." I should ask him what he means, but I'm not sure the answer is worth hearing. So instead, I ignore him.

"Not gonna charge you for today as it was only a quick look. But if the brakes start making a noise"—they won't—"then bring it back in."

Lowering the lift so the car is back on the ground, I turn, heading for the office. He has to realize I have no intention of continuing this conversation and he should just get in the car and leave, but nope, he carries on.

"Deep down, you have to agree with me. Why you've put up with his friendship so long is weird. I know you agree with what we've been telling him."

Agree with them? Weird friendship? What the hell is he going on about now? But this causes me to stop and turn to look at him. "No, deep down I don't agree with you and have no idea why you would think that having a gay best friend is weird—" But before I have the chance to say anything further, he takes a step forward.

"But you're an all-star football player. How can you accept this?"

Argh, so because I'm the football star, that makes me only want to be friends with straight people. The narrow-mindedness of these people is shocking.

Gritting my teeth, I respond, "I've known Addy has been gay a lot longer than you have. I don't care. He was my best friend then, and he's my best friend now." I take a deep breath to cleanse the anger out of me before I do or say something I'll regret. "Now, if you don't mind,"—I point to the other waiting cars—"another customer is due any second."

Finally listening to me, Chase walks around to the driver seat and gets in before carefully backing off the lift, into the yard, and turning it around. He accelerates out of the yard so fast it causes the gravel to spray out behind him, hitting one of the doors and making it ting. *Well, that explains why he had to brake hard if he drives like that.*

Turning to go back into the office, his words come back to me, "...agree with what we've been telling him," and I have a feeling Addy has some explaining to do.

Chapter 7 — Addy

Looking at the calendar announcement on my phone, I groan. One really shouldn't do that when it's saying *MOM'S BIRTHDAY DINNER,* and yet I do. I hadn't forgotten it was Mom's birthday, and I even got her a card. She'd stopped accepting gifts from me years ago, but she still gets a card even though a few years ago, when I had to go in the attic of the house for something, I found a box of cards, all addressed to Mom in my handwriting, and all of them unopened. Finding it had hurt. Not accepting the presents had stung, but now her not even opening the cards was just another blow. Why I kept putting myself through it, I had no idea, but I did. Sometimes I wish they had just disowned me; it would have been easier to deal with.

My groan had come out just as Mrs. Phillips had come up to the counter to order her coffee.

"That was a loud groan," Mrs. Phillips asks, looking up at me.

"Sorry, Mrs. Phillips. Let me get you your coffee." She has the same coffee as Mrs. Nichols. "Go take a seat, and I'll bring it over to you." She gives me a look before walking off, taking a seat next to her friend, then leaning over and whispering something, which causes Mrs. Nichols to look back at me.

Ignoring the pair of them, I pull out a mug and fill it with the coffee pot. Picking up both the mug and carafe, I walk over to the ladies and place the mug down on the table next to Mrs. Phillips.

"Do you need a top up, Mrs. Nichols?" I ask, hoping to distract her so she doesn't ask questions, a fruitless task, I know, but it was worth a shot.

"Gladys said you got bad news. Anything we can do to help?" she asks, smiling up at me. She's lying. She just wants to know what's going on in my life.

"Everything's fine," I reply, putting on the happiest smile. "Was just a reminder on my phone."

Unfortunately, she sees right through me. "A reminder on your phone made you sad?" I look over my shoulder to check if she can see the offending device.

"Mrs. Nichols, honestly, everything is fine. Now, would you like a top up?" But looking over to her cup, I can see that it's already three quarters full from the last top up. Figuring she won't want anymore, I turn to leave.

"Thank you, Addy, that would be lovely." Turning, I dutifully top up the coffee, which really wasn't worth it, but it was her way of keeping me close. She is *determined* to find out what happened.

"Now, Addy, you've not been happy since seeing that reminder, and don't try that fake smile on me. I've known you all your life. That smile didn't work when you were four, and it won't work now."

Sometimes having people who know you so well is a complete pain in the ass. "It was just a reminder that my mom's birthday dinner is tonight." I whisper quietly, finally admitting defeat and realizing it will be easier to just tell them and try to make a hasty retreat.

"Well, that does explain the groan," Mrs. Nichols states, clicking her tongue, her lips pursing together. Looks like she isn't impressed, either.

Mrs. Phillips leans over asking loudly, "What did he say?"

"Mom's birthday dinner tonight," Mrs. Nichols shouts at her, and I'm thankful there are no other customers in the place to hear my life being gossiped about. But I have a feeling the whole town will know by the time I come in tomorrow, which means there are going to be more ladies in the shop tomorrow checking on me.

"Oh my," Mrs. Phillips exclaims, giving me a look full of pity. "Addy, why do you put up with them?" she continues kindly.

"She is my mom. Family," I reply back with the standard answer I give if anyone asks me that question.

"Having the same blood doesn't make someone family," Mrs. Phillips states.

Her words stop me in my tracks. No one has ever said that to me before. Most of the time I just get a sad nod of the head or "you're right." I just stare at her, wondering if she's going to say any more, or if Mrs. Nichols is going to jump in and maybe call Mrs. Phillips out, but instead, she's nodding in agreement. These women continue to surprise me.

Walking back over to the counter, I replace the coffee pot and look over to the two ladies who appear to be deep in thought and have pulled out their knitting from somewhere. The clicking of the needles mixes in with the sound of their voices, not even following a pattern. The one time I tried to knit, it took all my concentration to just finish one row, and they're doing it like it's nothing. But it's still nice to watch.

Picking up my phone, I open the text app and fire off a message to Beau to let him know I won't be home till later.

Addy: Mom's birthday dinner tonight. Be home late.

Slipping my cell into my pocket, I try to figure what I can do to take my mind off this evening. Looking over the craft shelves, I decide to check my inventory and see if there is anything to order. And considering the two ladies currently in here, I'll check to see if they need anything but cross my fingers on no more questions.

Picking up a clipboard and a piece of paper, I make my way over and start with the needles, counting the stock and seeing if any sizes are missing or low. My aim is always to make sure some standard sizes are always in stock, the ones used for the most common patterns. Quickly spotting they are down, I make a note of the number and continue. The rest of the shelves are all well stocked, so what I was hoping would take me an hour or so ended up only taking me thirty minutes. Great.

"Excuse me, Mrs. Nichols, Mrs. Phillips. I'm doing a stock order. Is there anything you need me to get in for you?" I ask as I walk over to them.

"No, I think I'm fine, Addy. Thank you for asking," Mrs. Nichols states.

Casting my eyes over to Mrs. Phillips, I watch her as she looks in her bag, rooting for something, eventually pulling out a piece of paper that looks like it includes a picture of yarn in a bright green color.

"Oh, Addy. Can you get this in for me?" Mrs. Phillips asks, passing me the paper, and it does indeed include a picture of the yarn, and I have to hide the laugh which wants to bubble up.

"In this color?" I'm hoping she'll say this is the only picture she could find for the brand and that she is actually looking for another color because I have *no* idea what they could make with that.

"Yes, please. Isn't it lovely?" she replies, looking at the paper.

"It's um…" I pause to think of the right words. "Definitely interesting." Thankfully as I look closer, it's a brand I ordered before, which will make it easier. "Will get it ordered this afternoon, so it should be here in a few days."

"Thank you, Addy." She smiles up at me.

As I walk away from them, I can hear Mrs. Phillips behind me, thinking she's whispering again. "Such a nice boy. How that happened baffles me."

Slowing down, I wait to see if Mrs. Nichols answers her. "Don't you remember Mr. Walker? He was such a lovely man."

"God definitely took the wrong parent *that* night," Mrs. Phillips answers, causing me to almost trip over nothing. I've never seen this side of them. They are so mean toward my mother, and the thought makes me smile for the first time since reading the reminder.

Just as I place the clipboard on the counter, my cell vibrates in my pocket, so I turn my back on the two ladies so they can't see what I'm doing and ask more questions. It's a message from Beau.

Beau: Nice... not. Would say have fun, but it's your mom. Catch you later.

A few hours later, I'm walking over to my mom's place. It's a nice summer evening, the heat of the day having passed, but everything still has that warm glow about it. Much too warm for the dress pants and button-up shirt I have on, even if it is a short-sleeved shirt, which no doubt will be frowned upon.

Once outside my mom's, I take a deep breath and walk up the front steps, knock on the door, and, unlike Beau, wait for the door to be answered. You need to be invited into this house, even if you're the son of the owner. The door is answered by Chase, who has a huge smile on his face that drops the instant he sees who it is.

"Mom, Addy's here." But there's no warmth in his voice, and he begrudgingly steps back to let me in.

As I walk inside, I see Mom is sitting in her favorite chair in the corner of the living room. It used to be my dad's, but she started to sit in it soon after his passing. I like to think it was a way for her to keep him close. She looks up and smiles at me, but there is no light in her eyes. "Hello, Addy," she says, her voice just as dull as her eyes.

"Happy Birthday!" Going over to her, I give her the birthday card and watch as she tenses up as I lean down to kiss her cheek.

"How kind. If you don't mind, I'll open it later." Until I found the box, I had believed she'd wanted to open them in private away from the prying eyes of Chase. I now know differently.

"Yes, of course." Taking the seat next to her, I ask, "Did you get anything nice for your birthday?" trying to make conversation.

"Oh, yes." And she brightens for a minute. "Chase got me a new bible. It's beautiful." As she looks over to Chase, a smile spreads across her face, lighting up her eyes. "He is so thoughtful." But once she looks back at me, the smile vanishes.

"Is there anything I can do to help with dinner?" The answer will be no again. It always is, and yet I still ask every time.

"No," Mom states, and then because her manners kick in, she adds, "Thank you," but it seems as though she has to force those last words out.

The sound of a buzzer going off in the kitchen grabs all our attention. The room falls silent, eventually broken by Chase saying, "That's dinner."

All of us make our way into the kitchen, and I see the table set for three, which gets me thinking about Chase's reaction upon opening the door. Was he hoping I wouldn't be coming? I was a little later than planned but not more than a few minutes. In that time, had he thought I wasn't coming and seeing me standing there had extinguished that hope in one go? The thought made me very happy, but I made sure not to show it.

Taking a seat, I watch as my mom and Chase bring bowls and plates over to the table, setting them down. My mom shouldn't be doing this; I should be helping my brother, but that is another thing I stopped asking years ago.

When everything is on the table, my mom and Chase hold hands, bowing their heads in silent prayer. Both of them are reciting the same words; words that were drilled into me as a child, words which I repeat to myself now, finishing at the same time as them. But it is just another thing I'm not allowed to participate in anymore.

Helping ourselves to food, we just sit there, all eating in silence. No conversation takes place, Mom not asking me how I am, not asking how the shop is doing, because they both just don't care. Over the years, I've tried to make small talk, ask Mom about the church, how it was going, or asked Chase about himself, but each time I got one, maybe two-word answers. So, like everything else, I just stopped.

Once the plates have been cleared and removed — by Chase of course — I sit back and wait. Now that the meal is over, the questions will start, but on the bright side, it does mean that I'll be leaving soon. The moment Chase sits back down, as predicted, they start.

"You're still in town then?" Chase asks harshly. What a dumb question, but I nod all the same. "Have you thought about what we said at all?"

"Yes, but no, I'm not going anywhere," I answer him as calmly as I can.

"But you're an embarrassment to me and Mom," is his comeback, which is the same one he always gives.

A few months ago, out of the blue, I had been invited over for dinner. I stupidly thought maybe they'd had a change of heart and wanted to build some bridges, but I'd been wrong. Apparently my mom, Chase, and the church had decided I was somehow tainting the town and needed to leave. Yet it seemed nobody else thought this, not that I'd mentioned it to anyone. The coffee shop had been busier than ever. If, as they put it, I was tainting the town, surely the first thing to do would be to boycott the shop.

"Sorry you feel that way." I'm surprised that Chase looks shocked at my answer; it's the same one I've given every time he's said that.

"Don't you *care*? You're tainting this town and everyone in it!" The urge to roll my eyes at him is overwhelming, but I don't. Looking over to my mom, I see that she's just staring at me. She never talks or adds anything to Chase's speeches except for the occasional nod of the head. "Please," he says, " just leave town?"

"Madison Springs is my home. My livelihood is here, and my friends are here." But my answer is just being ignored again, as usual.

"You can move that shop anywhere; you only sell coffee. It's not complicated. And as for friends, if you mean Beau..." He pauses here and a smug smile spreads over his face. "He agrees with me."

What! Beau *agrees* with him. That's new. Gonna love to hear how he came to *that* conclusion. There's no way on God's green earth that Beau is going to agree with Chase. "Beau! He agrees"—I pause and point to him—"with you? How? When?"

The smug grin never leaves his face. "Took my car to his place. We've become friends and have been discussing you."

"Beau... friends... with you..." I find my laughter hard to contain. Chase has really finally lost it.

"Yeah, only today I was talking to him about you tainting the town," Chase says, enjoying this way too much for my liking.

"You spoke to Beau today and he agreed with you. What did he actually say?" I'm wondering what he could have said.

"Well, he had just finished looking at the car and was telling me there was no charge."

Oh my God, so Beau actually said nothing. "So, he didn't actually answer you directly," I say, trying to get him to realize what he just said.

"His silence spoke volumes. That's all I needed to know. Deep down, he agrees with me." Beau was right; my family really was bat shit crazy.

"If he agrees with you, then why the hell"—my mother gasps at my word choice—"is he still living with me?"

"Do *not* say that word in front of our mother," Chase says in a stony tone, suddenly getting angry. "He's only there to keep up the front of being best friends."

Finally, I lose my patience. "Beau doesn't agree with you. Hell, I'm surprised he even agreed to look at the car. But let me tell you something. I'm not going anywhere. So get used to it."

Chase stands up so fast he causes the chair he was sitting in to fall over. "Language like that is *not* tolerated in this house. *Leave now!*" His words are said through gritted teeth. Mom has gone as white as a sheet, but I know she wouldn't have disagreed with him.

"Happily," I reply, getting up from the kitchen table. I leave the house without looking back, not even bothering to say goodbye or wish my mom a final parting happy birthday. I'm walking as fast as I can back to the apartment to talk to Beau and get to the bottom of everything, anger bubbling up in me with every step down the sidewalk.

Chapter 8 — Beau

The slamming of the apartment front door has me sitting up in my bed. After getting back from the garage, I'd jumped in the shower and grabbed some food before retreating to my bedroom. It was the coward's thing to do, but I knew Addy's family dinner was going to end in a shitstorm, and if I'd been in the living room when he came home, I'd have wanted to pull him into my arms and never let go. My emotions were haywire as it was thanks to Chase, and I might not have been able to hide my true feelings as well as normal.

I can hear him pacing. Another bad sign. Whatever went down was worse than usual, which means I'm going to have to go out there and see if he's okay. Swinging my legs off the bed, I'm just standing when my cell phone rings, and for a split second, I sigh with relief that I can put this off for a few more minutes. Looking at the screen, Mom's name is flashing.

"Hey, Mom," I say, answering the call and plonking back down on the edge of the bed.

"Beau, I bumped into Gladys earlier. She mentioned something about Arden going over to his moms for dinner." She evidently isn't happy with this, either.

"I swear the women in this town can spread news faster than the internet," I say, chuckling to myself.

"Probably. You know what happened? Is he home yet? Did you say anything?" There's an impatient tone to her voice that wasn't there a minute ago, causing me not to answer right away.

"Sometimes I wonder if you wouldn't mind adopting Addy." Mom was supposed to laugh at my joke, but there was silence on the other end of the phone. Had I hit a nerve?

Mom and Dad have always had a soft spot for Addy and adopting him seems like a little much, but it does make me wonder. If anything happened between me and Addy, then Mom and Dad would probably not bat an eyelid; Addy would officially become one of the family. Just the thought makes my heart beat faster, my mind drifting off to images of all of us around the Christmas tree singing carols, which is a completely stupid daydream to have. We live in the real world and not some cheesy Christmas movie.

"Beau!" my mom shouts from the cell, reminding me I was in the middle of a conversation with her.

"Sorry, what?" I'm feeling a little guilty for zoning out.

"Arden? His mom's?"

"Right. I really have no idea. He's home, and from the pacing I can hear, it must not have gone well." There's no point in lying to her. She'll find out at some point.

"Knew it. That family is just…" Mom bites out before she makes a strange growl that turns into a huffing noise down the line.

"I know, Mom, but they're all the family he has," I offer to try and get her to understand why Addy puts himself through this.

"That isn't a family." Her annoyance is now clearly evident.

"Mom, let me go talk to him and find out what happened. If it's anything major, I'll let you know," I offer, hoping to get her off the line.

"Fine, but one more thing." From the sound of it, I'm not going to like what she says. "Was Arden's brother at the garage today? Please tell me you didn't have something to do with whatever happened."

Shit. "Yeah, Mom, he came to the garage. He wanted me to check the brakes on his car. How that could've affected tonight, I don't know and won't until I go talk to Addy."

"Fine. Just promise to call me later and give him a hug from me."

"I will. Bye, Mom," I say before hanging up the call.

Pocketing my cell, I gingerly make my way out of the bedroom and towards the living room, stopping in the entrance way and leaning against the doorframe while I watch as Addy goes back and forth. His face is contorted with anger and the color of a tomato.

Addy looks up at me, makes a huffing sound, then turns and walks back the other way, not saying anything.

"Looks like you had a nice time," I start out with, trying to make him laugh, but all it does is make him stop, look at me, and open his mouth just to close it and start walking again.

I don't think this is going to be as simple as asking him how it went. I think we're going to need a drink. Making my way over to the fridge, I open the door and grab a couple of bottles, then close the fridge. I'm just about to turn back to Addy when a thought hits me. We may both have work tomorrow, but something is telling me that something stronger than beer might be needed. Putting the bottles on the countertop, I open one of the kitchen cupboards and take out two glass tumblers. Leaning down to the bottom cupboard, I grab a bottle of bourbon from the back. After pouring a shot into each glass and leaving the bottle on the countertop, I pick up one glass and carefully hide it behind my back before getting the beer and going over to Addy.

As he turns and walks back to me, I hold out the bottle to him, not saying anything. He takes it from my hand and takes a swig. "You got anything stronger?"

Smiling at him, I hand him the bourbon and watch as he knocks it back in one go before handing the glass back to me. Going back into the kitchen, I refill his glass and stick my open bottle of beer in the pocket of my jeans. Picking up my own bourbon, I turn back to the living room. Addy has stopped pacing and has one hand on the back of the couch, still swigging his beer.

"Sit down," I tell him, thankful that he has stopped pacing, but he doesn't move. I give him a few seconds to see if he sits, but still nothing. "Addy," I say, adding a little force to my voice, "Sit. Down."

This time, the words seem to register, and he finally moves to the front of the couch and throws himself on the seat and takes another long swig of the beer. Handing him the glass of bourbon, I take the bottle of beer out of my pocket, place it on the coffee table in front of us, and then join him on the couch where I take a sip of my drink and enjoy the burn as it travels down my throat.

"Now, can you tell me why you're trying to walk a trench in the apartment?" I ask, trying for humor again.

Addy looks over to me, but there is no laughter on his face. "Has my brother been coming to the garage?"

Yep, this is not going to be good. Should have told Addy the moment he first came in. Taking a deep breath, I consider lying, but I know it wouldn't take long for the gossip tree to get to him.

"Yeah..." But before I am able to go on and explain, Addy is out of the seat.

"And you didn't tell me? What the... Why didn't you tell me he'd been there?" This reaction seems to be a little extreme for Chase just coming to the garage, but I'm going to have to tread very carefully on how to get the truth out of him.

"Addy, sit back down and I'll explain," I reply, looking him in the eye.

Taking the seat next to me, he takes another sip of his drink and looks over to me. "Explain," he snaps.

"So, yeah, Chase came into the garage a few weeks ago—"

"A few weeks!" Addy tries to interrupt, but I just shoot him a look to let me finish talking.

"He said he wanted me to look at his car. At first I was going to tell him to fuck off, but against my better judgement, I didn't want to turn a customer away. So I had a look—you should have seen the state of it! It was a death trap on wheels. Have to admit I considered telling him it was fine." I paused to take another sip of my beer. "Anyway, I quoted way over what it was going to cost to repair, thinking he would go elsewhere, but he didn't."

"So, you fixed his car?" Addy looked surprised.

"God, I was tempted not to, but that car shouldn't have been on the road." If anything had happened after I'd seen the state of the car, I'm not sure I could've forgiven myself.

"Wow." And I know why he thinks that, but regardless of what I feel about his brother, it's other people I was thinking about, too.

"Look, from the start I could smell a rat, but on each occasion that he came to the garage, he never spoke to me," I say.

"Not once. He didn't even bad mouth me?" It should be shocking that when Addy was talking about his family, he didn't even once consider Chase would ask about his health.

"Nope, not once. Until today." This statement causes Addy to look up at me.

"Today?"

"Yeah, he came into the shop today complaining about the brakes, and I humored him by taking a look. But he started going on about you and asking all these weird questions. In fact, I made him squirm." Taking another sip of the bourbon, I wait for my words to sink in and for Addy to ask about what was said.

"What questions?" I'm not surprised that this is the first thing Addy asked since I'd been waiting for it.

"Was all about how could I live with you because you're gay. It was so funny. I actually tried to get him to say the word, but unfortunately, he didn't." I finally allow myself to smile. "I couldn't wait to come home and talk to you about it. But then your message came through."

I had thought upon hearing what had happened at the garage would have lightened the mood, but Addy still looks just as mad.

"Did he mention anything else?" Addy finally asks.

"Like?" I question, confused at where Addy is going with this and think back to the conversation.

"Me, this town, *anything*?"

"Addy, what the fuck is going on? What the hell happened at the meal tonight?" Before I go any further with this conversation, I need to get to the bottom of what happened.

"Well, I was a few minutes late, so I think they both thought I wasn't coming, but other than that, it all started out as normal," Addy starts.

"In other words, your mom ignored you." Anger starts to fill me.

"Pretty much, but then they started on me again…" Stopping mid-sentence, he takes a large swig of his drink before looking right at me. "You didn't agree with anything Chase said today, did you?"

"*What!* Why in the hell would I agree with anything he said? He's crazy and full of shit." His family has really done a number on him tonight. I don't think he's ever asked me if I agree with his family.

"He said you did; that deep down, you agree with him." Okay, now Addy's earlier reaction makes sense, and I can't help but laugh.

"He thinks that deep down I don't like the fact you're gay. But I set him right on that. Told him to his face that I didn't care." But I don't add that I'd almost said the reason I didn't care was because I am, too.

"What about the town?" Addy whispers into his drink. Thankfully, he seems to be calming down.

"He never mentioned the town. Why?" The town's lovely and no one would say anything against him.

"He and Mom say I am tainting the town." Addy looks up at me, and I spot the worry behind his eyes before he looks away.

"They said that?" My heart rate increases, anger now raging through me. How the hell can someone say that to their own family? Looking at Addy, I can see him nodding his head in agreement. "Addy, no." Rising to my feet, I pace to try to calm myself, the irony that I am doing the same thing I tried to stop Addy doing.

Pulling out my cell phone, I pull up my mom's number and hit dial. I don't think Addy hearing how nuts that is from me is going to be enough, but hearing it from Mom might help, too.

"Hey, Beau. How is he?" Mom intuitively knows this will be about Addy.

"They did a number on him," I reply, telling her the truth. "They said he's tainting the town."

"*They said what!*" I have to pull the cell away from my ear as she shouts and can just about hear again by the time she calls my dad over and tells him, too.

"Mom, I'm handing the phone over to Addy." I give my cell to Addy, and he stares at it for a second before taking it out of my hand and putting it to his ear. He knows better than to go against my mom.

"Mrs. Johnson," Addy says into the cell, and I watch as he listens to whatever my mom has to say, wishing I had the thought to put it on speaker because as he listens. I watch the remaining anger melt from his features and a smile tug at the corners of his mouth. Damn, my mom is good.

"Okay, Mrs. Johnson. Thank you. Bye," Addy finishes before handing the phone back to me.

"What the he—" — I check myself before saying hell, as that wouldn't have gone down well with my mom — "heck did you say?" I'm hoping Mom will tell me, but she just laughs and says, "Some home truths," and wishes me goodnight.

Hanging up the phone, I look over to Addy, who still has the hint of a smile on his face, and decide to see if *he'll* tell me.

"What did she say? I've been trying to get you to smile all evening, and she manages to get it done in thirty seconds." But his smile is infectious and I find myself grinning back at him.

"She, um. Well, she called my family crazy. Then went on to say I should divorce them or tell them to stick it and watch the looks on their faces as half the town tries to adopt me." His smile grows as he repeats what my mom said.

Yeah, I think if I had heard that, I would've been smiling, too. "*Can* you divorce your family?"

The question finally breaks him, and he bursts out laughing. "No clue," he manages to get out, "but it's a lovely idea."

"So, are you going to listen to my mom? Stop seeing your mom and *definitely* your brother?" I kick myself the moment the question falls from my mouth, and Addy stops laughing.

"You agree with her." His features morph back into surprise. "I thought she was kidding around to just make me feel better."

"No, Addy. Mom and I have thought this for a while. We don't like how they treat you, and after hearing this, how they talk to you."

He bites his lips and takes a sip of his drink. "There's one more thing they've been saying."

"What is that?" I ask, and from the look on Addy's face, I already know I won't like it.

"Well"—he takes a deep breath—"normally once they've mentioned about tainting the town, they then say that I only own a coffee shop and it would be easy to open another in a different location."

"Open another?" I'm confused. Why would they suddenly be encouraging him to expand to another location?

"No, not open another location. They mean close to the one in Madison Springs and open somewhere else. They're trying to force me to leave town."

And just like that, my anger and rage are back and at a boiling point.

Chapter 9 — Addy

The moment the words are out of my mouth, Beau looks as angry as I feel. Where the hell did this come from? Is he angry with me or what my family has been saying? He knocks back the last of his drink and stomps off to the kitchen, coming back a few minutes later with more of the amber liquid in the glass but holding the bottle by its neck. Stopping in front of me, he tops up my glass but still is not saying anything to me, but the anger is clear in his eyes.

"Beau," I say gently, hoping he will talk to me, but he just looks over to me.

Deciding it might be best to let him process whatever he's feeling, I sit back on the couch, swapping my glass with the beer bottle from the coffee table. Taking a couple swigs of beer, I keep watching Beau, hoping the pacing might calm him, even though it hadn't really helped me.

Finally, he stops and turns to me. "How long?"

"How long what?" I ask, wondering where his train of thought is going.

"How long have they been telling you to leave?"

"Um..." If Beau has gone crazy just knowing that they told me to leave tonight, he's going to go postal when he finds out just how long it's been going on. Maybe I can throw him off "Not long. Can't really remember when it started."

"Bullshit," Beau snaps back at me.

So much for me getting him to ignore this.

"Beau, does it really matter?" I ask, pleading with him.

"Yes, Addy, it does." I'm not sure I have ever seen Beau this angry, but it feels like it's directed at me.

"Beau!"

"Tell me, Addy. I need to know how long this has been going on." From the tone in his voice, there is no way I am going to be able to get out of this.

Taking a deep breath and sip of the beer, suddenly wishing it were the bourbon in my hand, I mumble, "A few months, maybe six."

And as predicted, Beau goes nuts. He slams his glass on the coffee table, and if it's possible, he goes a deeper shade of red.

"Six months!" Beau yells at me.

"Beau, please. Why are you getting so angry with me?" This is my family's doing. I had taken no notice of them, so why is Beau?

"Why am I angry?" Beau asks, staring at me in shock. "You're kidding me, right?"

"No, I'm not kidding. You know it's my family just being their normal, crazy selves." I say, hoping that Beau will see reason, but it doesn't seem to happen.

"Addy, your family has been pulling this shit for six months and you didn't think to tell me?"

Is that the reason he's angry? Because I didn't tell him? But that makes no sense whatsoever. There was no reason for me to tell him, but then again, isn't that the pot calling the kettle black considering Chase had been to the garage and he never told me?

"Why didn't you tell me about Chase coming to see you?" I challenge, my anger flaring.

Beau just looks at me not speaking, and I wonder if he heard until he snips back. "That's different," *So he* did *hear me.*

"No. It's exactly the same," I counter, the anger seeping into my voice.

"Please tell me how it's the same. You kept this from me for months. Chase came to the garage *three* times," Beau snaps back at me.

"You know I don't have to tell you every aspect of my life." I blurt, regretting the words as soon as they come out of my mouth.

"True. But when your family is trying to make you leave, then yeah, that is something you need to tell me."

"And if you *had* told me you'd worked on Chase's car and spoken to him, I wouldn't have gotten as freaked out as you are."

"Did you actually listen to *anything* I said?" Beau demands, and I just look at him and shrug my shoulders. "Because if you had, you would've heard that today was the *first time we spoke about anything other than his car.* So please tell me when I would have had the chance to tell you."

Damn, he has a point there. I'd forgotten he'd told me he'd only spoken to Chase for the first time today, but surely he could've called or come to the shop or even asked me to come to the garage before going to my mom's.

"You could've called and told me," slips from my mouth before I can stop the words.

"I wasn't going to tell you over the phone."

"You could've come to the shop or asked me to come to the garage." But I'm getting the feeling now that this is going to be an argument that's going to go around in circles.

"Funnily enough, we both have businesses to run. I wouldn't expect you to close the coffee shop just to come talk to me, and I sure as hell hope you would feel the same about me closing the garage."

"Fine," I reply curtly because I know he's right, but at the moment, I hate that fact.

I lift the beer to my lips in an attempt to finish the rest of the liquid, but it's now warm and leaves a bitter taste in my mouth. Ignoring Beau, I swap out my drinks, loving how the bourbon burns away the taste of the beer, and I feel it as it travels through my body, giving me a distraction.

"So are you going to tell me why you didn't say anything?" Beaus demands, but it looks like he is finally going to stop pacing.

"This again?" I say and internally roll my eyes since Beau can't seem to drop it.

"Yeah, this again." Beau comes back over to the couch, again taking his spot next to me. "What would have happened to me if for some reason you'd listened to them and left?"

"Happened to you?" Did he think I was going to demand he come with me?

"Yeah. If you closed and sold the shop, I would've lost my home and my best friend."

"But I was never going to listen to them, so I never gave it any thought. That's why I didn't tell you."

Yet Beau's words hit home. It had never occurred to me how a decision like that could affect him. Even if it was something that would never happen. This was his home, but he didn't own it. Should anything ever happen to me, then Beau would be homeless.

"This will always be your home," I state, but I'm trying to work out in my mind how I can make it legal.

"Until you leave," Beau snaps back.

"Beau, I'm not going anywhere." Yet a pain I don't understand flashes through his eyes, but it's gone in a few blinks of his eyelids.

"But you could," Beau mumbles.

"My family isn't going to run me out of this town," I reply.

"Deep down I know that." The anger seems to have gone, but it's been replaced with this desolate sadness. "But it's made me think."

"About?" I ask, not liking the conversation taking a sudden change of direction.

"You aren't always going to be here, Addy. You could meet someone and then what happens? I don't have any legal right to stay here. Plus, you might want to live here."

It's wrong, and the moment it happens I know it's wrong, but a laugh bursts out of me at the mention of meeting someone. God, I wish I could tell him that he is the only guy I have ever wanted and there has been no one to light a spark in me like him, but stuff like that can't be said to one's straight best friend, so instead, a laugh is what happens.

"Not. Funny." The anger seems to come back in Beau's voice.

"Of course, it is." Which again was the wrong thing to say from the look that Beau gives me.

"Me being homeless isn't funny."

"You know you're just being stupid. You would never be homeless. You live in the same town as your parents." Again, completely the wrong thing to say. I didn't intend to make out that his worries were nothing.

"*Stupid?*"

"Beau, listen to yourself." Hoping that by saying it gently, he will actually listen to what he is saying because this conversation is starting to really frustrate me.

"No, *you* listen. You seem to think this is no big deal."

Getting to my feet, I look over to him and just walk away, heading to my room. The frustration is just too much. There's nothing I'm going to be able to say to him that will make him see reason, so the best thing I can do is just walk away.

"Where are you going?" Beau snaps out after me.

"My room till you can see sense," I snap right back at him.

I slam my bedroom door like a petulant child, but I'm trying to make a point that I'm pissed at him. Okay, more like frustrated, but it has the same effect. Flopping on my bed, I just stare at the ceiling.

A few minutes later, the sound of voices drifts to my room and I lift my head up to listen, wondering if Beau has asked someone to come over, but the voices change and I realize he must have put on the tv, which for some reason annoys me even more.

That whole conversation was weird. From the moment he got angry to the stupid idea I was going to leave. Beau should have been angry at my family, not at me. Yet I was the one he was yelling at.

His reaction was just so unlike him. Is there something else going on with him I don't know about? But then if there is, it should be something he talks to me about. Are we both starting to keep secrets from each other? Okay, I haven't told him my feelings, but that's different. We've always been open and told each other our concerns. But as I lay there on the bed looking up, I realize it never occurred to me that this is something I should have told him. Every other single time my family had done something stupid, I talked to him, but not this. Why?

Why? The word rattles around in my brain. Why didn't I tell him this? Slowly it dawns on me. It was for the same reason I got so worked up when Chase said Beau agreed with him. It scares me that Beau might agree with them. That's the reason. A deep-seated fear buried in the back of my mind I didn't even know was there until it slammed into the forefront.

The fear that everything I've worked so hard for and cherish could be fake. That behind my back, the town actually doesn't like me, and Beau only lives with me because the rent is cheap and someone his age shouldn't still be living with his parents. Had my family somehow worked this out and tried to use it against me? Yet, if *I* didn't know that was truly how everyone felt, how on earth could *they*?

Getting up off the bed, I start pacing in my room, not liking where my thoughts are going but unable to stop them. The distance in the room isn't enough. It feels as though the walls are closing in on me. I need to get out of here.

Grabbing some jeans and a t-shirt from my closet, I quickly change, slipping my feet into my deck shoes. Shoving my wallet into my back pocket, I walk out. Beau looks up as I walk into the living room but doesn't say anything until he spots me picking up my keys from the side table.

"Where are you going?" but it comes out as more a demand than a question.

"Out," is all I reply because I really don't know where I am going. "I'll be back later." And before he can say anything else, I leave, closing the door behind me and letting go of the breath I'd been holding.

Once out on the sidewalk, I look up and down the street wondering where to go. Do I go and get my car and go for a drive? That's what most people do in situations like this, right? They get in their cars and drive to clear their heads. Maybe I should have thought about this more before leaving, had a better plan in place. Instead, I'm standing on the sidewalk wondering what to do.

The warmth from earlier in the evening has dissipated, making it a pleasant evening. A great time to go for a walk, so I decide to head to the town square. It's only a few blocks away, but it might be nice to sit there for a while and listen to the evening.

Walking down the main street, I look at all the shops closed for the evening, smiling as I think about each person who owns them. Some live above their places like me, but most have got houses dotted around the town. It's nice to watch the mixture of light and dark of the building windows and streetlights as the darkness of the night chases away the daylight. The sky is a mixture of blues and purples, which is so beautiful. But it's also nice to have the street to myself since few of the town folk are going to be out and about at this time of evening. When I reach the end of the street, I turn toward the town square.

The square itself isn't that big, but it's a nice patch of green in an otherwise brick world. A few benches have been added over the years, most of them memorials for members of the town that have passed. The square is busier than I expected. With the rest of the town quiet, I'm surprised to see Mrs. Nichols and her husband sitting on one of the benches.

"Good evening, Addy," Mrs. Nichols calls over to me with a wave.

"Good evening, Mr. and Mrs. Nichols," I say as I make my way over to them. "Lovely evening."

In this town, you can't just say good evening and hope that's going to be the end of it. No, you have to make polite conversation, too.

"Yes, we thought so, too," Mrs. Nichols replies. "That's why we decided to come out for a walk. But it's unusual to see you out here. Is everything okay?"

That right there is a good question. Is everything okay? Well, no, not really, but I can't say this to Mrs. Nichols. The news would be all over town by the time I walked away and sat down. I go to smile at her but stop myself when I remember her telling me she could spot my fake smile. If I do that, I'm just going to give the game away.

"Everything is fine, Mrs. Nichols," I say instead, making sure my voice is as cheerful as I can without it sounding forced. "I just forget how beautiful the town is at night."

Mrs. Nichols looks around her and smiles, and I know she'll have forgotten that seeing me in the town square at night is strange.

"Yes, the town is beautiful." Looking over to her husband, she grabs his hand. "Time for us to go home, I think." She slowly gets up from the bench, turning to her husband. Mr. Nichols is a few years older than his wife and isn't as mobile or as spritely, so I rush over to help.

"I got this, Mrs. Nichols," I say, taking hold of Mr. Nichols' arm and gently pulling him to his feet, only letting go when I know he's steady.

"Thank you, Addy. This getting old lark isn't fun," he states as he takes the crook of Mrs. Nichols' arm.

"You're not old, Mr. Nichols. You're distinguished," I reply, smiling at him and laughing along with the laughter that erupts from him. "Have a nice evening."

As they walk away, I can hear Mr. Nichols talking to his wife. "Such a nice boy that will make someone a lovely husband."

Mrs. Nichols looks back over her shoulder to me and nods her head and says something to her husband, but she's now too far away to hear. I don't think it can be anything bad from the smile on her face. However, her husband's words have hit a nerve. Sitting on the bench they just vacated, I say the word, "Husband." It sounds nice on my lips, but this is something I've never even thought about. But maybe it's time. Time to forget about something that is never going to happen, and time to try to start moving on with my own personal life. If tonight has shown me anything, it's that we might already be drifting apart.

Chapter 10 — Beau

While staring at the images on the screen, I'm not really paying attention to what is on or being said by the actors. What I *am* thinking about is what the hell just happened. When Addy had gotten off the call with my mom, it felt like everything had been resolved. But then he mentioned the leaving town thing, and I'd lost it, and he still couldn't see why I was so angry.

Losing your best friend and home is something to worry over, but the fact he'd kept this information secret from me is what hurt the most. I'd thought our friendship had meant more than that. It did to me. But for him to say that my keeping Chase coming into the shop to myself was the same thing? What? Three times that had happened, and the one time we talked, I was coming home to tell him. So, yeah, not the same thing.

Looking down the hall toward Addy's room, I wonder if I should go down there and try to talk to him again, but I don't move from my position on the couch. Instead, I pick up the remote and change channels, hoping to find something to grab my attention and stop thinking about what happened.

The sound of Addy's bedroom door opening catches my attention, and it takes all the willpower I have not to look up at him as he comes into the living room. He's changed. Looks to be going out. Where on earth could he be going at this time of night? And he hasn't asked to borrow the car. Curiosity overtakes and I finally ask him in what I hope is a friendly voice, but the "out" I get in return tells me it wasn't as friendly as I thought, and I have to say that rankles me.

The apartment door slamming echoes around the room, and a part of me wants to chase after him, but that wouldn't be the behavior of a best friend. That's the behavior of a boyfriend. Plus, at least I have the apartment to myself. Normally a time I love. Getting to watch all the programs Addy hates or sticking a movie in that I know he wouldn't watch. But tonight, the emptiness of the place feels different.

Looking around the living room, I try to figure out what the difference could be. Everything *looks* the same. Nothing has moved. The only thing different are the thoughts in my head. If Addy were to leave either the town or move in with someone else, this is what it would be like every night if he allowed me to stay here. This is the emptiness I would experience every waking moment. It would be just me in this entire apartment.

Getting to my feet, I turn the tv off and go to my room, hoping the empty feeling stays in the living room. Flopping down on the bed, I stare at the ceiling trying not to think. But the silence becomes deafening, and I know I need to get out of this place.

Jumping off the bed, I quickly pull on my tennis shoes, grab my apartment keys, and leave. Once outside, I pause and wonder where to go and think maybe a walk to the town square would be nice, but I know I need to talk to someone who might understand, so I turn and head to my parents' place instead.

The walk to my parents, helped by the warm evening air, acts like a balm on my soul. After knocking on the front door, I try the handle. If it's locked, then they will be in bed or heading there shortly, but the handle turns easily, and I walk into the house.

"Beau?" Mom looks up at me as I walk in. "Everything okay?"

"Hey. Sorry to stop by so late. Had an argument with Addy," I reply to explain my sudden appearance at the house.

"Really?" she asks, her surprise deepening. "He seemed okay after he got off the phone with me."

"Yeah, he was, but there was something else he wasn't telling me." I say as I sit down in a chair opposite her.

Before I'm able to explain further, she calls out for my dad to join us and watches as he appears from the kitchen holding two glasses with a light golden liquid. My guess is it's my mom's favorite white wine in them.

"Hey, Beau. Didn't hear you." Mom gives him a look, and I try but fail to hide my snigger, causing Mom to shoot me a look, as well. Guessing Dad didn't hear Mom shouting I was here, probably too engrossed in the task of pouring wine, "We were just about to go sit out back and enjoy the evening before heading to bed."

"Beau and Arden have had an argument," Mom mumbles to Dad, which causes him to look over to me, surprise evident on his face, too.

"That's not like you. You want this?" Dad asks, handing me one of the glasses. "I can get another."

"Thanks, but I'm okay. Just needed to get out of the apartment." Dad hands one of the glasses to Mom and proceeds to sit beside her on the couch.

"Want to tell us what happened?" Dad asks but gives Mom a look I can't quite understand, so I decide to ignore it. Instead, I go over everything that happened from the moment Addy got off the call. Once my tale is finished, I sit back and wait for Mom and Dad to agree with me.

During the entire time I was talking, they just sat there and listened. Didn't make any noises or move their heads in agreement, but now that I've finished, they're both looking at each other, their faces a mixture of bemusement and worry. Both of them seem to want to say something, but neither of them goes first. Or maybe it's that neither one of them *wants* to go first.

"Beau," Mom finally says, going first but taking a sip of wine after she says my name, "sorry, but I think you might have overreacted."

"Mom!" I chastise, not believing what just came out of her mouth. How can she be on Addy's side in all of this?

"Your mom is right, Beau," Dad pipes up, and I can't believe that both my parents are on Addy's side in all of this.

"Arden doesn't have to tell you everything that's going on in his life. You don't own him," Mom gently continues, using her best, *I understand, really, I do* mom voice, while at the same time disagreeing with what I've said.

"I know I don't own him," I counter.

"Yet here you are sounding like you do." I'm left speechless, but her tone works, and the words filter into my brain. *Is that how I was acting?* But if I was, why didn't Addy just say that?

"He never said anything," I say, starting to feel rather foolish.

"Beau, he probably didn't even see it himself," Dad starts. "You guys have been very…" He stops and looks over to Mom as if he's trying to find the right word to describe our relationship. "Close" is the word he decides on.

"Of course we're close. He's my best friend." I'm beginning to think that Dad has completely lost it.

"Then maybe you need to start acting like it," Mom comes back with.

"I was," I counter, defending my actions yet again.

"No. You were acting like a jealous…" Mom looks over to my dad, which is really starting to piss me off. Each look is a silent form of communication only they know, but this time, I spot the very subtle nod of Dad's head. "Boyfriend," Mom finishes.

And there it is. The one word that shakes my foundations and stops me dead. Had I let my façade slip? Had I given the game away? Had I been acting like the jealous lover? Because I never meant for that to happen. Looking over to Mom and Dad, I find they are both looking at me, waiting for me to answer them, but the words have dried up in my mouth.

"Beau, are you okay?" Dad asks, concerned that I haven't answered them.

"Do you think Addy thought that?" I finally manage to get some words out of my mouth.

Yet this time, it's Mom and Dad who go silent, appearing confused by my words. I need to try to convey to them that I'm worried about giving the wrong impression to Addy because I'm straight and not because I'm afraid of what his reaction would be. That he would reject me.

"Um," Mom tries but doesn't add anything more.

"I'd hate for Addy to think that. It would make things very awkward." Again, they just exchange *the look*.

"Really?" Dad asks.

"Well, yeah. I don't want him to think that." And even to my own ears, this doesn't sound convincing.

Mom elbows Dad in the side in a shut-up gesture, or maybe a watch-your–words gesture. "Yeah, it wouldn't be right," Dad finally says.

"What should I do now?" I ask.

"Did he say when he was coming back?" Mom asks.

"No, just said later. God, I wish I'd realized that I'd sounded like that." If I had, the evening could have ended so differently.

"It will be fine. Give him some space, and the next time you see him, apologize for being a dumbass." This very sound advice is coming from my dad.

"Dumbass?" I'm not sure I've ever heard my dad say this to me before.

"Yep, you deserved it this time. Now, do you want some wine and all of us can go out the back," Dad asks, deciding that it's time to change the subject.

"Be nice to go out the back for a while, but think I'll just have some water." Because I really don't want to go back to the apartment just in case it's still empty.

"In that case, get your glass and come join us." Dad gets to his feet and holds his hand out to Mom, who takes it and gets to her feet, then both of them walk out the back.

Going into the kitchen, I walk over to the fridge, pull out a bottle of water, and go to make my way outside, but pause just inside the door as I hear Dad whisper to Mom, "You think they'll be okay?"

"Yeah, they will be." I wait for the, "They've been friends for too long," but it never comes, which makes the statement strange. But Dad's answer is just as odd.

"Arden's a good one. Beau should keep hold of him."

What!

I want to go out there and ask what they mean, but it would give the game away that I'd been eavesdropping, and from their hushed tones, this is something they don't want me to hear.

Opening the door noisily so they know I'm coming, I go out and join them. The backyard at my parents' place has always been a favorite part of the house. There's a large, covered deck that stretches the length of the house. On one end, there's a barbeque; in the middle, a table with chairs for four; and at the far end, a set of grey rattan chairs with a small matching table that is just big enough to hold our glasses but was mostly used as a foot stool by Dad. Mom and Dad had moved two of the chairs so they were closer to each other and placed another one just off to the side, giving us all a superb view of the garden.

"So, what did I miss?" I ask while sitting down.

"Dad was just saying how Arden is a nice boy." And I somehow manage to hide my surprise that they repeated some of the conversation.

"Considering the family, yeah he is," Dad adds, because how Addy hasn't become bitter over the years is still a wonder to us all.

"Losing Mr. Walker was hard on his mom," Mom states like this is a good enough reason for all the crazy that is Addy's mom.

"So did Addy," Is the only counter argument I have, but it's the truth, too.

"People deal with grief differently. Arden's Mom turned to the church."

"Mom, you're defending her," I say, looking over to Dad, both of us with knowing smirks on our faces when Mom finally figures out exactly how she sounds.

"What! Is that how it sounded?" she exclaims, and both Dad and I nod our heads in a yes.

"God, that woman is as crazy as a box of frogs." This statement leads to Dad and me laughing and then Mom joins in, setting the tone for the next couple of hours.

When I spot Mom yawning more and more, I know it's time to go home, having stayed longer than I intended. It's been nice sitting there chatting about everything. Them asking about the garage and then pretending to be interested as I explain about this new machine I purchased, then me pretending to be interested as Dad explained about his job. They'd offered for me to stay over, but I wanted to go home and clear the air with Addy.

Considering the amount of time I'd been at my parents, I was sure he would have been home.

Walking back to the apartment, I take the time to have a look around the town. It looks so different from the daytime, the lights from apartments dancing on the sidewalk, creating shadows even in the dark of night. When I get to our apartment, I look up and see the living room window shrouded in darkness, but that doesn't surprise me. Addy is probably in his bedroom, and from this angle on the sidewalk, you can't see his room.

Unlocking the apartment door, I walk into silence, but it doesn't feel like it did earlier. It has the feel of home again. Turning on the light, I place my keys on the side table.

"Addy?" I call out but hear nothing in reply.

"Addy. You home?" Again, silence.

Really, is he giving me the silent treatment? But I decide that I'm not going to stand for it. Walking to his bedroom, I see no light coming from under the door. *Odd. Did he go to sleep?* I gently knock on the door just in case he is sleeping. "Addy, you awake?" I ask as I open the door. His room is shrouded in darkness, but even in the dim light, I can see his bed is empty.

Closing the door, I go back into the living room and turn on the tv, sit on the couch, and check the time on my watch. It's not really that late being only eleven, but it's still late enough to worry that he isn't back yet. Maybe wherever he went he's lost track of time, so I'll just wait here for him.

Waking with a start, I wonder why I'm sleeping on the couch in the living room and then remember about Addy. Why didn't he wake me when he came in? Looking at my watch, I see that it's almost one in the morning. Creeping down the hallway, I quietly knock on Addy's door, but this time don't say anything. Opening the door, I stick my head in to still find the room empty.

Closing the door, I head back into the living room, turn off all the lights, and head into my bedroom. Turning on the bedside lamp, I quickly change, climb into bed, and turn off the light, hoping sleep takes me. But my worry for Addy is stronger than sleep. Flicking on the lamp, I pick up my cell and call Addy's number. It's not answered and clicks over to his voicemail. I consider leaving one but don't. Friends don't chase over friends... right?

Chapter 11—Addy

The walk to the town square was supposed to settle me, help me make sense of the evening, and yet I'm still sitting on the bench staring at the scene in front of me and still feeling as unnerved as before. This whole evening has made no sense at all, from my reaction to Beau thinking he somehow agreed with my family and then to Beau's reaction to finding out what they've been trying to do. He knows they've been doing and saying shit for years, so why was tonight so different?

The town is now covered in the darkness of night, and I hadn't even seen it happen. Maybe it's time to head back home and figure out, or maybe even fix, what happened between me and Beau, but I can't face getting off the bench and going home. Maybe a complete change of scenery might help, even if it is only for a few hours. Pulling my cell out of my pocket, I order a taxi. This might be a town in the middle of nowhere, but it has a great taxi service—strangely.

The nearest bar is on the outskirts of town and is normally frequented by people from a few of the other neighboring towns. It isn't a gay bar, and If I want that, well... I have no idea where I'd go, but it's a friendly place and that's what I need right now. The taxi driver drops me off outside, and I quickly pay and head into the bar. Thankfully, the place isn't busy, but it's not quiet either; it's a pleasant mix of both.

"Addy! Good to see you," the bartender shouts over to me, and it's nice to see that Justin is on duty tonight. We've known each other since high school, and I know he'll keep me company when he can, so I take a seat at one of the barstools that line the front of the bar. "Where's Beau?" he asks.

"We aren't joined at the hip, you know," I snap back at him, then instantly feel guilty. "Hey, sorry, Justin. Had a rough night."

Justin looks over and gives me a knowing smile. "Yeah, I heard. Dinner with your mom, right?"

"How do you know?" I ask, surprised the news has managed to travel this far out of town.

Walking up to me, Justin gives me a gentle smile. "Small town. Need I say more? Now, what can I get you.?"

"Yeah, small town." But I'm smiling at the thought myself now. "Just a beer. Anything you have on tap."

"Coming right up." Justin picks up one of the glasses and begins pouring my beer. "Here you go," he says when he finishes, handing me my drink.

"Thanks," I reply, enjoying the ice-cold liquid as it travels down my throat.

"So, what happened?" Justin asks, wiping down the bar in front of him. "Even if you're having a shit evening, it's even stranger to see you here without Beau."

"Evening with my family was the same shit, different day," I start, taking another sip of the beer. "Then argued with Beau about them afterward."

Surprise flashes in Justin's eyes. "You guys never argue. Don't think I've ever even seen you raise your voices at each other."

"Yeah. He was being an idiot, and I'm not going back to the apartment till he gets his head out of his ass."

Justin laughs at me. "Sure you guys will sort it out."

Before he has a chance to say anything more to me, a customer comes up to the bar, grabbing Justin's attention, and he goes over to serve them, leaving me alone with my thoughts. Justin's reaction to me saying I argued with Beau surprised me. Has he really never seen us argue? That can't be right.... But as I sit there sipping my beer, I look back at my friendship with Beau, and Justin *is* right. The last time we had an argument was when I'd spoken to him about coming out to my mom—which, in hindsight, might not have been the best thing to do. Not that I regret my decision.

So, that is making this evening more strange. Shit from my family is nothing new, but I'm actually annoyed that they have dragged Beau into this. When I came out to my family, I knew they were going to start doing or saying something, and I had told Beau this, which he just used as more of a reason not to tell them. It came as no surprise back then, so why is this time any different with my family? The only thing is they've gotten Beau involved, too.

Was Beau happy to sit on the side lines letting me deal with it and just being there when I needed to vent, but when he was suddenly personally involved by my family, it all became too much? But that doesn't make any sense either. Beau and his mom must have talked about me and my situation in the past for him to get her on the phone.

As I sit there sipping my beer, I don't think I am ever going to find the answers to what really happened tonight, and I'm just going to have to blow it off as something that occasionally happens in a friendship.

"Anyone sitting here?" An unfamiliar masculine voice from behind me asks.

"No. Help yourself," I reply with disinterest, not really paying that much attention to the newcomer but still wondering why he goes and sits on the stool right beside me when there are so many others available down the bar.

"Couldn't help but overhear, this Beau, is that your girlfriend?" The strange voice asks, but this time, I pay more attention to it. It's strong, warm, and with a little bit of a Southern drawl in it, but not strong enough that he spent his whole life there.

"What? Beau, my girlfriend?" But that's when it hits me. That is what's been bugging me. Beau standing there, demanding that I tell him something as if he were my boyfriend. Subconsciously playing with my emotions. He may not have even known it, but he was toying with feelings that he could never possibly give back to me. This is why I'd gotten so annoyed and needed to get out of the apartment.

"Yeah, I couldn't help but overhear you talking to the bartender." I finally look up at the friendly voice next to me, and my heart jumps into my throat. *Holy shit, this man is gorgeous.* Thick brown hair frames his face, and he has a strong jaw line with just enough stubble to make it sexy, and his eyes... hazel-colored irises stare back at me, his smile causing them to shine.

"Beau isn't my girlfriend." Smirking at the thought, I have never considered that Beau could be a girl's name, "He's my best friend."

"So, is there a girlfriend on the scene?"

Is this guy hitting on me? That hasn't happened in so long and I decide to see if I can have some fun with it.

"Nope, I'm perfectly single," I reply, making sure I don't mention any sex. Let's see if he can guess that he's much more my type than any girl ever.

"So, single?" the handsome man asks.

"Yep." And because I can't keep referring to him as "the handsome man," I hold out my hand in greeting. "The names Arden, but everyone calls me Addy."

The man takes hold of my hand in a firm shake that, if I'm not mistaken, contains a little squeeze, and because I can, I gently squeeze it back. "Well, pleased to meet you, Addy. I'm Jamie."

"Justin," I shout up the bar to grab his attention. "Another beer when you have a chance?" I ask while pointing to Jamie so he knows it is for him. Justin quickly pulls another glass, handing it over.

"So, are you new in town or just passing through?" I'm sure he bats for the same team as me, and a tumble in the stack might be nice, especially after the day I've had.

"Actually, I just moved to these parts. Got a place here in Madison Springs." Well, this is a surprise .

"Madison Springs?" I say, trying and failing to hide the surprise in my voice that someone moved here willingly. I love this town, but we really don't get many newcomers.

"Yeah, I passed through town a few years ago and fell in love with the place. I couldn't stand living in the city anymore, so I decided it was time to move." He pauses and has a look around the bar, checking to see if anyone might be listening before continuing, "But the gay scene seems to be a bit quiet. Thought there might be at least *one* bar nearby."

Throwing my head back and laughing, I have to place my hand on his knee to keep my balance and I can feel the warmth of his skin coming through his clothes. It brings me back to the conversation, and so I whisper to him, "You're looking at the only gay scene in Madison Springs."

"And what a good-looking scene it is." *Okay, that was definitely flirting.*

"Um, thank you." God, how lame was that? *I need to up my game.*

Looking over to Jamie, I spot him staring at me. "Wait, you look familiar. Have we met before?" Jamie questions, brow quirked.

Giving him a close look, I try to rack my brain, but he doesn't look familiar to me at all. Believe me, I would remember this man if I had met him before. "I would remember you if we'd met before."

"Maybe I've seen you around town on the few occasions I've popped in," Jamie says, and he doesn't stop looking at me.

"Maybe." But as I think about it, I don't remember the gossip tree mentioning someone new being in town. "How long have you been here?" I ask because the only way the ladies of this town wouldn't know is if it has been hours.

"Only a few days, but I've tried to keep a low profile. Didn't think about the whole gay thing when I moved to a small town, and I've been trying to figure out how everyone would react."

"Well, that explains it," I blurt, the words slipping out of my mouth before I'm able to filter them.

"Explains what?" he asks, giving me a quizzical look.

"How the gossip tree doesn't know about you yet." But he just gives me an even more quizzical look, and I know I'm going to have to explain. "The gossip tree is the old ladies of the town. They know and talk about *everyone's* business. If you've been keeping a low profile, they might not have picked up on you being here yet. Heed this warning: be prepared for welcome baskets and God knows what else."

"Noted," But a small worry line has appeared between his eyebrows.

"Honestly, you don't have anything to worry about. They are lovely, and if you're worried that they might not like that you're gay, then don't be. They'll probably spend most of their time trying to set you up with relatives."

I had timed the last statement just as he had taken a sip of his beer, which he then proceeded to spit all over the bar, making me laugh. I didn't think he was going to spray his drink everywhere.

"Relatives?" Jamie splutters.

"Yeah, I think I've been set up with two grandsons, one nephew, and I think there might have even been a great-grandson. They're all old romantics at heart." Even though one time, the person they set me up with hadn't even been gay, every single time I had had fun.

"Wow," is all Jamie is able to say, and I could say more, especially about some of the questions they can ask, but I decide to leave it as a lovely surprise for him.

"So, Jamie, what do you do for a living?" I ask, wanting to get to know this gorgeous man a little more.

"I'm a lawyer," he whispers like this could be a bad thing, which is just making me laugh again. I'm not sure a man has made me laugh like this in a long time. He has this strong, confident air about him, but every now and then it slips and a hint of insecurity escapes, and it's... lovely. Which isn't the right word to describe it but the only one I can think of at the moment.

"Lawyer. Impressive. So, are you planning on opening an office in Madison?" I'm keeping my fingers crossed that he is. It would be nice to bump into him more often.

"At the moment, the firm I work for is letting me telecommute, but it's not something I want to do long term. Honestly, I haven't thought about it."

"You move to a new town but don't make plans? You're one of two things," I say critically. The moment I decided what I wanted to do with my life, I was set. Not sure I could move to another town where I didn't know anyone without a plan for the future.

"Oh, and what are those?" Jamie asks, taking a sip of his beer but smiling over to me.

"Well, you're either very brave or very stupid," I respond, returning his smile.

"Which one do you think it is?" But the humor in his voice is making his eyes shine.

"Jury's still out," I say. The laughter that erupts from him sends a warm feeling all over my body. The laugh is just like him, deep and throaty and completely addictive as I start laughing along with him.

When we've finally stopped laughing, a silence comes over us, but it's not an uncomfortable one. More peaceful. The only other time I've felt this comfortable in silence has been when I've been talking to Beau.

"You know, the town could really use a law office. I think at the moment the nearest lawyer is the next town over," I suggest, hoping he won't mind me butting into his life.

"Really? I'd been trying to see if there was one in town but couldn't find anything."

"Yeah, the last lawyer died quite a few years ago, and not everyone wants to stay in or move to somewhere like Madison." Small town living isn't for everyone, especially some of the kids.

"Hmm," is all he offers. I'm not sure that Jamie is really paying too much attention to what I'm saying at the moment; instead, I have a feeling he's thinking about what I've already said, which I'm taking as a positive sign. Eventually, Jamie finally focuses back on me. "Sorry. I zoned, didn't I?"

"Maybe a little. What were you thinking?" I'm silently hoping he'll share what he was thinking about.

"Just the other day I spotted this great shop on the main street. It would be perfect for an office, but I didn't look into it. I'm now thinking I just might?"

The only shop on Main Street that could be used is right by my shop, which would be perfect. It really would give me an excuse to try and bump into Jamie more often.

"I know the one. It's just a few doors down from mine."

"You have a shop in town?" he asks, and I realize that we've talked about his career, but I've never mentioned what I do.

"Yeah, I own the coffee shop." And Jamie's face lights up.

"You own the coffee shop?" He seems so excited at this thought he's almost jumping up and down on his stool.

"Yeah," I say, repeating myself and chuckling.

"*That's* where I know you from. The coffee shop."

When the hell did I miss him coming in? But then, if it had been during a busy time, I can literally go from one person to the next and not really pay much attention. The only time I hate in the shop is when I don't have a chance to talk and meet new people. If I'd paid more attention that day, I could've known Jamie a lot longer.

"Your coffee is some of the best I've ever tasted," he states, and I realize that Jamie is still talking, so I look over to him. "What beans are they? South African? Indian? Oh, are they Rwandan?"

"You know coffee?" I ask, my mouth hanging open, and Jamie is finally laughing at something I've said.

I signal to Justin for more beers before I begin talking about my favorite topic, and just like that, the rest of the evening vanishes and Justin is coming up to us to tell us he's closing. *Where the hell did the time go?* And I realize that for the first time I haven't thought of Beau in hours.

Chapter 12 — Beau

Waking up the following morning, I lay in bed for way too long listening to the sounds in the apartment. I'm hoping to hear the sound of Addy moving around and try to ignore the relief I feel knowing that he did, in fact, come home last night when I do. Taking a deep breath, I gingerly get out of bed, throw on some sweatpants and a t-shirt, and head to the sounds of Addy in the kitchen.

"Morning," I say, Addy jumping at the sound of my voice. He apparently hadn't heard me come in.

"Jesus, Beau, you just scared the crap out of me!" Addy says, but at least he's smiling at me.

"Sorry. What are you doing?" I ask.

"Making coffee," Addy replies, pulling out mugs from the cupboard.

Making coffee? Addy never normally makes coffee during the week, preferring to go to the shop, have everything set up, and get his morning fix there. If he's making it here at the apartment, I have an awfully bad feeling in the pit of my stomach.

The kitchen in the apartment is just off to the side of the living room. It's not a bad sized kitchen for two people, but to make it a little more open, we'd knocked out the wall between the living room and kitchen and made a breakfast bar. When you look at it, it looks like a large window but without the glass . Yet for some reason, we kept the original doorway and door so we could still close off the room if needed.

Pulling out one of the bar stools, I lean against the breakfast island and look over toward Addy, who still has the odd smile on his face. *What the hell?*

"Late night last night?" I ask, thinking this is why he needs the coffee earlier this morning.

"Yeah, probably got in just after one." Addy still isn't mentioning the fight and is acting like nothing happened at all last night. Should I do the same, ignore it like he's doing? But I know I won't be able to.

"Where'd you go?" I cringe since I didn't mean it to sound so accusing. It was supposed to sound friendly, one friend asking another what they did, but even to my ears, I know I failed.

"Just the town square, but then went for a drink after that." The only place he would have been able to go for a drink is the bar just outside town, and I'm surprised at the pang of jealousy that hits, knowing he went there without me.

"Oh," I reply because I can't think of anything else to say.

"Justin asked how you were," Addy says, looking over his shoulder to me.

"That was nice of him," I reply rather flatly.

Addy turns towards me then, handing me a steaming cup of coffee, and then goes back to leaning against the kitchen worktop staring off into space. He isn't smiling anymore but still has an odd look on his face, almost dreamy. What on earth *happened* last night?

"So, um," I start, taking a sip of the coffee to disguise the deep breath I'm talking. But Addy cuts me off before I'm able to ask about last night.

"Shit, look at the time. I have to get going." Addy rushes past me, carrying his coffee cup, and just a few seconds later, I hear his bedroom door close.

Cupping my hands around the warm mug in front of me, I lean my elbows on the breakfast bar and wonder what the hell just happened. Why wasn't I able to get everything off my chest and why did he act as though nothing had happened last night? But the biggest question is why any of that is pissing me off so much. Do I really still want him mad at me? Because that isn't going to accomplish anything.

When I hear Addy's bedroom open, I wonder if he's decided to come back and talk, but I guess not since I just hear the bathroom open, then close, and the shower start. Looks like there's no way we're going to be talking this morning. Finishing my coffee, I make my way back to my room and wait. The moment I hear the shower turn off, I get my own shower stuff, and as soon as I'm sure Addy is back in his room, I make my way into the bathroom.

Closing the door behind me, I take a moment to breathe in the scent of Addy's shower gel lingering in the steam. It's one of the only reasons I was so quick to get in here after hearing Addy leave. The knowledge I would be able to smell him without giving myself away, and after last night, I need the calming balm for my soul.

Turning on the shower, it only takes a moment before it's up to the temperature I like, the steam already billowing out, dispersing the scent left by Addy. Jumping under the hot spray, I let the water thump against my muscles, easing the tension. Something must have happened when he went out last night. *Did he meet someone? But who?* Madison Springs isn't the hot bed of the gay scene. Maybe he spoke with Justin.

Shaking my head to try to stop overthinking what on earth is going on with Addy, I pick up my own shower gel, quickly lathering up my body.

As I step back under the stream of water, a thought hits that maybe I can catch Addy before he leaves for work. Quickly washing my hair, I turn off the shower, wrap a towel around my waist — droplets of water still clinging to my skin — and leave the bathroom, the steam following me in waves.

"Addy," I call out to see if he's still here.

"See ya, Beau," Addy shouts, closing the apartment door. He must have heard the shower turning off but still thought I was in the bathroom. For a split second, I consider running after him but what's the point? I'll pop over to the coffee shop at lunch time, and if he isn't busy, hopefully, I'll be able to talk to him then.

Going back to my room, I towel myself down, rubbing the towel through my hair before throwing it in the direction of my laundry basket. Walking over to my window, I peek out to check the weather, not worried about anyone seeing me in my nakedness: one, because at this time of the morning, it's doubtful anyone would be on the street, and two, my bedroom windows cannot be seen from the front sidewalk.

There's not a cloud to be seen in the sky, the color bright and inviting like those crystal-clear oceans you see in documentaries. But that also means it's going to be a warm day, and the garage can be very unpleasant on days like that. Picking out some sturdy cargo pants and a tank top with the Jackson Auto logo embroidered in the corner, I get dressed. When I get to the garage, I'll put on some coveralls to protect my clothes, and depending on the level of heat, I might keep just my underwear on. Sometimes it's the only way to keep cool.

Once changed, I pick up my keys and leave the apartment, walking to the garage. I can already feel the heat in the air. *Yeah, it's going to be a very warm day.* I begin to mentally go over the cars scheduled to come into the garage, thinking of anything that might be problematic in the heat, but nothing springs to mind.

The entrance to the apartment is at the back of the building so as not to cause confusion with the front store entrance. Walking around the side of the building and to the front of the shop, I can't help but look inside. A man is standing at the counter and looks to be chatting with Addy, who's smiling at him. Normally I wouldn't think anything of it — Addy smiles at everyone — but this is that same goofy smile he had on this morning. Is he smiling like that at the customer or is it still left over from last night? The urge to go inside is overwhelming, but I just keep pushing forward. Whatever or, more worryingly, *whoever* is causing the smile, I'm sure Addy will tell me.

Opening up the garage doors and locking them in place, I walk to another door at the back of the garage and lock that one open, too. Sometimes, if I'm lucky, having all the doors open will let through a cooling breeze. Going into the back room that doubles as my office and changing area, I pull off my cargo shorts and slip on my coveralls, but instead of pulling them up and slipping my arms in, I tie the arms around my waist just to keep cool, planning to only pull them on if I have work under one of the cars.

Before long, my first customer arrives, and thankfully, it's a bigger job — a full brake change, including the rotors, calipers, and pads on all four wheels, which will take me a good couple of hours and should take my mind off Addy. I let the customer know that the car should be ready about lunchtime, though I'll call them once I'm finished so they don't need to wait, I untie my coveralls and slip them up over my shoulders. I could use the lift and work quickly wheel by wheel but decide to use the car jack instead. The job might take longer, as I have to jack the car up and down each time, but that means I'm not standing for hours putting extra pressure on my knee. This way I can sit on a low stool I have, or sometimes I've even been known to just sit on the floor.

The job goes like a dream, the discs and pads going straight on with no complications. I got so lost in my work that I forgot all about Addy until the job was done and I looked at the clock in the corner and saw that it was well past one in the afternoon. I called the customer to let him know the car was done and ready for pick up but that I was heading out for lunch, and he agreed to come by in an hour.

Changing out of my overalls and back into my pants, I close up the garage, placing an OUT TO LUNCH sign on the front window. But my cell phone number is on the bottom stating to call if there's an emergency. Once done, I walk towards the coffee shop. The heat has built during the day, and I'm glad I changed.

I'm only a few shops down from Addy's when a movement inside one of the other shops catches my eye. Normally, I wouldn't have paid it any attention, but this particular shop has been closed for a while. Stopping, I stare inside to make sure nothing untoward is happening and spot two men talking; one I recognize as the realtor, and the other has his back to me. Realizing the shop is fine, I continue my walk to Addy's coffee shop.

The bell rings as I open the door, and I watch as Addy's head snaps up, a huge smile on his face that falters for just a split second when he spots that it's me before coming back, though not quite as big as before. *Was he expecting someone else?* But who?

"Hey," I greet, walking up to the counter, thankful that the shop is quiet at the moment.

"Hey," Addy replies blandly, following up with, "Coffee?" But he's already turning away from me and working with his back toward me now.

"Been busy?" I ask, going up to the end of the counter and leaning on it slightly to wait for my coffee.

"In this heat? Not really."

"You know you need to look into those iced coffees," I say, and Addy's head snaps over in my direction as he glares at me, causing me to laugh.

"Blasphemous," he states and pretends to shudder, which only causes me to laugh harder. When it comes to coffee, Addy thinks it should be served hot. He doesn't care what type of coffee as long as it's hot, but he point blank *refuses* to sell it cold.

"You know, I'm sure you could find one you like, or maybe you could add some iced tea." I'm trying to rein in my laughter, but it feels good to be laughing with him, or, well, at him.

"Iced tea?" Addy repeats, and I can't believe that he never thought of it before. "You might be onto something there."

"You could always ask Mrs. Nichols or Mrs. Phillips if they have a recipe they'd be willing to share. Could sell it as a local beverage then."

"Brilliant, you're a genius," Addy states.

"Really, it's only taken you till now to figure that out?" I retort, loving the joyful air between us at the moment.

"You hungry?" Addy asks, suddenly changing the subject.

"Well, I was hoping to get some food and not just a coffee."

Laughing, he hands me my coffee and nods his head in the direction of one of the tables. "Go take a seat, and I'll bring over a sandwich and join you."

There's no point in him asking me what I want. He already knows my favorite sandwich is a BLT, and I'd bet my bottom dollar that is exactly what I am going to get. Sure enough, five minutes later, he's walking over to me, a coffee cup in one hand and a plate in the other. Placing the plate in front of me, he then takes a seat opposite.

"Aren't you having anything?" I ask, surprised that he hasn't gone back to get his own meal.

"Had something earlier." And a gentle smile touches his lips again.

Biting into my sandwich, I almost moan. I have no idea how he does it, but Addy makes the best BLT. The lettuce is crisp, the tomatoes sweet and juicy, and the bacon adds a note of saltiness, countering the sweet. Swallowing down the first bite, I quickly take another, savoring the flavor before placing it back on the plate.

"Addy, look, I'm sorry about yesterday," I say quickly to get the words out.

Addy looks up at me and just smiles again. I don't think I've ever seen him smile as much as I have today. It should be making me happy that something out there is making my best friend happy, but it's not. All I can feel are pangs of jealousy.

"Water under the bridge, Beau. We're just friends, and I shouldn't have expected you to tell me every aspect of your life."

And, bam, just like that, it feels like a knife has been slammed into my chest, pain lancing through me. Yes, we're friends, but I'd gotten used to the closeness we shared. We'd felt like more than friends, but in that one sentence, Addy has shifted the goal posts.

"I still should have told you when Chase came in." But since the words struggle to come out, I pick up my sandwich, taking another bite, only now the flavor is gone and feels like sawdust in my mouth.

"Beau, you don't tell me about every customer that comes into your shop. Maybe I should've warned you about the shit my family had been pulling so you were prepared, and I'm sorry they dragged you into it."

Just as I'm about to answer him, Addy's cell phone beeps. I watch as he pulls it out of his pocket and catch the flash of *something* in his eyes as he reads the message before quickly typing out a reply and slipping it back in his pocket.

It's then I feel it, something in the pit of my stomach that tells me things have changed. The fear deep within me comes to life, igniting as quickly as a match to kindling and burning just as bright and hot. The fear that one day, Addy might find someone.... That's the only explanation I have for all of this. Someone other than me is making Addy happy, and no matter how much I want to deny it, it hurts. My heart is breaking in two, and there is nothing I can do or say to change it. Addy was never going to be mine, I knew that, yet there had always been this thin sliver of hope. But to actually witness it happening in front of me, it's a pain I never imagined.

Chapter 13—Addy

Before we left the bar last night, Jamie and I had swapped numbers. I'd hoped he would get in contact with me but hadn't been sure. There'd been a spark the night before, but it could have just been the surroundings. In the cold light of day, it could turn out to be nothing, so when my cell had beeped this morning and it had been a message, I'd almost jumped for joy. Most people would have been shocked that he had contacted me so soon, Me, though, I thought it had been awesome. It had been a simple good morning, but it didn't need to be anything more than that. In return, all he got was a simple good morning back. It had been the perfect start to the day.

The only issue had been Beau. I knew he wanted to talk about last night, but I just wanted to forget about it, and so after making the coffee, I'd bolted from the apartment as quickly as I could. It was the coward's way out yet again, and since I knew there was a craft class in my shop tonight and I wouldn't be home till late, I was hoping by the time I got home he would have decided to drop the whole matter.

The shop hadn't been open long when the ting of the bell had me looking to the front of the store, trying to hide the smile and failing when

I saw Jamie walk in. He explained that he'd called the realtor about the vacant storefront first thing this morning and had made an appointment to look at the space this afternoon, so he thought he'd venture into town and have a proper look around.

It had been a quick visit, but it just confirmed the attraction I felt for him. Was it anything like what I felt for Beau? No, but I had a feeling that it could be, given time, just maybe in a different sort of way, and I really hoped that Jamie would want to explore whatever was happening between us.

When he arrived at the shop just after midday, I knew he was interested in me, too. There was no way my coffee was that good, even though some of my customers might disagree with that statement. Initially Jamie had said he was just popping in to say hello, that it hadn't taken him as long as he thought to get into town and so had some time to waste. I couldn't control my laughter when I asked how much and he'd said an hour. Then he tried to defend it by explaining that where he's from, it would take that long just to get across town. I couldn't help the enjoyment of saying that he now lives in a small town and traffic is a lot different.

With it being so close to lunch, I offered to make him some food. The place had been quiet because of the heat, and it was nice to have someone in the shop. Making us both some lunch, I had placed it in front of him and asked if I could join him, and then just like last night, the time had flown by, and it was only when an alarm on his cell started beeping that we realized the time. Jamie had rushed off to look at the space, and I had gone behind the counter to wait for customers.

Not much time had passed until the door to the shop tinged again, and I had looked up, hoping to see Jamie standing there. For an instant, there was disappointment that it was Beau, which was a very odd sensation. Beau suddenly appearing had always made my heart beat a little faster or I would feel a flutter of butterflies in the pit of my stomach. Looking closely at him, they were there, but not as strong as they had been. It left me feeling happy that finally, after all this time, I was moving on, but also a little sad. Even though it would be something I never wanted to happen, there was a feeling that this was going to change our friendship.

I think he caught the flash of disappointment I'd tried so hard to hide, but he didn't say anything, and when he had laughed and joked with me while I had made his coffee, I thought he had gotten over everything from the previous night and we were back to normal. But that hope was short-lived. The moment I had sat down with him, he'd mentioned the previous night. I'd tried to blow it off — we really didn't need to know the ins and outs of each other's lives — but he'd become hurt. He might not realize he had shown it, but there had been a fraction of a second when pain had flashed through his eyes. Why, I don't know, but he seemed to compose himself after the fact, and we continued with his lunch till he had to go back to his shop.

The rest of my day had dragged by. Very few customers had come in for coffee, and most of them had actually come in to look at the craft shelves and enjoy a few minutes in the comfort of my air conditioning. A few purchased some items, but it still meant a really slow day. But it had made me think about Beau's idea about iced tea. Even though coffee was my passion, I still supplied tea for those odd people out there who didn't like coffee. The idea of selling iced tea had been growing on me, but it had to be a simple recipe.

Looking at the forecast on my phone, it showed that it was going to be warm for at least the next week, which wouldn't be good for business. Mrs. Nichols and Mrs. Phillips were going to be at the class tonight.... maybe I could ask them, as Beau suggested, for a recipe and try it over the next few days to see if it becomes popular.

Finally, it was closing time. Well, in the sense that I moved the sign to closed and locked the door. The classes always start an hour after closing to give me time to get the last of the customers out, wash and tidy any dishes, and move some tables around so they're in a row. The ladies liked to talk, and it was just easier this way. When they had first started, I kept the tables positioned as they are every day but soon discovered them shouting across the room to each other made it very noisy.

With one minute left to go, Mrs. Nichols is knocking on the door, asking to come in. She's always the first to arrive and most of the time the last to leave, helping me clear away any cups. I always tell her not to, but she does it, anyway.

"Good evening, Mrs. Nichols," I say, opening the door wide enough for her to come in.

"Good evening, Addy. It's been hotter than hell out there today," Mrs. Nichols states matter-of-factly. To look at her, she appears so sweet and innocent, yet that mouth of hers.

"It has been." I have to bite my lip to stop from laughing or smiling at her. "Mrs. Nichols, I wonder if I can ask you something."

"Of course," she says with a nod, and I wait until she's settled in one of the chairs.

Pulling out the chair next to her, I sit and say, "Mrs. Nichols, I've had an idea. Well, Beau did, actually." At the mention of Beau's name, a smile spreads across her face.

"Oh, Beau!" she says dreamily. "How is he?"

"He's good." But I leave out that she only just saw him yesterday. "Anyway, he came up with an idea for me to sell iced tea. What do you think?"

Mrs. Nichols' eyes light up at the thought, and I know this is going to be a great idea. "That is a *wonderful* idea. It would be lovely, especially on days like this."

"In that case, I was wondering if you have a recipe I could use?" I'm keeping my fingers crossed she doesn't turn around and say the recipe she has is a family heirloom and she's not able to give it to anyone.

"I don't, but Gladys has a lovely one, and it's pretty simple. It's the one I make all the time."

I'm wondering why she doesn't just give it to me and am about to ask when I open, then instantly close my mouth, knowing she will just turn round and say it wouldn't be hers to give.

"Thanks, Mrs. Nichols. I'll make sure to ask her when she gets here." Getting up from the chair, I make my way around the back of the counter and set the coffee for them. I always like to make sure it's freshly made. They probably wouldn't mind the stuff that's sat there most of the day, but I can't do it. So, they get freshly brewed coffee.

Soon after, the bell over the door doesn't stop ringing with everyone coming in, all of them shouting over a hello to me but then quickly chatting with all the other ladies sitting around the table. Once all the seats are full, I go over and click the lock on the door. These classes are private, and I don't need other people coming in and disturbing everything.

Mrs. Nichols looks to be heading the class today, so it's going to be a knitting lesson for sure. One of the ladies normally heads it, but I would say that ninety percent of the time, they end up knitting and talking no matter what the class is supposed to be. Honestly, if I were to look more closely, these had become more like meetings than classes.

Mrs. Nichols gives out a pattern she wants them all to work on and sits back down, but then quickly gets back to her feet again.

"Ladies." And they all turn to look at her. "Addy spoke to me earlier and told me he is looking to start selling iced tea." Before she is able to finish what she's saying, a round of applause breaks out, and when they have stopped, she continues. "He asked me for a recipe. Now I don't have one. I know Gladys does, but am sure he'll take any others to try, as well."

There is murmur amongst them all as they discuss the best option but eventually all agree that Mrs. Phillips' iced tea is the best and encourage her to give me the recipe. I heave a sigh of relief when she agrees.

"Addy, if you'll get me a pen and paper, I can write it down for you," Mrs. Phillips states.

Smiling, I pick up a pad of paper I keep behind the counter and take it over to her and watch as she writes down four ingredients—tea, sugar, ice, and lemon. From the way the ladies had been talking, I'd been expecting there to be more, and a complicated method to make it. Yet it all looks really easy, so I can make it the night before, which is perfect, and my brain is already working on how to change this up. I'm thinking I can add peaches instead of lemon, or maybe mint.

"Thank you, Mrs. Phillips," I say, taking the paper from her and walking behind the counter.

Leaving the ladies to sit, I lean back against the counter, pulling out my phone to check through my emails and look up every now and then to check on the ladies. But if they wanted me, they would just call me over.

After about thirty minutes, I've checked everything I can and decide to grab a coffee pot and have a walk around the table to check for refills. I've just filled up the last cup and am making my way back to the counter when their chatter hits my ears.

"Have you heard that a new lawyer is coming to town and taking over the old law firm space?" This stops me in my tracks, but of course, Jamie had texted me earlier to say he had decided to sign the contract for the storefront.

"Really?" Mrs. Nichols asks, sounding surprised, and considering she normally knows everything that goes on in Madison, Jamie really had been keeping a low profile.

"What do we know about this man?" Mrs. Phillips pipes up.

"Jamie is a great guy." The words fall from my lips before I can stop them, and everyone turns to stare at me.

"Jamie?" Mrs. Nichols questions.

"Um, yeah. I bumped into him last night. We got talking." I turn to walk away, mentally kicking myself and praying they'll drop it.

"Addy. Stop." There is no malice in her voice, but Mrs. Nichols is going to demand some answers. "Come back here, please."

Slowly turning, I make my way back over to them. "Yes, Mrs. Nichols?"

"I think you need to tell us what you know." And from the look on her face, I have no way of getting out of it.

"He moved here recently. Said he wanted to get away from the big city. And as I said, he was friendly. I think he'll be a good fit for the town." Thankfully, this seems to satisfy all their curiosity and I go to leave, but of course, they have to ask if he's available.

"Do you know if he's single? A lawyer would be a great catch for my granddaughter." Oh shit, this isn't my place to say, but how can I tell them he's not interested without outing him completely?

"Um, I'm not sure your granddaughter is his type." I answer, but I'm going to have to text Jamie the moment this is over and apologize.

"Addy, does he play for the same team as you?" Mrs. Nichols asks, always sharp as a whip.

"Um, yeah, he does." And I'm mentally apologizing to the universe for outing someone.

"And you met last night?" The innuendo is blatantly clear in the question.

"Mrs. Nichols, it was by accident. Honestly, we were just at the same place at the same time. A very happy coincidence." I stand there for a few seconds, and when no more questions are being fired at me, I turn to walk away.

"What about Beau?" Mrs. Nichols asks. Thinking I'm being asked the question, I turn to face them, but when Mrs. Phillips shrugs her shoulders, I realize the question wasn't for me. What a confusing question to ask, but that is something I can't dwell on at the moment. Instead, I'm pulling my cell out of my pocket, moving to the corner of the shop, and hitting the call button on Jamie's contact. This is not something to explain over text.

"Hello," I hear, the call being answered almost immediately.

"Hi, Jamie. It's Addy," I say.

"Your name *does* flash up on my screen, you know." And there is the hint of laughter in his voice.

"Yeah, sorry." Feeling an embarrassed blush hit my cheeks, I clear my throat and continue, "Look, sorry to call, but I didn't want to do this over text."

"You sound like you're breaking up with me when we haven't even gone on a date." There's still laughter in his voice.

"What?" His mention of a date throws me for a minute.

"Never mind. What's up?"

"Look, I am really sorry, but I think your secret is out. The ladies were talking about you, and I opened my mouth before I engaged my brain." Hoping this doesn't affect his opinion of me.

"I had a feeling they would learn about me, especially with me visiting the shop," Jamie replies.

"Um," I start, crossing my fingers, "they also know you're gay. Sorry. They were already trying to set you up with one of their granddaughters."

There is nothing but silence from the other end of the phone. Oh, this is not good. But then I hear a huge sigh and the words, "Thank God."

"Excuse me?" I wonder if I'd heard him right.

"It's been worrying me how to tell anyone. You doing it for me is a huge relief, and this also means I can ask you out without the town gossiping too much." And he really does sound relieved.

"Oh, they will gossip, anyway," I reply, laughing at him.

"Will that stop you going out with me?" Jamie asks.

"Nope," I reply, and both of us laugh on the phone with each other.

Chapter 14 — Beau

A week has gone by since the heated argument with Addy and everything seems to have gone back to normal, and yet it also feels so different. Okay, Addy seems different. *We* feel different. He's been going out more than usual and seems to be spending a lot of time on his cell. The constant beeping noise has really been getting on my nerves, and I've almost said something to him several times before the noise suddenly stopped. I thought that whatever he'd been doing had finished, but it took me a bit longer than was necessary to realize he'd just put his phone to silent.

Even now, when we said we'd have a movie night, he feels distant. We're drifting apart, and I hate it but don't know how I can stop it. It's my worst fear coming to life, and yet it's somehow inevitable. Deep down, I know that whatever he's doing on his cell is linked to someone who's more than just a random person. I knew that one day he'd meet someone, and they would see how amazing Addy is. One only has to spend five minutes in his company to see that. He might not realize that he's doing it, but every time he looks at his cell, a soft smile appears on his face.

Now. Now is the time I need to act. Now is the time to finally tell Addy how I feel before I lose him completely. Looking over to him, I take a minute just to take in his profile, and my heart starts beating a little bit faster.

Addy must have felt me staring at him because he turns to look at me.

"You, okay?" he asks.

This is it; Addy has given me the perfect in to tell him, but just as I open my mouth, the screen on Addy's phone lights up, grabbing his attention. He's too quick at picking up his cell for me to see any name on the screen, so I turn back to the movie. When I hear a chuckle escape from Addy, jealousy rips through me. Irrational, unadulterated jealousy. *I* used to make him chuckle like that.

"Sorry." The sound of Addy's voice brings me out of my thoughts.

"It's okay. Anything important?" I ask, nodding my head in the direction of his cell.

"Just a friend," Addy replies, but the way he says friend makes my jealousy flare even brighter.

"New?" I push, hoping that my tone is friendly but also realizing how stupid that question is. Of course they're going to be new.

"Yeah. They're new to town," Addy says, looking back at his cell, but I have a feeling he's being vague on purpose. "I met them when I went out for a drink last week."

Well, that ties into what's been happening this week and confirms that it is someone important on the other end of the cell. I know he's deliberately not saying if they're male or female, but why? Why would he want to keep this person a secret? Addy knows what Madison Springs is like. It won't take long for the gossip of a new person to make the rounds, but as I think about it, if they've been here a week and I'm only now just learning about them from Addy, then they're good at keeping a low profile.

"Wow," I say, the word slipping from my mouth.

"What's wow?" Addy asks, picking up the remote and pausing the movie that neither of us is really watching anymore.

"That there is someone new in town and the gossip tree has missed it," I state, making sure that I don't mention the sex of the person we're talking about even though I know that they're male.

"Well, they know someone is here," Addy says, which honestly surprises me.

"Really?" I think I'm going to have to visit Mrs. Nichols and see what she knows. "I haven't heard anything."

"Well Ja—" Addy stops himself from saying the name of the person. "Umm, they've been keeping a low profile. Mrs. Nichols knows there's someone new in town but doesn't know who."

Well, that is just... impressive. As much as I don't want to admit it. Managing to evade the gossip tree for this long, in this town, is just impressive. There is no other word for it.

"They're looking to open up the shop up the street from mine," Addy continues.

"The old law offices," I state.

"Yes," Addy confirms.

Well, that's just another kick in the gut. Not only must they be handsome — because to be able to turn Addy's head I know that they will be — but they're also smart, too. There is no way I'm going to be able to compete with that.

"Do you mind if we call it a night," I state, looking over to the paused movie. "I don't think either of us have been paying it much attention."

"You okay?" Addy askes, and I can hear the concern in his voice which just makes me feel worse.

"Yeah, just a little tired," I lie.

"But I haven't seen you much this week," Addy says, looking over to me and I have to bite my tongue to stop from snapping at him. *He's* the one that has been going out more this week, not me.

"We've both been busy," is what I say, instead.

Getting up off the couch, I make my way around him, but just as I'm passing him, he grabs ahold of my wrist, the heat of his touch traveling up my arm and causing my breath to catch in my chest. My brain is suddenly assaulted with images of Addy running his fingers all over my body, him trancing every inch of me. Exploring my body. And I know I shouldn't, but I yank my wrist away like his touch is burning me.

"Beau," he starts, but there is an edge to his voice now, "are you sure you're okay?"

"I'm fine," I say and turn to leave the room, but I can hear Addy calling my name again. I ignore him.

Walking into my bedroom, I close the door behind me, and even though I'm tempted to lock it just in case Addy decides to come talk to me, I don't because a part of me actually does want Addy to come and talk to me. Flopping down on my bed, I place a hand behind my head and just stare up at the ceiling.

I know I need to go and apologize to Addy; my behavior just then wasn't how a friend would act, but I can't. Well, not at the moment, anyway. Not before I get my head around what is happening. Closing my eyes, I hope sleep might come and take me away even though I'm not really tired, but instead, all I can see is Addy smiling at his phone.

Sitting up in bed, I know I need to get out of the apartment for a while. Digging my phone out of my pocket, I call for a cab. Maybe a couple hours at the bar will help. Maybe some different scenery and all that. Thankfully, I don't need to change after deciding to stay in the jeans and t-shirt I changed into after I got back from work. It might be hotter than hell out there now, but there's no way I'm wearing shorts. Since my accident, I can't bear people looking at my legs in shorts, looking at my scar. Feeling pity for me. So, I keep it hidden and have learned to live with sweaty legs in the heat.

Grabbing my keys and wallet, I walk out of my bedroom and am surprised to see Addy still sitting on the couch. I thought he would have retreated to his own room when I escaped to mine.

"I'm headed out," I say to the back of his head, watching as he jumps at the sound of my voice. He must not have heard me come back into the room.

"Shit, Beau," Addy says, looking over his shoulder to me. "You just scared the crap out of me."

"Sorry," I reply and just stand there for a minute, not saying anything because I just don't know what to say. I'm acting like a teenager when they find out their crush doesn't like them back. "See you later," I finally blurt out and walk out the door before Addy has the chance to invite himself along.

The cab is already waiting for me when I get outside. Opening the passenger door, I climb in the front. Being a small town, there's only one cab driver, and Hank and I have always found it strange for me to get in the back when the person driving is almost a friend.

"Evening, Beau. Where's Addy?" Hank asks, looking over my shoulder.

"Just me tonight," I reply.

"Oh." Surprise takes over his features. "Where we off to?"

"Just the bar," I say. Considering there's only one bar in town, there's no need for him to ask which one.

"You're unusually quiet," Hank states. "Everything okay?"

"Yeah." I know I should give Hank more than a one-word answer. If I don't, my shop is going to have a lot of walk-ins tomorrow because it won't take long for news to travel how I was quiet and everyone will suddenly be concerned.

"How's the shop?" Hank asks, and I know he's just trying to be polite and make conversation, but at the moment, I just don't feel like talking.

"Shop's good." I know I could add something about Hank's upcoming appointment, but again, the words don't come out. Thankfully, Hank seems to get the hint and stops talking to me, and honestly, I've never been so grateful that it doesn't take more than five minutes to get to the bar.

"Thanks, Hank," I say once we pull up outside the bar as I hand him some cash and get out of the car.

"No problem. Hope you feel better soon," Hank says, and I want to contradict him but don't bother.

Pushing open the door, I heave a sigh of relief when I see that the bar isn't busy. I'm really not in the mood for small talk, but I'm glad to see that it's Justin behind the bar tonight. "Beau! Good to see you, man. What, no Addy?" Justin asks.

"We aren't joined at the hip, you know," I fire back with more venom than I intend, and I'm about to apologize when I look up to see Justin smirking at me. I swallow the words, pull out a bar stool at the end of the bar, and sit down.

"Addy said exactly the same thing last week." His smirk is getting bigger. "So, I'm guessing you haven't kissed and made up yet," Justin says as he comes over with a bottle of beer in his hand, knowing what I want.

"Kiss and make up?" I question, wondering why he would choose those words.

"Yeah. You and Addy have been friends forever. Not sure I've ever seen an argument between the pair of you," Justin says, and he isn't wrong. "You guys are normally pretty close."

"Kiss and make up?" I repeat, his words still rolling around in my head.

Justin starts laughing at me "You know I don't actually mean kiss and make up, as in literally. I know you're not that way. I remember you in high school."

"Oh," I say, forcing a laugh out at Justin's statement.

"So, you still arguing over Addy's family? Why he still talks to them baffles me," Justin says.

"Me, too," I confirm. "No, this is something different." I wonder if I can talk to Justin about how I feel without actually giving away how I feel.

"So, what now?" Justin asks, leaning on the bar and looking over to me.

In my head, I go over everything I could say to explain what I'm feeling. The words, "Addy has a new friend, and I'm jealous," is on the tip of my tongue, but it just makes me sound stupid and maybe a little juvenile.

So instead, I say, "Nothing. I just needed a change of scenery."

"If you're sure." Justin says, and I have to say that is the one thing I like about Justin. Unlike other people in town, if he knows I don't want to talk, he won't push me.

"Yeah," I confirm.

"But I will just say this. You guys have been friends through some pretty tough times in your lives. Don't lose that friendship over something trivial," Justin states.

"Thanks, Justin," I say and take a sip of my beer, loving the feel of the liquid as it travels down my throat while his words run around in my mind. He's right. We have been through some incredibly tough situations where our friendship stood the test of time. When Addy's dad died, he could have easily pushed me away, as I could have done to him when I'd had my accident. But each time, we didn't. In fact, we did the opposite. We became closer.

The fact that Addy is keeping this person a secret should be all the proof I need that Addy doesn't see me as anything more than just a friend. Which makes me wonder if telling him how I feel would do anything but destroy what we have. Do I *want* to ruin our friendship over something as simple as his happiness?

The image of Addy looking at his phone with a smile on his face jumps into my thoughts, and for the first time I ask myself if I really don't want my friend to find his happiness because I have never been brave enough to come out or tell him how I feel. Did I honestly expect him to stay single for the rest of his life? One day, someone was bound to come along and sweep him off his feet. Doesn't he deserve that?

Do I want my best friend to be happy with me? Yes. Does the thought of him being with anyone else fill me with so much jealousy I could cry, again yes. But do I really want to deny my friend that happiness? No, of course not. For years I've watched him grow his shop, live for his business, never once thinking about himself. Survive the treatment from his family when possibly many others wouldn't. Maybe it is time for me to let him go. Time to let him find his own path without me.

But even just thinking this breaks my heart. I have spent my entire adult life dreaming of a future with him, so am I really prepared to let that go? Maybe instead of just letting him go, I should use this as the motivation I need to win his heart. Show him that we can be more than just friends, hopefully before whoever this *person* Addy is chatting with wins his heart completely.

"You look happier than when you came in."

Justin's voice pulls me out of my thoughts, but I don't answer him. Instead, I just pick up my beer and take another swig as I try to think of a plan to come out to Addy and win his heart.

Chapter 15 — Addy

I can't believe it; I have a boyfriend. Okay, so not an actual boyfriend. What I have is a potential boyfriend and that in itself is amazing. For years, the only person that I've been remotely attracted to is Beau. I could never have envisioned myself with anyone but him and now suddenly Jamie popped up. Am I attracted to him as much as I am Beau? Maybe not now, but there is *definitely* something there. Something I know could grow to be more.

I know that I need to tell Beau that I've met someone and yet for the past week, I've kept Jamie a secret. Why? This is a question I've asked myself a thousand times this week but still don't know the answer to. Over the years, I've gone on dates and had hookups. Mainly it was just to scratch an itch but also to make sure Beau never learned of my feelings for him. The dates never made it past the first one and hookups were just one-night stands, and they were never very often. But Jamie is different.

The texts we'd been exchanging with one another from that very first *Good morning* had been fun, and we texted almost every day. Nothing major. It would start with a morning message, asking what plans there were for the day. There had been no other phone calls other than the one I made when I had to tell him I had outed him to the town. But we had met up a few times during the week, and each time, the hours had flown by.

But even after all that, I should have spoken to Beau about Jamie and vice versa. Jamie knows that I have a best friend named Beau, but that's it. Jamie has never really asked about him, but then I suppose he wouldn't. One waits for the person they're with to tell them about their life and who they're living with, etc. It seems strange that we've talked about almost everything – music we love, films, TV programs — but we both seem to have avoided the conversation on families. Considering what Chase and Mother are like, it's not a bad thing, but why wasn't I forthcoming about Beau?

But Beau, he's different. He is something more than family, if that's possible, and he knows something is going on. He may not have said anything yet, but I know the constant beeping of my phone was driving him insane, so I had switched it to silent. But he still saw me paying attention to my phone and never once asked a question. Then his behavior tonight when he was acting so strange. Like we had argued and then he rushed out the door. It was almost like he was jealous, which is stupid. Does he think that Jamie is going to come in and change our friendship? Somehow take me away from him? That's never going to happen.

First things first, I have to talk to Jamie. He needs to meet Beau cause he's *never* going to meet any of my other family. So, I pull out my cell from my pocket and open the message thread with Jamie and send him a text.

Addy: You free tomorrow after work?

Then I just wait, staring at the cell and waiting for an answer. Normally Jamie replies pretty quickly, and just as I'm thinking this, the three little dots appear at the bottom of the screen, letting me know he's typing a reply.

Jamie: Of course. Everything okay?

Is everything okay? That's a very good question. Yes, no, I have no idea, are the answers that flash through my mind. Yes, because of Jamie. No, because I feel like I'm losing Beau. Which is stupid. A true friend will stay with you regardless of the situation, and Beau has proven that time and time again, so what would be so different this time? Is it because I'm scared that if Beau and Jamie meet and don't get along, I'm going to have to choose between the two of them? Am I scared of how Beau is going to react? This is the first time I will be introducing him to someone. But this just leads me to more questions, such as what do I introduce Jamie as? He isn't my boyfriend. Hell, we haven't even gone on an official date yet.

Addy: Yeah, lol. Just wanted to meet up.

This is the best reply I can think of. If I said I wanted to talk, it may have sounded more serious than what I intended. I need to think of this as giving him more information about, and being honest about, myself.

Jamie: Meet you at your shop.

Addy: Perfect.

Nothing is booked for the coffee shop tomorrow, so we can stay inside and have some coffee without the risk of being disturbed. Suddenly I'm nervous and excited all at once.

Looking at my watch, I heave a sigh of relief. It's finally time to close the shop. Today has been manic. The iced tea I put on the menu has been a great success. Now I'm going to have to think of a way of thanking Mrs. Philips for giving me her recipe because my profits have definitely increased. Maybe next time she needs me to order something, it can be on me. Or, well, the coffee shop, anyway.

The sound of the coffee shop door opening has me looking up, and I'm just about to let the customer know that we're closed when I see Jamie standing there, and I swear my eyes nearly pop out of my head. He's standing there in a deep gray, three-piece suit, jacket hanging open and exposing the vest, crisp white shirt, and black tie. Every other time, he's always been in jeans and a t-shirt. Have to say I much prefer this look.

I can feel the smile on my face as I look over at him. "Can you turn the lock and flip the sign around for me?"

Jamie just smiles back at me and nods his head, turning around to lock the door and flip the sign.

"Thanks. Give me five to just finish tidying some of the tables and then want the usual?" I ask, realizing that neither of us had even said hello to greet one another. "Hi, by the way."

Jamie chuckles at my statement, "Hi back, and yes, the usual would be great. Today has been manic."

"Tell me about it. Have a seat," I say, nodding to one of the only clean tables and turning around to grab a tray so I can clear the others when the sound of china clinking together catches my attention. Turning around, I see that Jamie has walked over to one of the tables, picked up all the mugs, and is currently making his way over to me.

"Careful." I call out, thinking that sometimes not every drink is finished, and I would hate for him to pick up a mug and spill coffee down the front of that wonderful suit.

"I got it," Jamie replies.

"Just watch out for coffee. Wouldn't want to ruin that beautiful suit," I tell him.

"Beautiful suit," Jamie states, a smirk touching his lips as he comes up to the counter.

I can feel the heat in my cheeks as I realize what I've just said and wonder if there's a way I can get out of this with my dignity intact. But there isn't. I've been caught. He knows I was checking him out.

"Yep, beautiful suit," I reply, taking the mugs out of his hands and placing them on the tray I was going to use.

"Well, I'm glad you like it," Jamie says before turning away from me and going over to one of the other tables that still has dirty mugs.

"Hey, I can do that," I shout after him.

"Yes, but the sooner this is done, the sooner we can sit down. Right?" Jamie replies while looking over his shoulder.

"Yes, but..." And my words fail me as I can't think of a counter argument because he's right.

"Well then, I'll clear the tables. Just tell me where to put the mugs, and you can wipe down the tables. Deal?" Jamie bargains.

"Deal," I reply, giving him what I hope is a grateful smile. "Just put the mugs on the tray, and I'll take them into the kitchen when we're done with ours."

Five minutes later, all the tables are cleared and wiped down, and the chairs all pushed under them. Jamie is finally sitting at one of the tables, having removed his jacket and placing it over the back of one of the chairs and unbuttoning his vest. His shirt is pulling across a particularly flat stomach, and it's very distracting, *especially* when I'm making our coffees.

When the drinks are finished, I carry them over to the table, placing one in front of him and setting mine down opposite him. I pull out the chair, sit down, and take a sip of my drink, loving both the warmth and bitterness that lingers once I've swallowed the liquid.

"You really do make the best coffee," Jamie states, breaking the silence that has descended over us.

"Thank you," I reply, not sure what else to say.

"You know, your text had some serious undertones to it," Jamie says, picking up his mug and looking over the rim at me.

"Well..." I start, "I did want to talk to you."

"Oh, about what?" Jamie asks.

"Beau," I say simply.

"Beau?" Jamie questions.

"Yeah, my best friend." I'm surprised he doesn't remember, but then I have only really mentioned him in passing.

"What about him?" Jamie asks, taking another sip of his coffee and waiting expectantly.

"Well, we live together." I state.

"And?" Jamie says, a look of confusion on his face.

"Umm, I just wasn't sure if you thought it was strange," I reply.

"Why on *earth* would I think that?" And the confusion on Jamie's face has now been replaced with amusement.

"Well, it's two guys living together," I say, stating the obvious.

"Addy, you do know that two guys can live together, outside of college, and it's fine?"

"Umm," Is the only thing I can think of saying.

"Is there anything more? You must be close if you live together," Jamie responds.

"Beau and I are very close," I confirm.

"Have you been friends long?" Jamie asks and seems genuinely interested in my answer.

"We actually grew up together and ended up going to the same college," I explain.

We both fall into silence again, just happily sipping our coffee. I can't believe that I was so worried about telling him about Beau. Maybe I'm not as worldly as I thought. Being concerned about two men living together is such a small-town mentality, even in a town as forward thinking as this one.

"So, do I need to get Beau's seal of approval before we can go on a date?" Jamie asks, his question taking me by surprise.

"Well, I didn't want to say, but Beau does give all potential boyfriends a two-hour written exam that must be passed in order to confirm the first date," I say, making a joke.

"Potential boyfriend?" Jamie says.

Oh, crap. I didn't mean to say that out loud. We haven't even been on a date, not to mention not even kissed. I shouldn't have said that, but I'm not sure how to get out of it.

"So, you see me as a potential boyfriend?" Jamie questions when I haven't responded to him.

"Maybe," I say, deciding to give him the honest answer.

"In that case I think I'm going to have to meet Beau and pass this exam. Do you know what the questions are about? Is there some study material I need to purchase or books that I need to read up on? I must be prepared," Jamie says, smiling over to me.

"Really?" I reply, laughing at the serious tone in his voice.

"Of course," Jaime replies, continuing the joke. "Who doesn't love studying and exams?"

"Said no one ever," I reply. "I'm not sure there is a person on the planet that has enjoyed studying, let alone taking exams.

"Yeah…" he says, but then I watch as a red tint appears on his cheeks.

"Oh my god," I blurt out, laughing. "*You*. You were being serious! You actually enjoy it. Don't you?" I say.

"Okay. Yeah, I do. Escaping into books, learning about the world. I love it," Jamie states.

"But exams!" I exclaim. "The pressure. Oh God no. I hope I never have to sit through another exam in my life."

"Yeah, I think I am a rare breed to like exams."

"Well, I think you are on your own there," I tell him, smiling at him.

Silence descends over us again, and we go back to sipping our coffee, which has cooled enough to make it easy to drink.

"So, do I really need to meet Beau before we go out?" Jamie asks as he places his empty mug on the table.

"No, you don't," I answer as I finish the last of my coffee.

"Good," Jamie says, a smile brightening his features. "So when?"

"When?" I ask, wondering what he's getting at.

"When shall we go on our date?"

"Oh." I laugh at my own stupidity. Of course that's what he meant when he said when. "How about this weekend?"

"Sounds good," Jamie confirms.

"There aren't really many restaurants in town. What do you feel like doing?" I ask,

"Well, how about you come over to my place. I can cook," Jamie replies,

"Aren't you full of surprises? Good taste in suits, like studying, and can cook," I say, because honestly, I'm surprised. There aren't many men I know who can cook. Beau and I get by, but I don't think we could say we are great cooks.

"Well, I try," Jamie replies.

"Sounds good. Saturday night work?" I ask.

"Perfect," Jamie says, leaning back in his chair.

And just like that, I have a date. The first date I've been on in a very long time, and a date that I'm excited about. That must be a first. I've also gone on some dates wanting them to fail, so of course they have, but this one I wouldn't mind working out.

"I better get going. Can I text you my address and a time later?" Jamie asks as he gets to his feet and pushes his chair under the table.

"Yes, of course. I really need to finish cleaning, anyway," I reply, getting up from my chair and, just like Jamie did, push it under the table.

Jamie turns and walks to the door; I follow him to make sure to lock it behind him. When he suddenly stops and turns to face me, I walk straight into him.

"Sorry," I mumble as I take a step back.

"It's okay," Jamie says but keeps staring at me, then he places a hand on the side of my neck and pulls me forward, licking his lips. I am completely transfixed, watching as the tip of his tongue runs over his lips.

Then his lips are on mine, and I wait for the spark that I knew would come when we first kissed and there is... nothing. I wrap my arms around him, pulling him even closer to me. I can feel his tongue running along my lips and I open for him. Our tongues start a dueling match as the kiss deepens and still... nothing.

We break apart, both of us breathing heavily as we stare at one another.

"See you Saturday," Jamie says, unlocking the door and stepping out. Locking the door again after him, I walk back to the counter, trying to figure out what I'm feeling, but all I get is... nothing.

Chapter 16 — Beau

Today. Today is the day I am going to talk to Addy. I know it's one of the days that he has nothing going on in the shop during the evening. My plan is to go there with the pretense of helping him clean up so he can finish earlier than if he had to do it all alone, and so I closed the garage a few minutes early and am now walking to Addy's shop.

I'm not sure I have ever felt so nervous, and I realize this is something I should have done a long time ago. I've wasted ten years just being his best friend when we could possibly have been so much more. Why? It's a question that I've probably asked myself every day since I figured out my feelings for Addy. I should have told him that I was gay in high school, especially once I witnessed how well everyone else took it when Addy came out, but I didn't. I told myself back then that there was no way I could be a football star *and* gay, and at the time I loved football more.

Turning onto the street Addy's shop is located, I spot a very handsome man in front of me wearing a particularly nice gray suit, and he's not someone I've seen around before. *Is he new in town or just passing through?* But now is not the time to dwell on the new stranger. The gossip tree will let me know who he is soon enough, but then I watch as he turns into Addy's shop, making me stop dead in my tracks.

This must be the person Addy has been chatting with...., But why is he going into Addy's shop now? Making my way to Addy's shop, I stand just out of sight and carefully peer inside. I watch as the stranger starts to clear the tables, taking a step back when he gets closer to the window and could possibly see me. I take a few deep breaths and then turn back to look. Addy is now wiping down all the tables, and it seems they're working together. Soon after, Addy is behind the counter — I'm guessing to make them drinks — and the stranger has taken off his jacket, placing it on the back of one of the chairs. Addy brings over two mugs and takes his place opposite the stranger. Everything in me is telling me I need to walk away, that this is a private conversation, and from the way Addy keeps smiling, one between friends bordering on something more, and yet I can't move, frozen in place.

I have no idea how long I've been standing there watching them, but with each smile that spreads across Addy's face, my resolve to tell him about my feelings disintegrates inch by painful inch. Just as I am about to leave, I watch as the stranger gets up and puts his jacket on. *He's leaving.* This should be my cue to leave, too, but nope, I still stand there and watch. The stranger walks to the front door with Addy following behind and when the stranger suddenly stops, Addy walks straight into him.

In the pit of my stomach, I know what I'm about to witness, but I still can't walk away. So, I stand there as the stranger places a hand behind Addy's head and pulls him forward. The pain that lances through me as I watch them lock lips is indescribable and then Addy pulls him tighter to him, and even with my heart shattering I can't look away.

I remain watching as they finally break apart, both breathing heavily. And that's the final straw. Turning, I walk away from my hiding place but have no idea where to go. I don't want to go home and be there when Addy returns. I could go to the bar, but I don't feel like being social with anyone. There's always my parents', but there would be questions there, too. *My garage.* It's perfect. There's a car I've been working on; I can get lost in my work. The best thing I can do is close the doors and escape from the world.

I move down the street and increase my pace, not wanting to wait around, and within minutes I'm back outside my garage, unlocking the door and pulling it open. Taking a step inside, I take a deep breath. The smell of oil fills my nostrils, and it's somehow calming. Something familiar in the turmoil that has engulfed me. Turning on the light, I close the door, shutting out the twilight and the rest of the world. I walk over to a locker, pull out some coveralls, and quickly pull them over my clothes, then walk over to the car sitting in the middle of the garage. I'd completed most of the tasks, but I still had to change the oil.

I have no idea how long I've been working in the garage, but when my legs start to ache, I know it's longer than I intended, but it's exactly what I needed. I was able to turn off all my thoughts about what I witnessed.

Picking up my cell, I see that I have two missed calls and five text messages from Addy. When I'd been putting on my coveralls, I'd taken my cell out of my pocket and left it on the side so as not to damage it. I'd also put it on silent because I knew Addy would be trying to contact me when he got home. Opening the messages, I quickly scan them.

Addy: Home from the shop.

Addy: Do you know when you're coming home?

Addy: Beau?

Addy: Is everything okay?

Addy: Beau, call me when you get this. Getting worried.

I know that I should reply to his messages, but I don't. Instead I close down the app and press the button to my voicemail and wait for Addy's voice to fill my ear.

"Hey, Beau, just to let you—" I hit the option to delete before listening to it all and wait for the next one to play.

"Beau, is everything okay? Haven't heard from you and getting worried. Call me when you get this."

I don't delete this message and instead hit replay and listen to his voice again, liking the edge of worry I can hear in his voice and knowing that he still cares, even if just a little. I listen to the message one more time before ending the voicemail and opening my contacts. I open Addy's number but can't call him. I know I should, but what's the point? I will be home in a few minutes.

Stripping off my coveralls, I hang them back in the locker since I haven't gotten them that dirty and can use them again tomorrow. After slipping my cell into the pocket of my jeans, I walk over to the door, pulling it open, and am surprised to see that it's dark outside. When I'd been looking at Addy's messages, I hadn't paid any attention to the time. Getting out my cell I check the time and the display tells me that it is ten pm. Well shit, no wonder he's worried. I thought I had only been a couple hours, but it's been almost five, if the clock on my cell is correct.

I quickly turn off the light and lock up before making my way back to the apartment, hoping that Addy hasn't called the cops yet, or worse, my parents. After the day I've had today, I'm not sure I could deal with them tonight, too. Yet I'm still not rushing to get home as the image of Addy kissing that stranger is lingering in my mind. I just don't understand why this person is affecting me so much. Over the years, I had gone to a few bars with Addy just to be his wingman, and even though Addy didn't know it, I enjoyed the bars as much as him. Addy used to find it amusing that I would be hit on by scantily-clad men, but it always felt good. And I'd watched Addy kiss guys while he'd been on a dance floor, and it had never bothered me before. Each and every one of those guys could have turned into something special, yet I always knew they wouldn't. This time, though, it feels different.

Turning the key in the lock once I'm at the apartment door, I take a deep breath. Addy is going to be pissed. I want to avoid him and go into my room and hide but I know he will be in the living room, waiting for me. And if I know Addy, he's been wearing a trench into the floorboards.

"Where the hell have you been?" Addy's angry voice travels across the living room as I walk in.

"Sorry, was at the garage," I reply, hoping this will be enough to prevent any conversation so I can escape to my room.

"Till now?" comes Addy's retort.

"Yes," I confirm, turning to make my way to my room.

"I messaged you," Addy states.

"Yeah. My cell was on silent. Just saw them now." Which is virtually the truth.

Looking up at his face, I can see the concern etched into his features, and I know I *should* apologize but as I look at him, the image of that kiss invades my mind again and I need to get away from him. Addy will never be mine now, and the sooner I can accept it the better, but until then, I'm going to have to stay away.

"Where are you going?" Addy demands.

"Bed. I'm tired," I reply.

"Beau?" Addy's voice suddenly changes, the concern from moments ago gone and replaced with uncertainty, so I turn to look at him. "Is everything okay?"

"Yeah, Addy. Everything's fine. Just got side-tracked with a car, that all," I reply,

"I wanted to talk to you," Addy adds.

"Can it wait till tomorrow? I'm tired and my leg is aching," I say, knowing full well that the moment I mention my leg, Addy will let me go.

"Yeah, it can wait," Addy replies. "Night."

"Night," I say back, quickly turning away from him and going to my room.

The moment the door is closed, I lean up against it and let out a breath I hadn't even realized I was holding. The whole conversation with Addy had gone exactly how I thought it was going to, and I know that surely this isn't normal for any friendship. Up until today, I never questioned how close we were; it was just us. But this, what happened tonight, wasn't right. The lines of our friendship have blurred. But blurred into what, I don't know.

Walking over to my bed, I flop down, place a hand behind my head, and close my eyes, but the image of the stranger in the smart suit pops up. If mine and Addy's friendship has changed to something else without us even realizing it, how am I supposed to compete with that stranger? That suit looked expensive and hugged his figure in all the right places. I would never be able to afford a suit like that.

With a deep sigh, I know what I'm going to have to do, and it's going to suck and hurt, but Addy deserves to find his happiness. After everything that happened with his dad and how his family have been, how could I deny him having that someone special? Someone who will make him laugh and smile like I saw today at the coffee shop. Closing my eyes, I bring up the image of Addy sitting in the coffee shop, his face smiling, and let sleep take me.

The following morning, I wake to the smell of fresh coffee wafting into my bedroom. I roll over and pull the covers over my head. I know I should probably go and talk to Addy, but I think he's going to tell me about the stranger, and this morning, I feel like too much of a coward but know that it will have to happen at some point.

Pushing back the covers, I get out of bed and walk over to a chest of drawers in the corner, open the top drawer, and pull out the first random t-shirt I come across and put it on, then take a deep breath and walk out of my bedroom.

Addy is sitting in the living room, staring at his cell and sipping his coffee.

"Morning," I say as I make my way over to the kitchen.

"*Jesus*, Beau! How the hell are you so quiet?" Addy exclaims.

"Sorry," I say with a chuckle over my shoulder to him.

"There's coffee in the pot," Addy says.

Going into the kitchen, I pull a mug from the cupboard and pour myself a cup, and this morning, I just want it black. Normally I might add some sweetener, but today I need the bitterness that comes with a good coffee. After I put the coffee pot back, I grab my mug and make my way back into the living room.

"How's the leg?" Addy asks as I take a seat at the other end of the couch.

"It's fine," I reply and take a sip of the coffee.

"Sorry about yesterday," Addy starts. "I know I overreacted, but I was worried."

"I know," I say, then add "You wanted to talk?" to get this conversation over with.

"Yeah," he says, and I watch as Addy takes a sip of his coffee before beginning. "I've met someone."

Bam. Just like that. Three words that I knew were coming but still suck.

"Have you?" I reply, trying to sound interested.

"Yeah. He's new in town. His name is Jamie," Addy continues.

So, the stranger in the nice suit is named Jamie... It oddly suits him, and when I look over to Addy, I realize he's still talking, and I have *no* idea what I've missed but make a point to listen to him.

"He's a lawyer and is opening up in the old law office." He pauses for a second and then says, "And we're going on our first date on Saturday."

"Addy, that's awesome. When do I get to meet him?" I reply, hoping that I've laced enough enthusiasm in my voice to fool him since all I really wanted to do was grunt. "How about you tell me more about him later? I need to get to work," I say, needing to get away.

"Yeah," Addy replies, and I'm not sure if it's to me or the coffee mug in front of him when he finally says, "I need to get to the shop myself."

I go back into my room, closing the door, but instead of getting changed for work, I go and sit on my bed, adjusting the pillows behind me. So, the stranger is a lawyer and named Jamie. The town's needed a lawyer, but why did he have to come to this town, and why now? Just when I was finally ready to tell Addy.

Picking up my cell from the bedside table, I open the internet search engine and type *Places to rent Madison Spring* and wait for the results to appear. I want Addy to be happy more than anything, but there is no way that I'm going to be able to sit and watch while he brings Jamie back to the apartment.

Our friendship needs to change again if Addy is getting his happy ever after. But the only way I can think of to do that is to give Addy his space, and the best way to do that is by moving out.

Chapter 17 — Addy

That kiss has been going around in my mind since the moment it ended. Why did I feel nothing? How can I be attracted to him and yet the moment we kiss, it felt like I was kissing a friend. Even when I deepened the kiss — nothing. I desperately wanted to talk to Beau about it, but relationships weren't something we'd ever talked about before because there had never been a need.

Relationships for both of us had never been in the cards. I knew my reasons, of course, but the fact Beau had never met anyone still confuses me. He was a catch for any woman, even I knew this. He ran his own very successful business and was kind, thoughtful and handsome. He would be the complete package in anyone's eyes, and yet he was single, and as far as I was aware had never had a girlfriend. I'd even wondered at one time if he were a virgin but then remembered he was an athlete in college – so yeah, he definitely would have gotten some action there.

But today, today I really wanted to talk to my best friend. Get his opinion on what was happening. I had also wanted to tell him about my date on Saturday, which I'd been so excited for right up until *the kiss*. That kiss changed everything. We had still been texting each other almost daily like before, but where the excitement had been there was now trepidation. Jamie was everything I had been looking for to finally try and get over Beau and move on with my life, but now... now I had no idea.

I had hoped to talk to Beau the night of the kiss, but he ended up working late, much later than I had *ever* known him to work before, and when he came home, he went straight to his room after our conversation and stayed there. I know I could have gone to his room, but he'd looked drained. I thought it best that he rested, and I knew I would catch him in the morning, but then when I did see him, the conversation was so generic. I told him about Jamie, and he *seemed* pleased... but then I didn't see him again last night. He'd said recently that he'd been busy in the garage, but I had never known him to be this consumed with work. But when I didn't run into him this morning, I knew that he must be avoiding me, but I didn't know why.

All I know is today is Thursday and I only have tonight and Saturday afternoon to talk to Beau, as tomorrow night the ladies are coming to the shop after hours. So somehow between now and then I need to find time to sit down with Beau. I know that he'll set me straight. Get me to look at the situation in a whole new light and then everything will be okay for tomorrow.

Remembering that I'm still at the shop, I look around and am thankful to find that it's deserted. When I look at the time, I'm surprised to see how late it is — the shop should have closed twenty minutes ago. Thankfully, there are no ladies coming in this evening. I'm not sure I could cope with dealing with them along with everything that's going on in my life. Flipping the sign to CLOSED and locking the door, I've walked just a few paces when a knock on the glass draws my attention.

Turning, I see Beau standing there looking at me. Rushing back over, I unlock the door, opening it wide enough for him to come in before closing it again and locking us in.

"What are you doing here?" I ask.

"Umm…" Beau starts, but he doesn't finish his sentence. He looks tense. I'm not sure I've ever seen him look like this, even when he was in the hospital.

"Do you want to wait while I clean up and we can go home together?" I prompt.

"Aren't you ready now?" Beau asks, managing to finish his sentence, and I can understand why he would think I would be ready. On any normal day, that would be the case. The shop isn't huge and doesn't take me that long to get everything cleaned up.

"No. I only just locked the door," I say.

"Was there a rush?" he asks, looking around at the empty tables.

"No. Just lost track of time," I explain.

"Oh," Beau replies, but he doesn't question me any further on why I lost track. "Want me to give you a hand?"

Before I can reply, another knock on the window of the door catches our attention, and I turn and see Jamie standing there. This is the first time I've seen him since the kiss, and my heart skips a beat at seeing him standing there, but I'm not sure if it's from excitement or something else.

Going over to the door, I unlock it once more and open it for Jaime, welcoming him inside. I look over to Beau expecting to see confusion written all over his face. I know he would be wondering why I let this complete stranger into the shop, but his face remains expressionless. Okay, his behavior is now completely odd and I'm going to have to get to the bottom of what's going on.

"Hi," Jamie says, and I wonder for a second if he is going to try and kiss me again, but he doesn't; however, I do catch when he looks over to Beau before looking back at me.

"Hey," I say back. This is *not* how I wanted Beau and Jamie to meet. The room already feels tense for some bizarre reason. I'd been hoping to arrange a meeting that involved beer so we could relax but that's not going to happen, so I just need to get this introduction over with.

"Jamie, this is my best friend, Beau. Beau, this is Jamie," I say in a rush and pointing between the two of them.

"You're Beau!" Jaime exclaims and a huge smile spreads across his face.

"Yes," Beau replies before hesitantly adding, "Nice to meet you."

"I've heard a lot about you. It's nice to finally put a face to the name," Jamie continues undaunted and appears to have missed Beau's apprehension. "Addy tells me that you have an exam that I'll have to pass in order to date him."

"Exam?" Beau repeats, confusion showing on his face over what Jamie is going on about.

"Sorry," Jamie says, looking at me and then over to Beau. "Thought it was a joke you knew about."

A silence takes hold as Jamie must begin to realize that I haven't mentioned him much to Beau, and I can't help but wonder what he's thinking. Is he hurt that I haven't told my best friend about him? Maybe he's wondering why I haven't said anything. Considering I told Jamie how close me and Beau are, it must seem strange that I haven't mentioned anything. I need to say something to break the tension that is starting to creep into the silence.

"Addy can be such a joker," Beau says suddenly, startling both Jaime and me. "What did he say?"

"Addy explained that you've been friends for a long time and that when someone wanted to date him, you gave them an exam."

"Really," Beau deadpans, giving me a look, a look I know only too well, and I have a strange feeling that he is somehow going to try and embarrass me.

"Yeah, but if he thought it was going to intimidate me, it backfired as I love exams," Jamie says.

"You love exams and want to date Addy," Beau starts. "You do know that Addy hates exams, school, and studying. How he managed to graduate high school and college is a mystery to me, and I went to school with him. "

"Growing up in the same town I would have guessed that you both would have gone to the same high school, but I had to admit I was surprised when Addy told me you went to the same college, too," Jamie states.

"It wasn't our plan," Beau states, "especially as I was playing football at the time. My plan was to go somewhere where I could play and hopefully one day get drafted, and in a bizarre twist of fate, we both got into the same place."

"Addy never told me you played football. Do you still play? What team do you root for?" Jamie blurts out, and I know in that instant that I have lost him to Beau for a while. Other than cars, the next topic that Beau likes to talk about is football.

"Before you two fall into the black hole that is football," I say, "did you want me for anything?" I direct my question at Jamie.

"Honestly, I can't remember now," Jamie replies, giggling to himself. "Must not have been that important, and if I remember, I can just text you later."

"Oh," Beau suddenly exclaims "So *you're* the texter."

"I'm the what?" Jamie questions.

"You're the one that made Addy's phone sound like R2D2 having an orgasm with the constant beeping," Beau states, and right there is the embarrassing statement I knew was going to come.

"Beau!" I exclaim, not quite believing that he said that.

"Addy!" he replies, and I know he is trying to match my tone of voice. A laugh from beside us has us both turning to face Jamie.

"What?" we both say at the same time.

"Nothing," Jamie says, but he's still trying to hold back a laugh. "But I can see why you two are friends."

"Look," I start, deciding to change the subject, "why don't we clear up this place and head back to the apartment. Maybe order a pizza, get some beer, and the pair of you can talk about football."

"Yeah, that sounds like fun," Jamie replies. "Be nice to make a new friend in this town."

Beau doesn't say anything but does nod his head in agreement, and so between the three of us cleaning the shop over the next ten minutes, we're leaving and heading towards the apartment. But the moment we walk through the door, Beau makes an excuse to disappear into his bedroom, saying something about grabbing a shower to get the smell of the garage off his skin. When I asked him about the pizza, he said to order him his usual and call him when it arrives. He apologized to Jamie, who said he understood.

When I hear the shower going a few minutes later, I hope that Beau is living up to his statement that he would be joining us when the pizza arrives and not retreat back into his bedroom like he'd been doing all week.

"So, what kind of pizza do you want?" I ask, turning to Jamie while pulling out my cell, ready to call in the order.

"When it comes to pizza, I'm *really* boring and like just plain cheese," Jamie replies.

"Cheese," I repeat. "Just cheese. Nothing else?" I'm not sure I believe that someone would order just a cheese pizza.

"Yep," Jamie confirms.

"Wow," I reply but decide not to tease him, no matter how much I want to. "So, looks like it's going to be one cheese and one pepperoni."

I quickly place the order, and just like with any small town, the moment they hear my name, they don't need the address. For those of us who grew up here, we know everyone's address.

"Didn't you need to give him your address?" Jamie asks after I hang up, and I can't help but burst out laughing.

"You've never lived in a small town before, have you?" I ask.

"No," Jamie confirms.

"You'll learn," I say. "Most of the townspeople will just give their name when they come to you and expect you to know where they live. There will be some who will take pity on you and give you their address, but they'll only give it once. But don't worry, just come see me and I'll point you in the right direction," I reply.

"Thanks for that," Jamie says.

"Beer?" I ask when there's a silence that has descended upon us.

"Please," Jamie replies, nodding his head at the same time.

"Take a seat," I say and point to the couch.

Turning away from Jamie, I walk into the kitchen and grab three bottles of beer from the refrigerator, taking off the tops and then carrying them two bottles in one hand and one by its neck in the other into the living room. When I walk back into the room, I see that Jamie has sat down on one end of the couch with one leg crossed over the other, and I have to say that he looks very relaxed. Going over to him, I place the single bottle down on the table where I know where Beau is going to sit and pass another to Jamie, who takes a swig before placing it on the table in front of him.

"Not sure if I've asked, but have you settled in?" I ask, mentally going over all the conversations we've had and not recalling asking this before.

"Pretty much," Jamie replies. "Everyone has been really nice, but that reminds me... Do you know a Mrs. Philips?"

"Oh no," I reply because I have an idea what he's going to say next. "She's a part of the gossip tree."

"Well, she came up to me the other day and as bold as brass asked me if I was seeing someone as her nephew is single."

"I warned you. That won't be the first or last time that happens," I state.

"To be honest, I'm a little surprised at how accepting everyone is here. When I moved, I thought I'd have to keep my sexuality a secret until I'd been here for a while," Jamie explains as he leans forward to pick up the bottle of beer.

"Yeah, I know what you mean. Small towns have reputations for being homophobic, but not here. There *is* a church on the outskirts of town that doesn't agree with the lifestyle, but most of the town aren't members. But there may be church members that come to see you, and they may even tell you to leave town."

But before I'm able to say that these people are most likely going to be my mom and Chase, the buzzer in the apartment rings, letting me know the pizzas have arrived.

"Beau, *pizza*," I shout and head to the door to grab them.

Walking back into the room, I see that Beau is sitting at the opposite end of the couch, beer in hand, and is intently listening to Jamie, which, considering I was out of the room for only about a minute, is impressive. Placing the pizza boxes on the table, I flip them open and pull out a slice of the pepperoni.

"Are you two going to eat or just spend the rest of the night talking about whatever you're talking about?" I ask, taking a bit out of my slice.

"Jamie played some football in high school," Beau states, and I have to stop myself from rolling my eyes. I should have guessed that *somehow* football was involved.

"Only because I thought it would be good on my college application. I soon discovered that I enjoyed watching it more than playing it."

The pair of them lean over and take a slice of their preferred pizza, and I see Beau clocking the cheese-only one and wonder if he's going to make a joke about it to Jamie, but he doesn't. Instead, the pair of them go straight back into the conversation they were having while I was out getting the pizza. A part of me should be happy that they seem to be getting along so well, but there is another part of me that if I stopped to think about it long enough, I would realize that I was jealous.

Chapter 18 — Beau

Well, damn it. I'd wanted to hate Jamie, but I couldn't. I'd thought that if I hated the man that had stolen Addy from me, it would make it easier, but in good conscience, I couldn't say that. When he arrived at the shop yesterday, I'd known who he was, of course. I just didn't know his name, and it took everything I had to keep my composure and not race out of the shop like the floor was on fire; but if I'd done that, Addy would have guessed something was up.

Yesterday I'd finally decided to go and tell Addy that I was planning on moving out. I was still looking for places and didn't have any viewings lined up, but my mind had been made up. I'd actually considered asking Mom and Dad if I could go back there, but Addy would have found that just too strange. Of course Jamie had turned up, and all the plans to mention something disappeared. I couldn't discuss something like that in front of Jamie. I'd hoped that it was going to be a fly-by visit, but of course Addy just had to invite him back to the apartment.

I was able to make a hasty retreat, citing needing a shower, which wasn't really a lie, but I knew that it took me a lot longer than usual, only just getting changed when the pizza arrived. My plan had been to eat a couple slices and then escape to the bedroom again, but then Jamie had continued the conversation about football, and I honestly lost track of time. It had been so nice to talk about one of my favorite topics with someone who wasn't my dad. Addy watches the odd game with me, but he doesn't have the same passion. So, yeah, I ended up talking to him for a while and decided that he was a nice guy, but I was also aware that Addy would be getting very bored and he deserved some time alone with Jamie. Addy hadn't confirmed that they were a couple to me, but from the way Jamie kept glancing at him, I knew it wouldn't be long till they were.

Making my excuses, I retreated to my bedroom, throwing my cell onto the bedside table but still too wide awake to sleep, so I'm just lying on my bed staring at the ceiling, thinking back over the events of the evening. Up until meeting Jamie, I had no idea what I'd been planning to say to Addy, but watching the pair of them together, I knew I had the perfect excuse. All I needed to say was that I was giving him the space to develop their relationship without having to worry about whether he was disturbing me or not. Addy would most likely call bullshit and tell me it was fine and try to persuade me to stay, but it would only be delaying the inevitable. If things with Jamie went well — and by the looks of it they would — eventually they'll want to move in together, and as Addy owns this apartment, it would be logical for them to both move in here.

Addy could rent the apartment to me and move in with Jamie, but I know that I couldn't stay here. This place would feel wrong without Addy, and it would never feel like my place. It would always be Addy's. Looking around the now-dark room, it dawns on me that this really is the end of an era. For over ten years we've spent so much time together, and maybe I'd gotten complacent, but I was happy. Yes, I would've wanted more with Addy, had the opportunity to feel his naked body next to mine, wake up with him encircled in my arms, but too much time had passed. I had firmly enshrined myself in the friend zone.

I can still hear the slight mumble of voices coming from the living room, telling me that Jamie is still here. I wonder if Addy is going to ask him to stay over, the thought sending shivers down my spine. I don't need to hear Addy having sex. It was the one unspoken rule me and Addy had: we never brought dates home. If we met anyone, we would always say we had a roommate and hopefully go to the other person's house. Which had definitely been needed in my case as I could never bring a guy home. Getting off the bed, I walk over to my dresser in the corner and pick up some headphones that I left there. They're noise canceling ones that I treated myself to a while ago but didn't really use often, but they will be perfect for tonight.

Walking back over to the bed, I place them on the bedside table so I can grab them quickly if any noises start to drift into my bedroom. But at the moment, it sounds like they're still just talking. Picking up my cell, I open the internet search engine, starting my search again for places to rent, but just like the other day, there are very slim pickings. Maybe I'm going to have to move outside of Madison Springs, which wouldn't be ideal for commuting back and forth to work, but it could be a stop gap while I waited for something to become available here. Widening my search, I am disappointed to see that there seems to be even less available further out. I'm just going to have to keep looking, and the moment I like something, jump on it, I suppose.

Turning off my phone, I place it back on the side table, lean against the pillows, and am met with silence. The mumbling that had been coming from the living room has stopped. I wait for a few minutes to see if I can hear anything coming from Addy's room but again nothing, so I decide to brave going back into the living room.

Getting up off the bed I walk over to the bedroom door, and as quietly as possible open it just a fraction, pausing to listen but still nothing. Fully opening the door, I walk out on tiptoe, hoping this will somehow give me silent stealth abilities. When I get to the entryway to the living room, I stop and peer over to the couch and see that it's just Addy sitting there, alone.

"I know you're there," Addy suddenly says but doesn't look in my direction.

"Sorry. Wanted a glass of water," I say, hoping Addy doesn't see through my lies.

"Bullshit," Addy snaps.

"Excuse me?" I'm caught off guard at the harsh tone in his voice.

"You wanted to see if Jamie was still here," Addy states, finally looking over to me.

"Well, of course." I confirm. "Didn't want to disturb you. It looked like it was turning into a date," I add.

"Well, for your information, it wasn't a date. Our first date isn't until Saturday evening," Addy states, anger still lingering in his voice, but I have no idea why he would be angry with me.

"Really?" I ask in surprise, especially after witnessing that kiss the other day.

"Yes. If you hadn't been acting weird, I'd been planning on telling you," Addy says, looking away from me.

"I've been busy," I lie again.

"Beau, what the fuck is going on with you?" Addy snaps, his head shooting back in my direction, and I can feel my anger growing now, too. I've done nothing. Well, that isn't exactly the truth. I have been avoiding him, but for a very good reason.

"Nothing is going on with me," I say, trying to add as much conviction to my tone as possible.

"Stop lying to me. You've been avoiding me for days," Addy says, and I watch as a flicker of hurt flashes through his eyes. "I've been wanting to talk to you. Tell you about Jamie."

"He's a nice guy," I add, hoping that will placate Addy.

"How would you know?" Addy demands. "You hardly spent a lot of time together."

"Addy, you're the one going out with him, not me," I say. "You don't need my approval." Which is true. As long as Jamie makes Addy happy and treats him well.

"We aren't going out," Addy says, and I have to bite my tongue against saying anything because that kiss would contradict that statement. There was no way that kiss was anything other than romantic.

I wait in the entranceway to see if Addy adds anything more to that statement, but he remains silent, so I decide now is the time to tell him about moving out. Especially as he's already angry at me.

"I actually wanted to talk to you about something," I say, going over to the couch and sitting in the seat that Jamie had been in.

"About?" Addy asks, looking over to me.

"Well," I start, taking a deep breath and wishing I had a beer to wet my suddenly bone-dry mouth, "I think it's time for me to get a place of my own," I say.

"What!" Addy explodes, jumping off the couch, and I flinch at the harshness in his tone. If I thought he was angry before, that was nothing to what he is now.

I open my mouth to start explaining my reasoning when the look Addy gives me has me closing my mouth and just staring at him as he glares at me. He opens his mouth to say something but snaps it closed, turns on his heel, and storms away to his bedroom, slamming the door behind him.

Okay, I knew he was going to be pissed, but I wasn't expecting that reaction. I've never seen him that angry in all the time that I've known him. Even when his mother and Chase started being dicks, I didn't see him get this angry. This is one hundred percent not normal friendship behavior, and yet I still go over to Addy's bedroom door and raise my hand to knock to check that he's okay. But I lower it before doing it. Addy is going to need his space. Maybe we will be able to talk about it in the morning.

Making my way to my room, I close the door behind me, and unlike earlier, I get ready for bed. Climbing under the covers, it takes me a long time to finally drift off to sleep, but my dreams are plagued with images of an angry Addy. Him telling me to get out of the apartment, that I am no longer welcome here. Images of Addy in Jamie's arms. Jamie kissing his neck and whispering to me, "You lost. He's mine now," which makes me wake with a start. Picking up my cell, I check the time and see that my alarm will be going off soon, so there's no point in going back to sleep and I decide to go get some coffee. I will miss Addy's coffee first thing in the morning.

Getting out of bed, I sniff the air, waiting for the smell of freshly brewed coffee to hit my nostrils, but there's nothing. Rushing out of my room, I find the living room vacant, and when I enter the kitchen, the coffee pot is empty. Looking up at the clock on the kitchen wall, I check the time again, thinking that maybe I misread it in the bedroom and it's earlier than I thought. But no, the time was right. Addy should be up by now; even though it's a Friday and the ladies will have a class tonight, Addy will still go to the shop early.

Worried that maybe for the first time ever he's missed his alarm, I go over to his room and knock on the door, only to be met with silence. Giving it a few more seconds, I knock again, but this time open it while saying his name, "Addy," but his room is empty, and if it wasn't for the fact that his bed was rumpled I would have said that he hadn't slept there.

Shit.

I thought Addy would have calmed down enough for me to talk to him this morning. Clear the air between us. Make him understand. I could go to the shop, but it's not the ideal place to have that conversation, plus I have to get to the garage. I am going to have to wait until tonight to talk to him. Going back to the kitchen I start making some coffee, which I'm awful at.

Getting to the garage, I go straight into the office and check my schedule and groan when I see that the first appointment I have is Chase. Not how I wanted to start my day. Hopefully he won't mention Addy because I don't think I'm in the mood to deal with him, and I might not be able to hold my tongue today.

"Beau!" The sound of Chase's voice drifting through the garage has me rolling my eyes, and I have to take a few deep breaths before plastering a fake smile on my face and leaving the office.

"Chase, what can I help you with today?" I ask looking over to him.

"There's a red light on the dash," Chase says.

"Okay, let's have a look." Walking over to Chase's car, I have a quick look at the dash and see the oil light. Normally that would indicate that the engine oil was low, but I'd made sure to top it up the last time he was in. Popping the hood of the car and securing it, I pull out the dipstick and can see that the oil is indeed low.

"Anything serious?" Chase asks.

"Not sure. Let me just top up the oil and then can you drive it onto the lift." I say and spot the worried look that flashes over Chase's face.

I top up the oil and direct Chase to drive the car onto the lift. Once Chase is out of the car, I slowly begin to raise it.

"So, I heard that another homosexual has moved into town," Chase states, and any hope I had that this was a genuine car appointment vanishes.

"Is there?" I'm trying not to engage in this conversation but instead look at the plug on the oil pan that, if I'm not mistaken, looks like it's been tampered with. "Have you taken the car anywhere else recently?"

"No," Chase answers, maybe a little too quickly. "Does Addy know this newcomer? His name is Jamie," he adds.

"Addy is allowed to make friends," I state, and I can feel that I'm beginning to lose my patience.

"Yes, but not in this town. The pair of them should leave and go taint somewhere else," Chase says, and I cannot take it anymore.

"No. The only people who should leave this town are you, your mom, and that god awful church," I snap, and I have to admit that I get a small thrill when I see the look of shock on his face.

"We aren't going anywhere," Chase states. "We're going to stay and make sure we preach God's truth and make sure Addy and this Jamie know that the town doesn't approve of him, or people like him."

"You're joking, right?" Not sure I'm believing what Chase is saying.

"No. Our church is just voicing what the town is too scared to say out loud," Chase replies, and I know I need to get this man out of my garage, so I lower the car.

"All done. No charge," I say, not wanting to talk anymore.

"That's it?" Chase asks.

"Yep," I say. "Have a good day," I finish, walking away. I know I should stay and direct him off the lift, but I really can't stay in the same room as him for much longer.

"Beau, I know deep down you agree with me. I know you believe homosexuality is a sin. Please help me clean up the town." Chase says walking over to his car, but his words hit home, and anger fills me.

"Chase," I say, looking over to him.

"Yes?" he replies, looking hopeful.

"One, next time you want to talk to me, don't deliberately drain the oil. Two, Addy is loved in this town, and they definitely don't care that he's gay and he'll never be forced out. And third, I don't believe, nor will I ever believe, that homosexuality is a sin, and you know why? It's because I'm gay, too. Now get out of my garage and don't come back. You're not welcome here."

Staring at Chase, I realize what my anger made me say. I just told Chase that I'm gay. The first person in the world I told was Chase. My only hope now is that he doesn't go straight to his brother and tell him. Suddenly, I'm very pleased that Addy has a class tonight.

Chapter 19 — Addy

I have never been so angry with Beau as I am today.

What the fuck was that last night? He wants to move out? Just like that, completely out of the blue. I could tell that he wanted to talk to me about it, but last night I couldn't. I'd just needed to walk away. I thought I would have felt better enough this morning to maybe sit down and discuss what the hell was going on. But I had a crap night's sleep and just decided to get to the shop. I hadn't even bothered to make us coffee. What was the point?

Madison Springs was dead at this time of the morning and so instead of going straight to the shop I decided to take a walk. It would give me the time to think about what on earth was going on with Beau. He has been acting so strange recently, and I have no idea what happened to change our friendship, but something did. Now Beau is wanting to move out, and the thought completely scares me.

Beau has been there through everything, and it's the thought of him not being there that scares me the most. I wonder if this is what it feels like when a relationship ends? Do you feel like your world is coming to an end? The thought suddenly has me stopping in the street as it dawns on me that this is exactly what me and Beau have had – a relationship. I always felt our friendship was different. I lost count of the number of people that came up to me in college and asked if we were going out. I'd always laughed it off, explained that Beau was straight and that we were just close because we'd grown up together.

So the emotion I thought was fear was, in fact, pain. Pain that what we had was coming to an end even though there isn't supposed to be anything coming to an end in the first place. Beau hasn't died; he'll still be in my life, just not like he is now. I suppose that's something I'm just going to have to accept.

Turning around on the spot, I make my way back to my shop. It's still early, but I may as well open — it might take my mind off things — but I know that I'm definitely glad the ladies have a class tonight, giving me that little extra thinking time since there is no way that I can talk to him about Jamie. Not yet, anyway. Maybe I should cancel my date with him on Saturday night… it just doesn't seem fair if the spark isn't there. Why did he have to kiss me? Up until that point, everything had been going so well.

Walking onto my shop's street, I spot a figure standing outside my shop and groan. Why is Chase standing outside my shop? He never comes here, so this can only mean one thing – trouble.

"Morning Chase," I say as I unlock the front door. "Did you want a coffee?" Which I already know the answer to but still ask, anyway.

"Not from you. God knows what you would infect me with," he snidely replies.

"Then what do you want?" I ask.

Chase looks up and down the street and doesn't speak until he sees that it's empty. "What have you done to Beau?"

"What do you mean?" I'm confused by the question.

"He just kicked me out of his garage and told me my business is no longer welcome there," Chase replies.

I almost want to fist pump the air on hearing this. Whatever Chase said to piss Beau off must have been bad for him to refuse to work on Chase's car anymore.

"You've infected him with your ways and destroyed him," Chase continues. "And I hear there's another homosexual in town. Are you determined to ruin this town?"

"Chase, people are allowed to move into town," I state, "And last time I checked, Beau was a grown adult who was able to make his own decisions."

"You wait till I tell the congregation what you've done," Chase continues. "You know everyone in this town hates you. Just you wait till they find out what you did to Beau. You really should leave before something bad happens."

"Excuse me? Was that a threat I just heard?" The sound of Jamie's voice makes us both jump.

"Who the hell are you?" Chase demands.

"I'm the person who just heard you threaten Addy in broad daylight." Jamie continues, "And I also happen to be a lawyer. So, if anything happens to him, his friends, his home, or his shop, then I'll be coming after you with the full extent of the law."

"You don't scare me," Chase counters, standing up straighter and pushing out his chest.

Jamie stands to his full height and takes a step closer to Chase, who flinches slightly. "You don't scare me either. Now if I were you, I would leave before I call the sheriff."

"Remember what I said, Addy. Leave," Chase states one more time before turning around and storming away.

"Hey. You, okay? What the hell was that about?" Jamie asks, a concerned look on his face.

"It's nothing. Chase has been spouting that shit for months. Most of the time I ignore it," I explain.

"You know that's harassment, right?" Jamie asks.

"It's just Chase being Chase. Like I said, I ignore him most of the time." I say.

"If you're sure… He's the first homophobic person I've met in this town," Jamie says, looking in the direction that Chase went.

"He's a member of the church I mentioned. The one on the outskirts of town," I tell Jamie.

"Oh. Why is he coming after you?" Jamie asks.

Taking a deep breath, I wonder how this is going to go down. "Chase is my brother," I state and walk into my shop and behind the counter without waiting for a reply.

"Your brother!" Jamie exclaims. "Wow. I wasn't expecting that answer from you. So, I'm guessing the family doesn't approve," he continues as he follows me into the shop.

"You could say that. My dad died when I was in college, so he never knew, but I came out soon after. Our relationship has been very strained since then." I explain, hoping that Jamie will finally drop the conversation. Thankfully he must catch a glimpse of something on my face because he doesn't say anything more.

"Want your usual?" I ask.

"Are you even open yet?" Jamie asks.

"Technically, no." I reply, but give him a smirk as I turn away and start to make his coffee, handing it over when it's done. "No charge today. The look on Chase's face was priceless."

"Promise me that if he starts talking that shit again, you'll come and see me," Jamie says, almost pleading.

"I promise, but I think today only happened because Beau pissed him off," I explain.

"Beau's a nice guy. It was nice to meet him. I had fun last night," Jamie states, taking a sip of his coffee.

"Sorry about him having to crash." I'm not sure why I'm apologizing for Beau, but somehow I think it was needed.

"Oh, no need. He was tired. I understand. He has a very physical job," Jamie says, and I can't believe how understanding he's being. "Anyway, I have to get going. Thanks for the coffee. See you tomorrow night. I'm looking forward to it."

"Yeah, me too," I reply, even though I am not entirely sure what I'm feeling about tomorrow night. Jamie is a nice guy — just look how he defended me against Chase. Maybe I should just go tomorrow and see what happens...

Shaking my head to try and clear the thoughts of Jamie, I start to get the shop ready. Setting up the tables, getting trays of cups prepped, and starting to brew a jug of filter coffee for those customers who aren't as adventurous and like the simpler things. But the moment I'm finished, the conversation I had with Chase starts to spin around in my mind.

What was he going on about with me infecting Beau? Infecting him with what? Chase really has lost it. It was bad enough when he was coming after me, but it looks like Beau is going to start getting it, too, which is just another topic to add to the list we already have. Pulling out my cell, I decide to send Beau a text. We need to talk.

Addy: We need to talk.

I don't pocket the cell and wait, hoping that Beau has his cell on him for a change and am rewarded when Beau replies a few minutes later.

Beau: Yeah. Tonight. Will be home when you get back.

Feeling a little better now that I'm finally going to be able to ask Beau what the fuck is going on, I get on with my day, keeping my fingers crossed that it goes quickly.

By the time closing time arrives, I feel like I've been in the shop for an eternity. The day has dragged so much. This morning I'd been so looking forward to the ladies coming in so I could avoid Beau, but now I want to get home and talk to him. I quickly move the tables around to make the bigger table that the ladies like and keep my fingers crossed that maybe they wouldn't stay that late tonight. As if they can hear my thoughts, Mrs. Nichols and Mrs. Phillips walk through the door together.

"Good evening, ladies," I say as I pull out a chair for each of them to sit.

"Good evening, Addy," both say together before taking a seat.

"I'll just go get you your coffee," I say and walk away.

Grabbing two mugs and a jug of freshly filtered coffee that I make especially for the ladies, I make my way back over to them, placing a mug in front of each of them and pouring in some coffee.

"Are you okay, Addy? You don't seem yourself tonight?" Mrs. Nichols asks.

"Just a lot on my mind this evening," I say honestly.

"This anything to do with your brother?" Mrs. Philips pipes up, looking up at me from her seated position.

"My brother?" I question.

"Yes," Mrs. Philips confirms. "Me and Mr. Philips decided to go for a walk this morning before the town was fully awake and we saw you talking, and he did not look happy."

"My brother was here this morning talking his normal crap," I say, not worrying about any language that might offend because honestly, I think these ladies could make a sailor blush.

"If he mentioned the town hating you, please ignore it. To be frank, the townspeople are getting more and more disillusioned with that church. I know a few members who have left," Mrs. Nichols adds.

"Yes, I know, Mrs. Nichols," I say. "Thank you. Is Gladys joining you this evening?" I add to change the subject.

"Yes," Mrs. Phillips confirms, so I make my way over to the counter and grab another mug, taking it over to the seat that Gladys normally sits at, and when she arrives a few minutes later, I go straight over and pour a coffee.

"Have I missed anything?" Gladys asks Mrs. Nichols and Mrs. Philips.

"We were just discussing why Addy looks so sad this evening," Mrs. Nichols answers.

"Really? What's up, Addy? It's not like you to be melancholy," Gladys asks.

"Apparently, he has a lot on his mind," Mrs. Philips replies for me.

I love these women more than anything. Maybe I could talk to them about Beau. It surely couldn't do any harm.

"Well, Beau has decided he wants to get a place of his own," I say to them.

"Really?" The three say in unison, and it's almost laughable.

"And I have a date tomorrow night with Jamie," I add.

"A date?" And that's Mrs. Nichols questioning this before adding, "You don't seem that excited about it."

"I don't know what I feel about it," I tell them honestly. "I was when we arranged it, but then Beau started acting weird and me worrying about him took over."

"Does Beau know about the date? Or Jamie?" It's Gladys asking this time, but the three of them share a look like they know something.

"He knows about Jamie but not sure on the date. Why?" I know I mentioned the date to Beau so why I said this I have no idea, but I'm suddenly intrigued that they might know something I don't.

"Have you considered that Beau might be jealous?" Mrs. Philips asks gently.

"Jealous? Of what?" I ask, very confused.

"That you might have met someone," Mrs. Philips continues.

"But just because I've met someone, it wouldn't stop Beau being my best friend," I tell them.

Mrs. Philips opens her mouth to say something else when Mrs. Nichols reaches out, touches her hand, and shakes her head in a 'no' gesture, which confuses me even more, but I decide to ignore it.

"You and Beau have been friends for a long time. Didn't you ever think that one day either of you might meet someone?" Mrs. Nichols asks.

"Umm, not really." I reply.

"You love him, don't you?" Gladys suddenly asks, taking me completely by surprise.

"Of course I do. He's my best friend," I reply.

"We aren't talking about that type of love, and you know it," Mrs. Nichols states, pursing her lips, and I stand next to the table as the three women in front of me don't say anything more but just keep staring at me, waiting for me to answer. Do I lie to these women or finally admit out loud to someone other than myself?

"Yes," I whisper in answer to the original question.

"Oh, Addy. I really think you need to talk to Beau. How long have you loved him?" And I'm not sure who asks as my emotions are now all over the place.

"It's been a while," I say, not wanting to admit quite how long it's actually been.

"Why haven't you mentioned anything to Beau?" And this time I can see that it's Gladys asking me.

"Cause he's my best friend, and I couldn't lose him. With him being straight, I didn't know how he'd cope knowing that I loved him more than just a friend, even a best friend."

Gladys opens her mouth again to say something, but just like before, Mrs. Nichols stops her. What the hell is going on? I wish they would just tell me what they know.

"Addy. Just talk to him. Everything will be okay in the end," Mrs. Philips adds. "Now ladies, I wanted to ask your opinion on a pattern I found," she says, looking at the other two, which is my cue to walk away.

Thirty minutes later, I pick up the coffee pot and make my way over to the table and see that the three of them are huddled in closer, whispering to each other.

"I just don't understand. They both clearly love each other deeply," Gladys is saying.

"Coffee?" I ask, and the three of them jump in their seats and a blush is touching all their cheeks.

"Thank you," Mrs. Philips replies, and as I walk away, I feel them all watching me. I have to wonder if they were talking about me and Beau. But why would they think he loves me? These ladies do get some strange ideas.

Chapter 20 — Beau

From the moment Addy sent me the text this morning, I've been clock watching, hoping that each job I had would take me hours so the day would just pass me in a flash. Of course, it hadn't, and when I eventually got back to the apartment and found Addy not there, I remembered that Addy had the ladies coming in tonight, so I was left alone with only my thoughts for company. Which in my current state was not the best idea because all I can see is that kiss I witnessed between Jamie and Addy. Addy taking that step closer to Jamie, deepening the kiss, and me wishing with every fiber of my being that it was me who Addy was kissing.

Pulling my cell from my pocket, I check the time and see that it's seven, which means that Addy should be back soon. Heading over to the kitchen, I grab a couple of beers, bring them back into the living room, place them on the table, and sit down. But within seconds, I'm back on my feet. Yeah, I can't just sit and wait, so instead I pace. Pacing helps. It's giving my legs something to do. And then I start counting. Ten steps, turn... ten steps turn... and I keep doing this till I hear the key in the lock, when I move quickly over to the couch and sit. I don't want him to see me pacing.

"Hey," Addy says as he comes in through the door, placing his keys into a bowl we have on a side table by the door.

"Hey," I reply and pick up my beer and take a sip. "Beer?" I ask as I point to the other bottle on the table.

"Thanks," Addy replies, taking a seat next to me, picking up the bottle, and taking a huge gulp. But then silence descends, and I can feel the tension between us. In all our years of friendship, I've never felt this when I've been with Addy, and I'm not sure if I should go first or wait for him.

"Long day?" I ask when I see him take another long drink from his beer.

"Yeah," Addy says but doesn't add anything more.

"How come?" I prompt, hoping we can talk about mundane stuff before anything else.

"Well, let's see," Addy starts, "you dropped this bombshell last night that you're moving out, you're only cordial to Jamie, oh, and then to top it all off, I had a run in with Chase this morning outside the coffee shop."

Chase. Shit, he did go straight to Addy after I kicked him out of the garage. I should've known he'd try and cause trouble straight away, but did he out me? Yet if he did, I think Addy would be more pissed than he is.

"Chase," I say, trying to keep my voice as even as possible. "What did he want?"

"He came to the shop, bitching that you kicked him out of the shop, that there was another gay in town, and that I had infected you. So, the normal bullshit."

"He said there was another gay in town?" The bastard told Addy about me. Just kicking him out of my shop wasn't enough. I should have kicked his sorry excuse for an ass right across town.

"Yeah, think he was talking about Jamie. But he actually said I was tainting this town," Addy says, looking down at his beer bottle.

"But do you know what he meant by saying I was infecting you?" Addy asks.

"No," I say, but I have a feeling that Chase was trying to say that Addy had infected me with homosexuality, so he did try to out me to his brother without actually saying I was gay, which, by some kind of miracle, failed as Addy had no idea what was going on. We fall back into a silence, and I take another sip of my beer while Addy just stares at his bottle.

"What the fuck did you say to him, anyway?" Addy suddenly asks.

"He came to the shop saying there was a warning light on in his car. It didn't take me long to realize that he'd deliberately drained oil from his car in order to make the check oil light come on," I explain.

"He did what?" Addy interrupts.

"He did it so he could come to the garage and talk shit about you and Jamie. I'm guessing that bit, but I just had enough. I called him out on draining the oil. Called him, your mom, and their church god awful and said they need to leave town and not you. Then I kicked him out of the garage and told him to take his business elsewhere," I explain.

"Wow. Wish I could have seen his face. But that explains why he was so pissed," Addy replies.

"Sorry, it wasn't my intention for him to come after you. I was tired of his shit," I say.

"Yeah, I know. Anyway, I think that Chase might be staying away from me for a while, thanks to Jamie."

"Jamie?" I question.

"Yeah. For the first time, Chase actually threatened me this morning. Unfortunately for him, Jamie overheard him. It was quite a sight to witness Jamie putting Chase in his place," Addy says, and I'm certain I can hear a tone of admiration in his voice.

"Jamie's a good guy," I say, trying to take any bitterness out of my voice. Addy deserves a good guy. Someone to stand up for him, and it looks like Jamie did just that.

"How would you know?" Addy snaps back at me.

"Hey. We talked the other night. He was cool," I say, trying to defend myself. Admittingly it was only about football, and if I was asked about him, all I could say was who his favorite football team was.

"You spoke to him about football," Addy says, confirming my own thoughts. "And then the moment food was done, you escaped to your bedroom," Addy retorts back.

"And?" I ask, wondering why Addy was pissed that I left them alone. Surely he would've wanted some alone time.

"All you can say is, 'And?'" Addy coolly replies.

"I thought you would've wanted to spend alone time with your boyfriend," I counter.

"What? Jamie isn't my boyfriend," Addy says, "We haven't even gone on a date yet."

"Really?" I ask in surprise, considering all the texting they've been doing.

"Yeah. We go on our first one tomorrow night," Addy says.

"But I saw you…" I start to say but stop when I see Addy staring at me. "Never mind," I finish.

"Saw what?" Addy prompts.

"Never mind." I say again.

"No! Saw what?" Addy demands.

There is no way I'm going to escape this now. "Saw you kissing," I mumble.

"Oh," Addy replies and finishes the rest of the beer.

"So yeah, I wanted to give you some space," I repeat.

"Is this why you want to move out?" Addy asks.

"Maybe," I confirm.

Addy suddenly gets up off the couch and starts pacing in front of me, and I have to bite my tongue to stop myself from saying, "Count to ten and then turn." But then he stops and just looks at me.

"Beau, what the fuck is going on with you?" Addy blurts. "You've seen me kiss guys before."

"Yeah, in clubs," I say, "but this was out in public."

"It was one kiss that hasn't been repeated," Addy shouts, and I can see that he's getting more and more worked up. "We haven't even gone on a date, and you've already decided that we're dating."

"Addy," I start to say.

"No, Beau," Addy says, holding up a hand to stop me from talking. "There is more going on here, and you better fucking tell me what it is."

"There's nothing more," I lie. "I just thought it best to give you your own space."

"Bullshit. Suddenly you decided that it's time to give me space. You didn't even do that when we were in college," Addy says as he starts pacing again.

"We've grown up since we were in college. I just thought it was time we had our own space," I say again.

"If you aren't going to talk to me, then what is the fucking point of me even being here?" Addy says. "I've needed my best friend the last few days, and you decided that we needed time away from each other. Thanks, Beau."

Addy suddenly turns to walk out of the room, and I'm on my feet and grabbing his arm to stop him. What the fuck is he going on about — he needed his best friend. But the moment my skin touches his, a shock shoots up my arm, and I instantly yank my hand back.

"What the fuck is that supposed to mean?" I demand, standing in front of him. "I will always be your best friend," I tell him.

"Could have fooled me," Addy spits back. "After that kiss with Jamie, I needed my friend. I needed to tell someone about it. I need to tell you about it."

Oh shit. I was worried he was going to say something like that. That's the one thing I definitely don't want to talk about.

"Sorry," Is the only word I get out before turning to walk away.

"No!" Addy says, grabbing my arm this time. "Like fuck you get to walk away."

Looking at his hand on my arm, I'm filled with a jealous rage. "Yes, I fucking do. Do you think I wanted to hear all about an amazing kiss with Jamie?" I shout at him.

"What the fuck are you talking about, Beau?" Addy asks, seeming not entirely sure what I'm going on about.

Pulling my arm out of Addy's grasp, I scream, "I love you, Addy." Oh shit. Those were not the words I intended to come out of my mouth, and I just stand there, staring at Addy, who doesn't seem to be reacting like I thought he would.

"Beau, I love you, too. You know that you're my best friend," Addy says gently, misunderstanding my meaning. Now more than ever I need to get away from him.

As I try to move around him, I can feel the tears coming. I thought the moment I said the words out loud Addy would understand and then we'd kiss and the universe would align, that everything would fall into place. But that was only a fairy tale, a stupid dream. Instead, he's just looking at me, a confused expression on his face, and I've never wanted to be further away from this man in my life. My dream is laying in tatters around me. But with every sidestep I take, Addy is still blocking me.

"No!" Addy shouts at me "You are not going anywhere."

"Addy, please let me through," I beg, trying to stop a sob as I feel a tear run down my cheek.

"Beau, please. What's wrong?" Addy says more gently and reaches out a hand to stop me.

"Just let me go," I ask. I need to get away from Addy, from this apartment. Hell, at the moment, I want to get out of Madison Springs.

"No," is all Addy says, and when I try to move around him again, he blocks me. So both of us just end up standing there facing each other. Neither of us says anything, but then I'm not sure I have anything else to say.

"Beau," Addy tries again a few minutes later.

"I think it's best I leave," I tell him.

"Just like that," Addy says, anger lacing his voice again.

"Yeah. I'll go stay with my parents and collect the rest of my stuff in a few days," I say again. This time, instead of trying to sidestep Addy, I turn around and walk around the back of the couch, but Addy is faster and is standing in front of me again.

"So just like that, you're letting a kiss destroy our friendship?" Addy demands.

"Addy," I try, and I know what he's saying is right, but what more can I say?

"You don't get to say Addy in that pleading voice like it's the answer to everything," Addy states.

Suddenly I've had enough and push Addy. He stumbles back but composes himself quick enough to push me back with a lot more force than I was expecting.

"What the fuck, Beau?" Addy asks, but I just ignore him and try to push him out of the way, which, considering I'm bigger than Addy, shouldn't be an issue. But Addy is standing firm. "No," Addy shouts.

For a second, I stop trying to push him out of the way and wait for him to relax, then I strike and push him, but this time I keep going until I've pushed him up against the far wall beside the hallway entrance that leads to the bedrooms. My aim was to use his surprise at being pinned against the wall to my advantage and get down the corridor and into my room before he could stop me. Instead, I'm transfixed. I take a step back, both of us breathing hard, but Addy is staring at me, confusion written all over his face, then he unconsciously licks his lips and I snap.

Pressing him against the wall again, I move in closer and connect my mouth with his. This is not how I envisioned our first kiss, but then I realize that Addy isn't kissing me back. Shit. The one thing I was frightened about is coming true. Our friendship isn't going to survive this. I'm just about to stop and take a step back to apologize, when I feel Addy's tongue run over the seam of my lips, asking me to open for him.

What the... opening my eyes while our lips are still locked together, I see Addy staring at me. I thought what I was going to see was hatred, but what I'm met with is wonder and something else. Closing my eyes, I open my mouth, granting Addy permission. His tongue sweeps into my mouth and a duel with my own starts, and I can taste the beer we'd both been drinking. Addy pushes himself off the wall, never breaking our kiss, and wraps his arms around me, pulling me closer to him. Our chests are molded together. He runs his hand up my back and grabs my neck, pulling me further into the kiss. Suddenly he spins us around and pushes me up against the wall. In this position, I can feel his hard on against my own, and I start grinding into him. I'm not sure which one of us moans first, but it's the catalyst to bring us back to reality and make us both realize what just happened.

Addy jumps back, his lips red and swollen, his breathing fast, and his hard on clearly evident in his pants. And that's when I realize the gravity of the situation – holy fuck, Addy kissed me back.

Chapter 21—Addy

What the fuck just happened?

I keep staring at Beau and I know I'm breathing hard and fast, but I can't take my eyes off his lips. They're red and swollen, because of me.

We kissed. Holy fuck, we kissed and my God, I felt it. That's how a kiss is supposed to make one feel. Because Jesus, I felt that in my toes. When he pushed me into the wall, I wasn't sure what he was going to do, but kissing me wasn't at the top of that list. At first it took me what felt like a minute to realize what he was doing, and then he shifted ever so slightly. I knew he was going to pull away, and I just couldn't let him do that.

I wanted more. I wanted to let him know that I wanted this kiss, too, so I'd licked his lips. When he opened his eyes, I saw the hint of surprise at my request and something else. But before I was able to figure out what, he had closed his eyes and opened for me. The taste of beer lingered, and I could feel his stubble against my skin. The tingles that traveled all over my body got my dick's attention. I hadn't wanted him to know how aroused I was, so I thought if I shifted positions I could hide it, but the opposite happened. The next thing I could feel was him hard and grinding against me. The moan that came from him was like music to my ears. Beau was enjoying it, but it was this thought that had me jumping away from him.

Beau just kissed me.

"Beau," I whisper.

"Sorry," Beau whispers back and tries to move away. Quickly, I grab his arm to stop him.

I place a hand on the side of his face and feel him as he leans his head into it. I run a thumb over his cheek and decide to risk it. I lean in again and place a kiss on his lips. Gentle, soft, and then he kisses me back.

"Beau," I whisper as I break the kiss, his name hovering above our lips. "What was that?"

"Addy, I'm sorry," Beau says back, casting his eyes down.

Sorry? I thought that he enjoyed that kiss as much as me. Why is he suddenly saying sorry? Oh, crap, is he regretting it already? Instantly I remove my hand from the side of his face. Was it a spur of the moment thing? Just something that happened due to the heightened emotions?

Taking a step back, I drop his arm that I hadn't even realized I still had a hold of. "You're regretting it, aren't you?"

Beau's head snaps up to look at me. "God, no, Addy. I'm not regretting it."

"Then why the fuck are you saying sorry?" I ask.

"Jamie," is the only thing he says.

Fuck. I'd forgotten about Jamie. My thoughts had been consumed by that kiss. Beau mentioning Jamie's name has me suddenly comparing both kisses, which I know isn't something one should do, but I just can't help it.

When I'd met Jamie, the attraction had been there, and I thought that when we kissed there would be sparks... Of course there would be. Jamie and I were attracted to each other, so of course the kiss would be amazing, and then it wasn't. Even though the feeling wasn't there, I couldn't deny Jamie had been a great kisser. But when I compared it to Beau kiss, it was like an amateur now. No one had ever kissed me like Beau had just done.

Even the one-night stands I'd had over the years, some of which had been very intense, were nothing like that kiss. I swear my lips are still tingling. But what the hell does that mean for us? What does it mean for our friendship? Has this changed everything?

Every time I imagined an occasion where Beau kissed me, there were no complications or questions that needed to be answered. In my daydreams, Beau would come up to me and say, "Addy, I want to be more than friends," then he'd take me into his arms, kiss me, and that would be that. We would seamlessly shift from friends to lovers. But real life doesn't work like that.

"Excuse me," Beau whispers, and I take a step back, giving him space. He immediately takes a sidestep and disappears down the corridor to his bedroom. I want to shout after him, ask him all the questions that are racing around my head, but I stay silent.

Pulling out my cell from my pocket, I check the time and wonder if it's too late to drop Jamie a text to see if I can come around and am surprised to see how late it actually is. There is no way I can go over tonight. I can't close the shop on a Saturday, which means that I'm going to have to leave it till tomorrow night. Great. Not the ideal time to tell someone that you kissed someone else.

Putting my cell back in my pocket, I take the empty beer bottles into the kitchen, turn off all the lights and make my way to my bedroom. A light is shining from underneath Beau's door so I know that he's still awake. I go up to his door, raise my hand to knock but lower it again. I want to talk to him so badly but know if I go into that room tonight everything would change more than what it already has, and until I talk to Jamie that is not something I can do. Turning around I walk over to my room, and before entering give one last look toward Beau's room. The light suddenly goes out and my heart sinks.

The following morning, I wake early and when I leave my room, see that Beau's bedroom door is wide open. Sticking my head in I see that it's empty with the bed already made and for a split second, I want to see if his clothes are still there. Last night he had said he was going to leave before our kiss, but at the last moment I chicken out. I would prefer to believe that he is still here at the moment, plus maybe he's in the kitchen.

But the moment I enter the living room, I know that Beau isn't in the apartment. It's just too quiet. I had hoped to see Beau this morning since last night had ended so suddenly. The kiss hanging in the air between us. Without thinking I glance over to the wall, the image of Beau pushing me against it, the pause before he kissed me, and even just imagining it, I can feel the tingles all over my body. Shaking my head to rid myself of the image, I get on with making myself some coffee. Dwelling on that kiss is not going to help me today.

The one good thing I know is that Saturday is my busiest day of the week. With most of the town not working and the weather still dry, the townspeople like to go out and about, which should mean I'll be busy enough to forget about everything that is going on in my life at the moment so I cannot wait to get to the shop.

Of course, that doesn't happen. The shop is busy just like I thought, but every time the shop door opened, I would look up to see who it was, never sure if I wanted it to be Beau or Jamie to walk through the door. Which meant that I was mentally exhausted as I locked the door at closing time. All I wanted to do was go home and go back to bed but I had to get ready for my date.

Jamie had texted me his address telling me to get there at seven. So, I suppose I could go home and have a nap for an hour, but I was too worried about sleeping through any alarm I would set, and I needed to talk to Jamie tonight.

Walking into the apartment I'm greeted with the same silence as this morning. Beau is still not here. Pulling out my cell, I go to text him and ask him if he's okay but don't. Instead, I lock the screen and put the cell back in my pocket. I want to talk to Beau once I can tell him that nothing has happened or is going to happen with Jamie.

Going into the kitchen I brew myself a strong coffee and take it into my bedroom to drink slowly while I get ready to go to Jamie's. I had decided to dress casually with maybe a touch of something smart. Pulling on my blue stone wash jeans, I grab a light blue t-shirt, pulling it on. Then I put on my brown Chelsea boots. Walking over to the wardrobe that sits along one side of my bedroom wall I open the door to reveal a full-length mirror and check out my outfit. Pulling my dark grey suit jacket off the hanger I slip it on, and my look is complete.

My original plan had been to drive to Jamie's tonight; it would have meant that I couldn't drink and if the evening went downhill, I had an easy escape. But after the events of the last twenty-four hours I decided to walk. It gave me more thinking time and I could still leave whenever I wanted, plus the evenings were a lot cooler now.

Dead on seven I am ringing the doorbell for Jamie's, the smile on his face as he opens the door racks me with even more guilt. He's a great guy and didn't deserve this treatment. He is also dressed very similarly to me. Blue jeans with a dark grey t-shirt with matching grey socks. Well, it is his house, he doesn't have to put shoes on.

"This might sound strange, but do you mind taking your shoes off?" Jamie asks a little sheepishly.

"Of course," I say, slipping off my boots and placing them off to the side.

"Thank you. Just have a thing about shoes in the house." Jamie explains.

Looking around me I take in my surroundings. In front of me are some stairs with a hallway leading to the back of the house, which Jamie is currently heading down. Quickly following him I pass a couple rooms to my right. One is the living room where I spot two couches facing each other and the next room is a dining room. There is a huge table, but I can't see any place settings, making me wonder where we are eating.

Reaching the back of the house I walk into a huge kitchen. One half of the room is the prep area and on the other side there is a beautiful wooden table and chairs set for two people.

"Hope it's okay that we eat in here," Jamie says when he catches me looking at the table.

"Yeah, of course," I reply.

"Take a seat. Want a glass of wine or beer?" Jamie asks.

"Beer would be great," I say, but honestly, I want something stronger to give me a little dutch courage, but instead I walk over to the table, pull out a chair, and sit down.

Jamie walks over to the cupboard, opening it up to show a fridge inside, and pulls out two bottles, bringing one over to me.

"Will the food be long?" I ask, wondering if I have time to get this over with before we eat.

"We have about ten minutes," Jamie replies.

"In that case, can you sit for a minute?" I ask.

"You sound rather serious," Jamie says, pulling out the chair opposite me and sitting down.

"Yeah," I say and take a sip of my beer.

"Okay," Jamie replies. "I'm getting worried."

"Look, I'm really sorry, but something happened last night that I need to talk to you about," I start.

"With Beau?" Jamie asks.

"Um, yeah. How did you know?" I ask.

"Tell me what happened, and we can go from there," Jamie responds, ignoring my question.

"Okay..." I say, hesitating a moment before I tell Jamie about the argument between Beau and me. "It got heated, and, well, it ended with Beau pushing me against a wall and he, umm... He kissed me, and even though it took me a split second, I kissed him back."

Jamie looks relieved for a second and then bursts out laughing. "Jesus, Addy. You just scared the crap out of me."

"What?" I ask, completely confused by his reaction. "I feel so guilty. We kissed and organized this date and then I kissed someone else."

"Can I ask you something?" Jamie continues.

"Of course," I reply.

"How long have you dreamed about that kiss?" Jamie asks.

I consider lying to him but decide that it's better to be truthful. "Since I was sixteen," I tell him.

"Thought so," Jamie states, giving me a smile. "And what about Beau?"

"What about Beau?" I ask, confused by the question.

"How long has he wanted to kiss you?" Jamie explains.

"No idea," I tell him.

"Interesting," Jamie states at hearing this, but he doesn't explain any more. I know I should ask him what he means, but I'm more interested in how well he's taking all this.

"You're being very understanding about this," I say instead.

"Did you enjoy our kiss the other day?" Jamie suddenly asks.

"It was nice," I reply, as I don't want to hurt his feelings.

"Nice. The one word everyone wants to hear when discussing a kiss." Jamie chuckles.

"Sorry," I say because that's the only thing I can think of.

"Okay, I'm going to be brutally honest with you Addy," Jamie starts, and I'm not sure I'm going to like where this is going. "When we met in the bar, I was totally attracted to you. I've loved the texts and spending time with you, but that kiss... I felt like I was kissing a friend, and not in a good way."

What? I wasn't expecting him to say that, and before I can stop myself, I burst out laughing. "Yes." Because that's exactly what it felt like.

"So, to be honest, you telling me about Beau is kind of a relief as I think we were destined to be friends. Now, tell me what happened last night after the kiss."

"Nothing," I tell him, still not able to believe what Jamie just said. The relief had been instant.

"What?" Jamie says, and he genuinely looks surprised.

"Yep. Beau mentioned your name and vanished, and I haven't seen him since," I explain.

"But that makes no sense," Jamie says, but I don't think he's actually talking to me, more out loud.

"What makes no sense?" I ask.

"Beau just walked off. I thought he would have been thrilled to have finally kissed you," Jamie says.

"Why? You know that Beau is straight, right?" I say to Jamie.

"You sure about that?" Jamie asks.

"Of course," I say. "If he was anything other than straight, he would have told me," I reply.

"Look, I'm not a hundred percent sure, but I think Beau likes you. I only had to spend ten minutes with him to know that."

"Well of course he likes me. We're best friends," I tell him.

Jamie gives me a look as if to say 'you sure about that?' but doesn't question me any more about it. I know if Beau was gay, he'd have told me long ago. There's no way he'd keep something that big from me.

"What do I do now?" I suddenly blurt.

"What do you mean?" Jamie asks.

"Mine and Beau's friendship," I explain.

"I can't answer that. That's something to talk to Beau about," Jamie says gently.

He's right. I know that. That kiss changed everything, and we can never go back to what we were before.

Chapter 22 — Beau

Last night did not go as I planned at all. I knew it was going to be a tough conversation, but it escalated so quickly. I thought that once I explained the reasoning behind my leaving, Addy would understand, but it somehow made things worse. Then I'd screamed, "I love you," and he still didn't seem to understand. In that second, my heart broke. I needed to get away from Addy. For the first time since we'd become friends, I couldn't look at him. It just hurt too much.

Why I'd thought I was going to get a different response from him, I don't know. He'd never even hinted that what he felt for me was anything but friendship. Then again, why would he? In his eyes, I'd always been the straight best friend.

But then he wouldn't let me leave the room. The one thing that I needed in that moment, and he wouldn't give it to me. Then it got heated. I was just so angry that I couldn't escape that I felt the only option I had was to move him out of the way – physically. I've always been the stronger of the two of us and thought that I would be able to push him out of the way easily, but somehow, he stood firm. He had to take a step back, but that was to steady himself more than anything. What I hadn't been expecting was the force in which he pushed me back. It proved just how angry he was.

That's when the wall caught my eye. If I could drive him over toward the wall, I could escape down the hallway to my room and lock the door. Addy wouldn't be able to follow me. The plan nearly worked until I had Addy up against the wall. His breathing had already increased, he had this almost startled look in his eyes. Basically, he looked stunning, and I couldn't stop myself. I'd already told him I loved him; may as well completely destroy what little shards of friendship we had left.

His lips felt amazing. Even though this was not how I imagined our first kiss going, his lips felt better than anything I could've dreamt of. They were soft yet firm, but then when he didn't kiss me back, I didn't know what to feel. This had to mean the end of our friendship, but then Addy kissed me back. Running a finger over my lips, I swear I can still feel Addy there. Like he left a permanent imprint of himself on me.

But Addy kissing me back wasn't the only thing I remembered. The feel of his dick as it rubbed against my own had felt so good. He was long and hard, and I had to fight every instinct in me not to run my hand up and down his length or even pull down the zipper of his jeans so I could take his dick into my hand. It would've been amazing to watch Addy as I caressed and teased him, watch him come undone in my arms. Instead, I'd remembered Jamie and broken us apart. I knew how guilty Addy would feel with just kissing let alone if we'd done anything else.

I apologized, of course. This was all my fault, and he then had the nerve to think I regretted the kiss. That kiss I would cherish for the rest of my days, but Addy had seemed to have forgotten all about Jamie till I said his name. It was then that he finally let me go.

I had paced back and forth in my room for what felt like hours. I had no idea what I was supposed to do now, but the one thing I knew for sure was that there was no way I could face Addy and needed to get away. I could go to my parents but arriving in the middle of the night would have made them ask questions I didn't want to be asked. So instead, I waited till I thought Addy had been asleep, grabbed a spare pillow and a blanket, and snuck out of the apartment. Driving to my garage, I opened up the doors and drove the car in — making sure to securely lock them again afterward — and climbed into the back seat where I fitfully slept for a few hours.

The following morning, I'm sitting in my car outside the garage just staring at my cell. Addy would've realized by now that I wasn't in the apartment. I thought he might have texted me to see if I was okay or even ask where I was, but I'd heard nothing. A part of me — and I am not sure how big that is — is disappointed. This ended up with me pacing in my room the night before when I'd gotten up after my fitful dreams. I'd convinced myself that Addy must have felt something to have kissed me back like that. But the lack of text proves I'm wrong again.

The reality of the situation is beginning to sink in now. The fear I'd had for all these years is coming true. Addy is never going to see me as anything but a best friend. And yet, even though it was something I knew and tried to condition myself for, the pain of that rejection still hurts. This leaves me no alternative but to move out. Addy has his date tonight, which means that I'll be safe to go and grab a few belongings to keep me going. Then, once the dust has settled, I can get the rest of my stuff.

There's a motel just on the outskirts of town not far from the garage, which is mainly used by tourists. I can go and stay there. I'd become the topic of the local gossip for a few days, but if I go back to my parents, I'll have to face the same gossip, anyway, so may as well endure it in a motel room by myself. Now I just need to find something to keep me occupied for the rest of the day.

Normally I don't like to work on the weekends, which I understand annoys some of my customers, but I like to make sure that I have time for me. If a customer is truly desperate and in need, I'll work late during the week, but that rarely happens. Today I will be making an exception. Doing stuff will not only keep me busy but also keep my mind occupied and off my sexy best friend, or ex best friend or whatever he is.

At the moment, I feel like I'm going around in circles. My thoughts are on a constant repeat. I've felt like this before, and it's unnerving, though it's never been a person who's made me feel like this before. The kiss in that moment was everything, but I can't even begin to explain to myself why. The tender kiss Addy had brushed over my lips but then he let me leave. He asked me if I regretted it, but I never asked him if he did. Now that time has passed, does he regret it? Is he comparing my kiss to the one with Jamie? Was Jamie's kiss better?

Shaking my head, I climb out of my car and head over to my office. Luckily, I keep a change of clothes here for emergencies. Working in a garage means one never knows when one may spill something or kneel in something that can easily seep through coveralls to the clothes underneath. Stripping down, I then pull on the jeans, black t-shirt, and coveralls, then turn on the radio, searching the stations until I find one playing music that meets my mood before getting to work.

The day passes by in a flash, and it's only when my stomach complains loudly that I realize I haven't eaten yet. Food has been the last thing on my mind, and my first instinct is to check the time to see if Addy is still open and go there. But then the image of our kiss flashes in my mind, somehow morphing into the one of Addy kissing Jamie, and I know I can't go there, not yet anyway.

Checking my cell, I can see that it's just after five, so Addy would be closed. He figured out a long time ago that there was no point staying open late since business always quieted down later in the afternoon. But it also means that Addy will be heading back to the apartment. I can't stay in the garage for that much longer. It's a great hiding place, but I really need to get food. My original plan had been to get my stuff and then go to the motel, but if I go now and get checked in first, I can see if I can get a pizza ordered to the room, then relax a while before going to get some stuff. It also means there is less of a chance of Addy spotting me.

Making my way through the town as quickly as possible, I keep an eye out just in case Addy or Jamie see me, not that Jamie knows my car. Thankfully, luck is on my side, and I don't see either of them and am able to get to the motel. In fact, the town is remarkably quiet, which is a bonus. If any of the gossip tree ladies had seen me, it wouldn't have taken long for them to ask my parents where I was going, which would have resulted in a phone call I wasn't ready to deal with.

Pulling into the motel parking lot, I'm surprised to see that it's relatively empty. We're still at the height of the tourist season, so I figured it would be almost full. Madison Springs isn't on many of the major routes, so nothing normally books out, but this is still quiet.

I pull into a space outside the reception, and for a minute I just stare at the door. It's been a long time since I've stayed anywhere other than my parents' or the apartment. I can't actually remember the last time I stayed somewhere by myself. It's going to be a very odd few days. Taking a deep breath, I get out of my car, and within a few strides I'm pushing open the door, causing an electric chime to go off, which makes me jump. The lobby is bigger than I expected. To my right is a couch with a coffee table, and to my left is a wooden counter that runs almost the entire length of the room except for the small section used as the entrance to get behind the counter.

"Good afternoon. Can I help you?" a familiar voice asks.

"Justin?" I say, surprised to see him behind the counter.

"Beau?" Justin questions like it's not me standing in front of him,

"What are you doing here?" I ask. I didn't know that Justin worked here. If I had, I probably wouldn't have come to this motel.

"I'm friends with the owner and help him out sometimes," Justin explains. "What are you doing here?"

"Um, I wanted to book a room for a few days," I state and don't miss Justin's eyebrows shooting up in surprise.

"Oh, okay. Let me see what we have," Justin replies, turning to a computer and tapping on the keyboard. "You're in luck," he continues. "Looks like we have a few rooms free."

"No offense, but have you seen the parking lot? It's empty," I deadpan and am thankful when he laughs.

"Looks can be deceptive," he states. "We could have had a bus load of people in."

"Good point," I respond, because I hadn't thought of that.

"So does you needing a room have anything to do with the fact you look like shit?" Justin asks.

"I was working all day," I reply, hoping this will stop the questions.

"On a Saturday?" Justin questions.

"Yeah," I say but don't add anything more, and Justin doesn't push me anymore.

"Room 10," Justin says, sliding a key card across the counter to me. "It's on the bottom floor in the far corner. Your car won't be easy to spot there," Justin explains, and without me even having to say anything, he must know that I'm hiding.

"Thank you," I reply, giving what I hope is a grateful smile. "Is it okay for me to order pizza to be delivered here to the front desk? Don't want it coming to the room."

"Yeah, no problem," Justin says. "I'll drop it over to you when it arrives."

"Here," I say, going over to the counter and giving Justin a twenty. "That should cover it."

I don't say anything more and turn to walk back out of the lobby, but then a thought hits me, and I turn back. "Hey, Justin?"

He looks back up at me. "Yeah, Beau?" he says.

"Do me a favor. If anyone asks, don't tell them I'm here," I request.

"Wasn't going to," Justin says with a smile.

Just as I turn to leave, Justin calls me this time. "Beau" — I turn back to look at him — "I'm working at the bar tonight, if you want to come and have a drink. I'm a good listener."

"Thanks, Justin. I might take you up on that," I reply, knowing full well that I won't. Tonight, I just need solitude and my own company.

Getting back into my car, I drive to the furthest corner of the lot and park, and as Justin said, I can only just barely see the main road from here, making my car virtually invisible, and I can't help but smile. Justin really was a good friend for doing that and not pressuring to find out why I was hiding.

Opening the door, I look at the room. As motels go, this is a nice one. In the middle of the room is a large bed with a bedside table on each side containing a lamp. Opposite the bed there is a dresser that's holding a television, and there's even one of those pod coffee machines that Addy hates. Throwing my keys onto the sideboard, I go over to the bed and move the pillows around so I can prop myself up on the bed, then I pull out my cell and order a pizza. Once ordered, I close my eyes, needing to rest them for a few minutes. The next thing I know, I hear a knocking on the door. Looking around, I'm disorientated for a second. I must have fallen asleep and don't know where I am, then I remember the motel and the pizza. Rushing off the bed, I open the door to see Justin standing there.

"Sorry," I say. "Fell asleep."

"Not surprised," Justin says. "Here's your pizza and the change."

"Nah, you keep it. Call it a delivery fee," I reply, taking the pizza out of Justin's hands.

"Thanks. So maybe I'll see you later," Justin states before turning away and making his way back toward the front office before I've even had a chance to thank him.

The next few hours drag. I ate the pizza and channel hopped but nothing caught my attention. All I kept doing was looking at the clock. I wasn't sure what time Addy's date was, but I knew that once he finished work, he'd want to get home and shower, so I guessed it would have to be around seven or eight and would only leave the sanctuary of the motel room at that point.

When eight o'clock finally arrives, I make my way to my car and drive to the apartment, letting myself in.

"Addy," I shout just to make sure that he isn't there, but I still wait a few seconds to make sure he doesn't respond.

Satisfied that Addy isn't here, I go down to my room and pull out a gym bag, placing it on my bed. Pulling out my jeans, t-shirts, socks, and underwear from the dresser, I place them all into the bag. Going into the bathroom, I grab my toiletries and stuff them in the small travel bag before placing that into the bag and zipping it up.

Picking up my stuff, I walk out of my bedroom and through the apartment before pausing by the front door and having one last look around. It feels so cold and empty and not the happy, homey place of before, and that thought is cold and sobering. Slowly opening the door, I walk out without looking back.

Chapter 23 — Addy

This evening had gone better than I'd expected. I'd been dreading telling Jamie what happened between me and Beau. I thought he would throw me out of his house while calling me a few choice words when just the exact opposite happened. We both agreed that we were attached to each other but not in a romantic way, and we were definitely better off as friends. With that established, we both relaxed, ate, drank, and had fun. I'd even joked that I couldn't wait to tell the ladies that we hadn't worked out. Watching the color drain from his face had been comical, and once I finished laughing, I promised I wouldn't but warned him that it wouldn't take long for them to find out, so to be ready for the matchmaking to begin.

In all honesty, I don't think either of us paid much attention to the time, and I'm not sure why I checked my cell — maybe subconsciously hoping for a text from Beau — but I was surprised to see that it was just after midnight. Jamie had offered to order me a cab when I explained that I had walked, but I declined. It was a lovely evening, and the walk home would burn off the alcohol I had consumed.

Getting back to the apartment, I had hoped to find Beau awake since on occasion the pair of us can be night owls, but the place was eerily quiet.

Going to my bedroom, I look over to Beau's room to see the door closed and there is no light coming from under the door, and I ignore the pang of disappointment I feel. I've waited long enough to talk to him about how I feel, waiting one more night isn't going to hurt.

Closing the bedroom door, I strip my clothes off, leaving me naked except for my boxers, pull back the covers, and climb into bed just laying there. Normally, even when getting in this late, I would have jumped in the shower, but that would be because Beau was awake. But he's sleeping, and I wouldn't want to wake him. So instead, I enjoy the peacefulness around me and think about me and Beau and our kiss. There was no mistaking what that kiss meant; no way he could deny it as platonic. You do not get that hard for someone you only see as a friend, but I'm not sure how we plan to navigate the change in our dynamic. Closing my eyes, I drift off to sleep with the image of Beau pushed up against a wall and our lips crushed together.

The following morning, I wake and listen for sounds of Beau in the apartment. Sunday is the one day I keep the café closed just to give myself the day off, but the apartment sounds strangely quiet. Getting out of bed, I open my bedroom door and look over to Beau's. The door is still shut, and it's unusual for him to sleep in, but then again, he has been working hard this week. I really need a shower, so hopefully it won't disturb him now.

Going into the bathroom, I turn on the shower and leave it to warm up while I grab a towel. When the bathroom is finally filled with steam, I climb under the water, loving the heat as it hits my skin. Turning so that my back is massaged by the jets of water, I tilt my head back and close my eyes. Picking up my bottle of shampoo, I quickly wash my hair and then, just because I want to smell like Beau, I go to pick up his shower gel but grab thin air. Looking over to where Beau keeps his shower gel, I find an empty space. His shampoo is missing, too, and a cold fear washes over me.

Grabbing my own shower gel, I wash in record time. I rip my towel from the rack, wrap it around my waist, not caring that I'm still dripping water all over the floor, and go over to the bathroom cabinet. As I thought, his toothbrush and toothpaste, gone. Flinging open the bathroom door, I rush down the hall to Beau's room. Knocking on the door, I wait a few seconds before knocking again and turning the handle while saying his name. "Beau?"

His room is empty, his bed not slept in. I know he keeps a gym bag in his closet, and even though I know I shouldn't, I walk over to see if it's still there. My heart sinks when I realize it's gone and so are some of his clothes. Beau left without saying anything to me... but why? Considering most of his stuff is still here, he's planning on coming back. But when is he planning to come back?

Going back to my room, I pick up my cell from the bedside table and dial his number.

"Come on, Beau, pick up." But the call just connects to his voicemail, so I hit end call. I wait a few minutes and try his number again, but this time it just goes straight to voicemail.

What the hell is going on?

Drying myself off, I pull on boxers, jeans, and a t-shirt and try Beau's number again, and just like last time, it goes straight to voicemail. I'm starting to get really concerned now. Is he okay? Has he gotten into an accident somewhere? But then why when I first called him did it just ring with Beau not answering?

Pulling on some sneakers, I run out of my room, grab my keys from the side table and am out the door. I don't care that my hair is still wet from the shower. I need to find Beau and make sure that he's okay. Once in my car, I drive over to his garage. It looks deserted as I stop the car outside the double doors. Getting out of the car, I leave the driver's door open and the engine running. If Beau is hurt, then I might need to get him to a hospital quickly. Trying the doors, I find that they're firmly locked.

"Beau," I shout. "You in there?" I try to listen for any noise on the inside, which is nearly impossible with my car engine running, but I have to reason that if Beau was inside, the doors would be open. So if he isn't at the garage, the only other place he can be is his parents. Well, at least he's going to be safe, but I need to get over there and get him to explain why he left.

Getting back in my car a little calmer now, I drive over to Beau parents, but the moment I pull onto their street, I can feel my anxiety increasing again. Their driveway is visible from the street so any cars parked there can be spotted immediately. I can see Beau's parents' car, but there is no sign of Beau's. Now this could mean that he's gone somewhere this Sunday morning, but I have a feeling that isn't the case now.

Pulling up into the driveway, I park the car and make my way to the front door. Taking a deep breath to try and calm my racing nerves I ring the doorbell.

"Arden!" Beau's dad says. "What are you doing here?"

"Good morning, Josiah," I reply, but I have to bite my tongue for a second to stop myself from saying, 'please call me Addy,' because no matter how often I've said it, they've never shifted. I tried to keep calling them Mr. and Mrs. Jackson in retaliation, but that didn't last long.

"Josiah, who's at the door?" I hear, and Beau's mom appears behind her husband.

"Arden!" she exclaims.

"Good morning, Debra," I start, and I'm just about to ask about Beau when Debra is turning to Josiah.

"Josiah, why are you standing here talking on the doorstep.?" she asks, scolding her husband, and I almost feel sorry for him.

"Please, come inside, Arden," Debra continues, and before I can protest, she's pulling me inside the house. "Have you had breakfast yet? Or do you want a coffee?" she asks, going into motherly mode.

"No, I am fine, thank you," I start. "Who I really want is to talk to Beau. Is he awake?" I ask.

A look of confusion passes over both of their faces, and they turn to look at each other before turning to look back at me.

"Beau is here, right?" I ask.

"No, he's not," Josiah states.

"Oh," I reply because there is nothing more I can think of to say. If he isn't at the garage and isn't here, then where the hell is he? Pulling out my cell, I open my contacts and hit Beau's number again, and it goes straight to his voicemail. But unlike last time, I leave a message.

"Beau, can you call me when you get this? Please?" And then I hang up the call.

"Is everything okay, Arden?" Debra asks, and I hesitate for a second. Should I tell them that their son is potentially missing? Because I'm not a hundred percent sure that he is. It's just that I don't know where he is or where he's staying, but these are Beau's parents... they've been there for me through everything, and I couldn't lie to them.

"To be honest, I'm not sure," I say.

"Look, let's go into the kitchen," Debra begins, "and you can explain what's going on."

"Okay," I confirm.

Following them into the house, I marvel both at the similarities and differences to Jamie's house. Just like Jamie's, the moment you walk through the door, you're faced with a large staircase that turns just before you reach the top. To the left of me is a huge sitting room with two massive couches, one on each side of the room with a coffee table in the middle, but I think if you go into any house in Madison Springs, the living room will be set up this way. It's like an unwritten rule that every living room should look like this. In one corner of the room, I can spot a bookshelf, but instead of containing books, it contains pictures documenting Beau's life, and it's also my favorite thing in this house.

To the right of me is the dining room, complete with a large dining table that's currently set up to seat six people, but I know that the table can be made bigger to seat eight. I've spent many a happy hour at Thanksgiving or Christmas seated at that table with people who loved and supported me and didn't care that I was gay. All they cared about was if I was happy and behaving myself. The rest of the layout is basically the same as Jamie's. A corridor leading to the back of the house where the eat-in kitchen is.

Suddenly I stop dead in my tracks. What do I do if I've lost all of this? I thought that kiss had changed things between us. Changed us from friends to something more, something wonderful. But with Beau leaving, am I wrong? I won't be able to go back to what we had before. I'd never be able to hide what I'm feeling. But it's not only Beau I would lose. I would be losing this, too. I would be losing my family, and before I can stop it, a sob escapes my lips that has Debra stopping and looking at me. Mom hearing at its best.

"Arden." She rushes over to me. "What's wrong?" She asks as she pulls me into the best mom hug.

"I don't want to lose this," I say between sobs, wanting to shake myself for getting upset.

"Lose what?" Debra asks gently.

"This." I repeat.

Gently letting me go, Debra keeps her arms around my shoulders as she steers me into the kitchen, and just like Jamie's, one end of the room is a kitchen and the other contains a small table and four chairs where most of the meals are eaten. Debra pulls out a chair and places me in it.

"Josiah, coffee," Debra orders and pulls out the chair opposite me and sits down.

We sit in silence while Josiah makes the coffee, bringing over a mug for each of us, then his own and a jug of creamer. He pulls out the chair next to Debra before sitting down.

"Now, Arden. What is going on and what don't you want to lose?" Debra asks.

Taking a sip of the coffee, I recognize the taste anywhere, "My beans!" I say.

"Wouldn't use anything else, but don't change the subject." Josiah says.

"Sorry," I start, "I don't want to lose this. Don't want to lose you guys. You and Debra have been more of a family to me than my own."

"Why on earth would you lose us?" Debra asks gently.

"If me and Beau stopped being friends," I tell them honestly.

"Okay, you're starting to confuse us now, Arden," Josiah says. "Has something happened?"

I want to tell them about the kiss that happened, but I don't want to out Beau to his parents if he is gay or tell them he is when he isn't because at this moment in time, I have no idea what his sexuality is. They wouldn't care, I know, but it's not my place to out someone.

"Beau and I got into an argument Friday night," I tell them, which isn't a lie. "Out of nowhere Beau told me that he wanted to move out."

"What?" Debra says, sounding surprised.

"So, he hasn't mentioned anything to you?" I ask, looking between the pair of them.

"We haven't spoken in a few days," Josiah says.

"Anyway," I continue, "we almost got into a fight when I wouldn't let him leave." I'm feeling embarrassed that I just told Beau's parents that we were physical, and not in a good way.

"You and Beau, fighting?" Debra says and she's still sounding surprised, and I just nod my head in agreement.

"Then what happened?" Josiah asks, and I wonder how I can navigate the kiss scene without actually telling them we kissed.

"Beau pushed me into a wall," I respond, which isn't a lie since he did. "Because it took me by surprise, he was able to get to his room."

"Are you okay? How hard did he push you?" Josiah asks, and I know he is annoyed, maybe even angry with Beau, and I'm going to need to diffuse that.

"I was fine. It wasn't hard, and it didn't hurt me. It was more that he took me by surprise, plus I pushed him back, too," I tell him, and the look he gives is the look only a dad can give, and I'm instantly apologizing. "Sorry."

"Then what happened?" Debra asks.

"Nothing," I confirm. "We both went to bed and that was the last time I saw or spoke to him. Then this morning, I noticed some of his things were gone. I tried to call him, but each time it went straight to voicemail."

"Josiah, can you go give him a call?" Debra asks her husband. "But don't tell him Arden's here." This statement takes me by surprise, but I don't say anything. I just watch as Josiah leaves the room and hear the sounds of the stairs creaking as Josiah goes upstairs to get his phone, and a few minutes later, we hear him as he comes back down, talking as he walks.

"Hi, son, your mom and I want to know if you and Arden would like to come over for some food this evening?" Josiah asks, and I wish I could hear Beau's reply, but whatever it is, Josiah's brows pull together. "That's a shame. But you can still come, right?" Josiah asks. There is silence again before he says, "Great," and ends the call.

"He answered straight away, didn't he?" I ask, and Josiah nods.

In that instant, I know that Beau is avoiding me.

Chapter 24—Beau

I pull Addy closer to me, his arm laying across my chest and our legs entwined together, just wishing the alarm would turn off, but my alarm doesn't normally sound like that. Opening my eyes, I stare around the room that looks completely different. I even turn my head to see if the alarm is waking Addy, but the space next to me is empty and the bed covers don't look like mine. Then I remember I'm staying in the motel, and Addy isn't with me. I realize it had all been a dream, and sadness washes through me. But I don't remember setting an alarm last night. Looking in the direction of the sound, I see my cell is ringing, Addy's name on the screen.

If he's calling me, then he must have figured out that some of my stuff is gone and is now wondering where I am. Opening up my contacts, I go to Addy's number and hit block. I know that it won't take him long to figure out that I'm avoiding him, but I need to get my emotions under control and have to figure out where our friendship goes from here. We can't go back to the way we were before, but I really don't want to lose him from my life, either. But God, everything is a mess. Why did I have to kiss him?

Rolling over onto my side, I put my cell back on the bedside table but continue to stare at it. I know he'll be trying to call me again and that he's probably starting to get worried. I also know that I should call him and tell him that I'm okay. I know I'm being a completely shitty person because I'm not talking to him. It's just that I'm not sure I can handle hearing his voice. I hate feeling this way, but I've been in love with Addy for so long, I always thought that we would be end game.

The plan had always been that one day I would sit him down and tell him I was gay. Then apologize for not telling him sooner but hope he understood my reasons. I would then declare my feelings. He, of course, would have said the same back to me, and that would be it. We would have gone from friends to lovers, transitioning seamlessly, but real life had other ideas. Instead, I declared my feelings by shouting them at him across the room.

Shaking my head, I try to rid myself of the same thoughts that have been plaguing me for days... hell it's more like years. All they do is go around my head, never changing. If Addy doesn't have the same feelings for me, the outcome is always going to be the same. I knew this, so why am I surprised? Why am I hiding in a motel room, licking my wounds? Wounds that were truly inflicted by me.

My cell ringing on the bedside table finally gets me to stop thinking about Addy, especially when I see the name Dad light up the screen.

"Morning," I say when the call is connected.

"Beau," Dad says, and for a split second I think he sounds surprised that I answered. Shit. What the hell do I say to him?. "Yeah, that would be nice, but Addy already has plans tonight," I lie when he asks if we're both coming for dinner, but then again, I might not be lying. He could have another date with his boyfriend. Dad says that's a shame, and again I think there is something underneath his voice that I'm not catching, but I decide to ignore it, and when Dad asks again if I'm coming, I confirm straight away.

With plans made for this evening, that means I just need to find something to occupy my day today without actually going into town. Addy is probably already going all over looking for me, and I don't want to risk running into him. So, I have two options: hide in this room all day or drive to another town. But that also runs the risk of Addy seeing my car and following me. So really, the only option that I have is to stay here.

A knock on the motel room causes me to jump out of my skin. What the… Going over to the door, I look through the peephole to see Justin standing there, so I open the door.

"Hey," I say once the door is open.

"Morning," he replies. "So I figured that, as you're hiding, you'd probably be at a loose end," He finishes.

"I am not hiding…" I start, but when Justin just shoots me a look while raising an eyebrow, I stop talking.

"I need to go to the wholesaler for some stuff for the bar and thought you could come along," Justin finishes.

"Oh, yeah. That would be cool," I say, because it's definitely better than staying in this room all day. "Give me five to get dressed. Come on in."

Opening the door wider, Justin comes in, closing the door behind him, and just stands by the door to wait for me. I grab my gym bag and head into the bathroom, changing into some jeans and a t-shirt. Coming back out of the bathroom, I throw my bag on the bed and pull on my boots.

"Okay, I'm ready," I say to Justin, making him jump. He was so engrossed looking at his phone that he hadn't heard me come in. He looks up, a wry smile touching his lips, and if I'm not mistaken, he looks me up and down. Did Justin just check me out?

"Cool, let's get going," Justin says as he pockets his phone and opens the motel door. Picking up the room key, I slip it into my pocket and follow Justin out the door, closing it behind me. Justin had parked his pickup next to mine and was already getting into the driver's seat. Wow, he can move fast when he needs to.

Opening the passenger door, I climb in. The moment I sit down and click in my seatbelt, Justin starts the engine and pulls out of the space.

"I'm not going to drive through town, so you won't need to hide in the foot well," Justin says, giving me a quick glance.

"Umm, thanks?" I say.

"Want to talk about why you're hiding from Addy?" Justin continues.

"Who said anything about me hiding from Addy?" I counter.

"Seriously," he says, chuckling to himself. "You remember we live in a small town, right? Where everyone knows you. So it doesn't take a genius to work out that that is who you're hiding from."

"Is the town already talking?" I ask, horrified that the gossip could already be starting.

"Well, no," he confirms, and I heave a sigh of relief, "but it won't be long till they do."

"Yeah, I know," I say.

"So, do you want to talk about it?" Justin asks, and I know it would be so easy for me to tell him everything. Actually tell someone I trust that I am gay and have been for as long as I can recall, but I've already blurted it out to Chase, and really, the next people I want to tell are my parents. They need to hear this from me and not someone else in town even though I know Justin wouldn't say anything.

"Not really," I tell him.

"No problem. So, you watching the game later?" he asks.

And just like that, the conversation about me hiding in the motel is over, and it remains like that for the rest of the day. The drive to the wholesaler was fun. We talked about the football season, teams, and players we thought were doing well, which, of course, led to us talking about the teams that weren't doing so good and it took my mind off Addy completely. By the time Justin was dropping me off outside the motel room, I realized I hadn't thought about what was going on with me for hours. It was the perfect escape.

"I'm working the bar tonight if you want to come by," Justin says as he pulls into the parking lot and up alongside my car.

"Thanks, but I am off to the parents tonight," I tell him and climb out of the pickup. "Hey, Justin?"

"Yeah," he says and looks over to me.

"Thanks for today," I tell him.

"Anytime," he replies, giving me a smile. I never realized how handsome Justin was, probably because I spent so much time with Addy. In fact, I'd spent so long fantasizing about Addy that I neglected my other friends. I remember me and Justin being good friends in school, and so I make a mental note to make sure to spend more time with him.

Opening the motel door, I throw the key onto the side table, slam the door behind me, and walk straight into the bathroom. Turning on the water, I stand there with my hand under the jets until I can feel the warmth coming through. Stripping off, I get into the shower, letting the water wash over me. The heat feels amazing on my skin, and the jets of water are powerful enough to feel like they are massaging my muscles.

It's only when the water starts to turn cooler that I realize how long I've been standing under the water, not really thinking about anything in particular, just enjoying the water flowing over my body. I quickly wash my hair and body before the water gets cold. Wrapping a towel around my waist, I lean down and pick up my discarded clothes and walk out of the bathroom and over to my bag that's still on the bed, throwing the clothes from the bathroom beside it.

Pulling out a fresh pair of underwear, I slip them on and root around for another pair of jeans. Dammit, I must have forgotten to pack them. Which means that I'm going to have to go back to the apartment earlier than I intended. Pulling the jeans that I wore earlier out of the pile, I slip them on and just grab a clean t-shirt from the bag and pull it on.

Once dressed, I pick up the motel room key and head out to my car, sending out a silent plea that, as I drive through town, Addy won't still be out looking for me. Pulling out of the lot, I drive through town quicker than I should, but from what I can see, not many people are out and about. Pulling into my parents' driveway, I park behind their car and make my way over to the house. Before opening the door, I take a deep breath. Tonight, I planned to tell Mom and Dad everything. I know they need to know what's going on with me and they need to hear that from me.

Opening the front door, I shout, "Mom, Dad!"

"We're in the kitchen," Dad shouts back.

Going to the back of the house, I walk into the kitchen and find Mom and Dad already sitting next to each other at the kitchen table. Both have very odd expressions on their faces.

"Everything okay?" I ask, going over to them, pulling out a chair, and sitting down.

"It will be when you tell us why you're avoiding Arden," Mom starts.

"What?" I splutter.

"Arden came by earlier. Looking for you," Mom states. "He hadn't been able to get ahold of you, and yet when your dad called your cell you answered right away."

Oh shit. Addy was here. Then they already know that something is going on. Surely, he wouldn't have told them about our kiss. I know that he loves my parents, but would he out me like that?

"Umm," I start.

"Umm nothing. Arden said that you got into a fight." And this time it's Dad talking to me.

"What exactly did Addy say?" I ask, needing to know what was said.

"Just that you got into a fight. You pushed him into a wall and then vanished," Mom says, and I can't help heaving a sigh of relief. Yes, Addy told them virtually everything that had happened, but he left out the most important part. "But there was more to it than that, wasn't there?" Mom asks.

"Yeah," I confirm.

"Think that you better give us your version of events then," Dad says.

"To be honest, Dad, what Addy said was right. We fought, and I did push him into the wall, but what he didn't mention" — and I pause here and take a deep breath — "We kissed." I wait for the shock and questions to come, but they just sit there looking at me.

"Did you hear me?" I ask, wondering if they somehow missed what I said.

"That you kissed Arden?" Dad asks, wanting me to confirm my question.

"Yes," I confirm.

"We heard you," my mom confirms.

"I thought you would be shocked." I state, their reaction completely confusing me. "I just told you that I kissed a boy," I add at the end, but they still just sit there. Looking the same as before.

"Why on earth would we be shocked?" Dad asks, and this time he glances over to Mom, who shrugs her shoulders.

"Because it's a boy?" And I take another pause and add, "And not the first. I'm gay."

"We know," Mom says.

"What?" How the hell can they know I'm gay? I've been so careful.

"Beau, you have never brought a girl home. In fact, I can never remember you even telling us about a girl you liked. Then there was Arden," Dad says.

"What does Addy got to do with this?" I ask. Every time I had this conversation in my head, it never turned out this way. It was usually my parents jumping to their feet hugging me, telling me they love me regardless. Not them saying, "We know."

"Well, your friendship was always a little.... umm, odd," Mom says.

"Odd?" I question. It didn't seem odd to me. "We're just close."

"Beau, there is close, and there is you and Arden." Dad continues, "We just always thought that something was going on."

"With me and Addy?" I ask, completely dumbfounded.

"Yes," they say in unison.

"But you never said anything," I tell them, stunned that they have known all along.

"Beau, that wasn't our place," Mom says and gets up from the chair, walking around the table and pulling out the chair next to me. "We knew you would tell us when the time was right."

"Oh," I reply because I can't think of anything else to say.

"Can I ask you something?" Mom asks me gently.

"Yeah," but I think I know what she's going to ask.

"Do you love him?" She says, and I was right.

"More than anything," I confirm, and a sob catches in my throat as I say the next words. "Do you think he knows? Because he has a boyfriend, and I don't want to make things awkward for him."

"A boyfriend?" Mom says, shocked, and looks over to Dad. "Since when?"

"Few weeks, I think," I say.

"Beau, honey, I'm not sure where you got that idea, but I think you need to talk to Arden," she continues.

"Addy will never see me as anything more than a friend," I say, hating the words.

"Are you sure about that?" Mom says.

Looking up at her, I see the seriousness on her face. Does she know something I don't? I shrug my shoulders because suddenly, in that instant, I'm not sure of anything.

Chapter 25 — Addy

The second Josiah confirmed that Beau had answered his call, I knew that my friendship with Beau was over. When Josiah had ended the call to Beau, I'd pulled out my cell and called his number, and just like before, it had gone to voicemail. With every call I'd made earlier, I had thought that maybe his cell had died or maybe he was out of signal range, but if he's answering calls from his dad, then it can only mean that he had blocked my number. If one ever needed proof that a friendship was over, blocking the number was definitely it.

Debra had promised to talk to Beau and find out what was going on, but they didn't know about the kiss. They just thought that we were two best friends arguing. But it was so much more than that. Driving back home from their place, all I could think about was how empty the apartment was going to feel. A part of me still wanted to go and find Beau, confirm that he was okay, but there really was no point.

Now it's Monday morning, and I'm lying in bed, staring at the ceiling, the silence of the apartment almost deafening. And yet I don't want to get out of bed. I don't want to go to the shop and pretend that everything is fine. I don't want to listen to customers, and I definitely don't want to deal with the ladies tonight.

Throwing back the covers, I know that I can't stay in bed all day. If I don't open the shop, more questions will be asked than if I open and am grumpy. Dragging my feet into the bathroom, I quickly shower and try not to stare at the spot where Beau's shower gel would normally sit. Like that reminder that he isn't here.

Once back in my bedroom, I stand in front of my closet for a long time, trying to decide what to wear. I really want something that reflects my mood. Maybe black from head to toe? But I don't. Instead, I just pull out a white shirt and black trousers. It's what I normally wear, and yet this morning, even deciding that was difficult. I slip on some loafers and head into the living room. Maybe a coffee will help… but as I enter the kitchen, I can't even face making one. I just need to get out of this place and open the shop early, so I grab my keys from the bowl and leave.

The street looks to be quieter than usual this morning, but then again I am getting to the shop earlier than usual, too. But it feels good to be out of the apartment and away from the memories of Beau. Opening the shop door, I flip the sign to OPEN, head behind the counter, and busy myself with getting everything ready.

When everything is set up, I go over to the window to see if the town is getting busier and see it's slowly waking up. But then I spot Chase. He's on the other side of the road. He looks over to the shop and glares at me. Normally seeing me standing on my own would have made him come over and torment me, but today he doesn't. He just keeps on walking. Maybe he's listened to Jamie and is going to leave me alone. Finally, after all these years, he will leave me alone. All those times he told me to leave this place.

Looking around the street, I am bombarded with memories of Beau, the mischief we got up to when we were younger, and I can't look at them. Turning away, I walk back over to the counter and pour myself a coffee.

What would it be like to live here and not live with Beau? To not see him every day. To watch him move forward. To find someone else. Would that be something I could cope with? Would I even be able to find someone and move on?

Chase's words come unbidden to the front of my mind... "Leave this town." Every single time I'd heard them, I'd said I would never leave this place, but now, today, those words might be right. If I leave, then maybe it can be the fresh start that I need. There is really nothing to keep me here. My family has wanted me to leave for years. They probably wouldn't even want to know where I was going. I'd miss Josiah and Debra, of course, but I can come back and visit, and it might even help mend me and Beau. I know we'll never be close again, but I can come back at birthdays, holidays, etc. and celebrate. We can have a normal friendship.

The more I think about it, the more it feels like this could be the solution to everything. Pulling out my cell, I open the internet search engine and type COMMERCIAL PROPERTIES TO RENT and wait for a website to load. I know that this isn't something that is going to happen overnight. I'm going to need to work out how much capital is needed. What I'm going to need to sell this place or if I can keep this open and maybe get a manager in. Opening the first website on the list, I scroll down all the listings. Most are for large warehouses, but right at the bottom, a listing catches my eye. It's a café to rent, which means I wouldn't need to do much to get it up and running.

I've just opened the listing to get more information when the front door opens, and when I look up, I see Jamie standing there.

"Good morning," I say to him, putting the cell on the countertop.

"Morning. God, I'm glad you're open early this morning," he replies.

"Usual?" I ask, and he nods in agreement, so I turn to the coffee machine and start making his coffee.

"Thinking of setting up a chain?" Jamie suddenly asks.

"Excuse me?" I wonder what he's going on about as I hand him his coffee.

"Shop listing," Jamie says, pointing to my cell. When I placed it on the counter, I mustn't have locked the screen, thus showing the whole world what I was looking at.

"Maybe," I confirm.

"Well, that would be exciting," Jamie says. "I can help with all the legal work. Would you get people to train here?" And I think that he's more excited than me at the thought of me opening another store.

"The idea only just came to me," I tell him honestly. "But I was thinking I would possibly open it and get someone else in here."

"You would leave?" The astonishment is clear in his voice.

"I haven't decided yet," I tell him.

"Oh," he says, then looks around the store before looking back at me. "Has this got something to do with Beau?"

"Maybe," I tell him truthfully.

"Has something happened?" Jamie asks.

"If you classify him blocking me as something, then yes. He came back to the apartment when I wasn't there and took some of his stuff. So yeah, something happened," I tell him.

"Have you spoken to him at all?" Jamie asks.

"Not since Friday night," I confirm.

"Maybe you should before you make any rushed decisions," Jamie continues.

"I know that you told me that you thought Beau liked me on Saturday night, but all of his actions are telling me otherwise," I explain.

"Addy, have you stopped to think that maybe Beau is thinking the same as you at the moment? He thinks that we're together, and he's hurting. My guess is that he's trying to figure out how to navigate this world without you," Jamie says.

"I just don't understand," I say out loud. "If Beau likes me, then why hasn't he told me?"

"Only Beau can answer that question," Jamie says gently. "But my guess is it's for the same reason that you're too scared to tell him how you feel. You were so shit scared of losing each other that you kept it hidden."

"But we've ended up losing each other, anyway," I tell him.

"I don't believe that," Jamie says. Looking at his watch, he looks back up at me. "Look, Beau should be at the garage right now. Go and talk to him. I'll mind this place."

"You can't make coffee," I say, looking over at the machine.

"You have the filter jug ready," Jamie says, pointing to the pot in the corner. "If anyone comes in, they can have that. You only charge five dollars for it, right?" Jamie asks, and I know that I am not going to win this argument.

"You're a very good lawyer," I tell him.

"I know. Now go." And Jamie is basically pushing me out the door.

I have no idea why I'm even listening to Jamie, but I am, and for the first time since Friday night, I'm filled with hope. Does Beau like me? Have we both had feelings for each other all this time? It would certainly explain why we are so close. Getting to the back of my building, I jump in my car and make my way to Beau's garage. It would only take me ten minutes to walk, but I need to get there quicker than that.

Pulling into the street where Beau's garage is, I see a pickup truck parked outside, and I stop the car and wait. I don't want to talk to him while he has a customer, and the wait shouldn't be too long. The person is either dropping off or picking up. I think the truck belongs to Justin, as I'd seen it at the bar a few times when I'd been there, but I hadn't realized that he brought it to Beau to look at.

Five minutes later, I'm still sitting here watching and waiting for Justin to leave, but finally they both emerge from the garage. Justin has a huge smile on his face, and I'm not sure I'd noticed before, but he's quite a handsome man, but all I can see is Beau. Looking over to him, I watch as Justin says something to Beau that causes him to throw his head back and laugh, leaving him with a breathtaking smile that causes my heart to skip a beat. What did Justin say to make Beau smile like that? I keep watching as Beau takes a step towards Justin and pulls him into a hug.

I didn't know that Beau and Justin were that close, or maybe I should be asking when they got that close. That hug looks very friendly. Had I missed my chance completely? He thought that Jamie and I were an item and had gone on to find someone else. I keep watching as they break apart and Justin gets into the pickup and drives off with Beau standing there waving before he turns and walks back into the garage.

I start the engine, but instead of driving over to the garage, I turn the car around and head back into town. There's no point in me stepping in and spoiling something for Beau. He looked so happy a few moments ago, there's no way that I can take that away. But at least I know something for certain: I'm not going to be able to stay in this town.

Parking the car back at my apartment, I sit for a few minutes just trying to get my thoughts together. How can so much have changed in forty-eight hours? Was Jamie right that the reason Beau and I got into this situation was because we were too scared to come clean to each other? Maybe one day we will be able to find out.

Walking into the shop, I see Jamie leaning on the back counter looking at his phone.

"Been busy?" I ask as I walk, making him jump, and he almost drops his phone.

"Nope. I sold a grand total of two," Jamie says. "But I have a feeling you are going to be busy later. A few customers weren't happy when they saw me standing here."

"Thanks for the heads up," I tell him.

"So, what happened?" Jamie asks as he walks from behind the counter and I swap places with him.

"Nothing." I state.

"Nothing. He wasn't there?" Jamie asks. "I can come back at lunchtime and cover again if you want to try then."

"No, he was there," I say.

"So, what? He didn't want to talk?" Jamie asks.

"When I got there, I spotted Justin, you know from the bar, pickup outside," I explain. "I didn't want to talk to him while there was a customer and so waited. Anyway, a few minutes later they came out and looked pretty friendly. So, I turned tail and came home. "

"They were kissing?" Jamie states, sounding surprised. "Wow."

"No, they weren't kissing," I say.

"Right. So, what were they doing?" Jamie asks, giving me a look.

"Hugging," I tell him. "But I know for sure now that I cannot stay here."

"Hugging?" Jamie asks. "But I thought Beau was straight?"

"Yes," I confirm but then add, "I'm not sure what his sexuality is."

"So you're telling me that you're basing your decision to leave town on a hug," Jamie deadpans, and honestly, when he says it like that, it does sound like a rather stupid decision.

"You're leaving town?" The voice of Mrs. Nichols makes both me and Jamie jump.

"Good morning, Mrs. Nichols," I start.

"Do not 'Good morning, Mrs. Nichols' me," she starts, and in the corner of my eye I can see Jamie biting his lip trying to stop himself from laughing. "Did I just hear you say that you were leaving?"

"Umm," I start. "I'm thinking about it," I confirm. There is no way that I can live here, too..

"This your doing?" Mrs. Nichols demands, looking at Jamie. "You go on a date together and suddenly he wants to leave town."

Jamie starts looking slightly affronted, the laughter from a moment ago gone. "This has nothing to do with me, I promise. We decided we were better off as friends," he says, putting his hand up defensively. But then he looks over to me, and with a smug look on his face, says, "But I do know who's causing this."

"Oh really," Mrs. Nichols states. "And who might that be?"

Jamie looks back over to me, the smug grin still there, but he now has a wicked glint in his eye, too. He's beginning to enjoy this too much, and he knows full well what will happen the moment he opens his mouth. I try to plead with him silently to not say anything, but it's a lost cause. He looks down to Mrs. Nichols, gives her his breathtaking smile, and just says one word.

"Beau."

Chapter 26 — Beau

God, I missed my coffee. Okay, scratch that: I missed good coffee. This morning while I was getting ready for work in my room, I made myself one of the pod coffees. Which was okay, but it was nothing like Addy's coffee, and that's what I really wanted this morning. I know I could have gone to his shop — actually gone and spoken to him — but I couldn't. Something was still holding me back from repairing our friendship.

The one thing I'm certain about over the last few days is that I miss Addy and the friendship that we share. But I've also come to the realization that I would miss Addy being in my life more than I would hate seeing him with someone who is making him happy. The only thing that I've done the last few days is act like a spoiled kid who's had their favorite toy taken away from them. What I should have been doing is rejoicing in the happiness my friend had found, not focusing on what I was losing. Maybe I should have been looking at what I was gaining — the potential new friend in Addy's boyfriend.

The one thing I know I need to do in order to start the healing process is to finally come out to Addy. If coming out to my mom and dad is anything to go by, then it's probably not going to come as much of a surprise. I still can't believe I've been so scared to tell them and they already knew. I spent years wondering what they would say when I came out, and they just presumed that something was going on with Addy. Like I would keep something that huge from them.

The sound of a vehicle pulling up outside the garage pulls me from my musings, and I wipe my hands on the cotton cloth I keep in my coveralls. Standing by the doors, I recognize Justin's pickup.

"Morning," I say as Justin gets out and walks over to me.

"Morning," he replies.

"What can I do for you this morning?" I ask.

"Well, I was wondering if I can book this thing" — Justin points to his truck behind him — "for a tune up?"

"Yeah, of course. Let's go into the office and see when I can fit you in," I say.

After we go into the garage, I schedule his truck, giving him an idea of how long it will be off the road and the rough estimate but also saying that I don't stock parts, so if it needs anything, I'll have to order it. Justin seems happy with the price, but as we're stepping back outside, I have a question.

"How come you are bringing it to me now?" I ask as we walk.

"Well, um..." Justin replies, not looking at me.

"You didn't think I could handle your truck," I say to him.

"No," he tries to argue, but I can see the pink taint his cheeks, proving that I'm right, and I can't help but throw my head back and laugh.

"Sorry," he mumbles.

"Hey, it's okay," I say, and I'm not sure why I do it, but I take a step forward and pull him into a hug and am surprised when he hugs me back.

We break apart, and I watch as Justin gets into his truck and drives off with me giving him a wave. I honestly had forgotten how cool Justin was. I really do need to make the effort to be more friendly with him.

But just as I'm turning to walk into the garage, I spot Addy's car parked up the street. I'd recognize that vehicle anywhere. Maybe he's coming to see me, and I don't want him to know that I've spotted him, so I keep walking inside the garage. But no sooner am I inside the garage then I hear the engine start. I hold my breath, waiting to hear the gravel crunching outside as he pulls in, but it never happens. So maybe he wasn't coming to see me.... But then why was he parked on the street?

For the rest of the day, this question plays in my mind. Why was Addy there? But then, more importantly, why didn't he come into the garage? The only reason he would've been parked on the street was to see me. There aren't any other businesses around me that Addy would need to go to. The only way to find out why he was there is to actually go see him. I'd been wanting to, anyway, so this seems to be the perfect excuse. It's getting close to closing, so maybe I can shut up early and be at the apartment when he gets home.

The sound of the gravel outside my door draws my attention from the tidying I was doing. Maybe Addy came back now, knowing that it was coming to the end of my day. Walking over to the doors, I see Mrs. Nichols parking her car. Her car was only in last week, and she drives so carefully that I'd be surprised if there was anything wrong with it.

"Mrs. Nichols," I say as she gets out of the car and walks over to me. "Lovely to see you. Is everything okay?"

"Don't start with the 'lovely to see you,' young man," Mrs. Nichols starts.

"Is everything okay?" I ask, surprised at how annoyed she sounds.

"No, everything is not okay," she snaps back.

"Is it the car?" It only came in for a checkup the other day, and I'd made sure all the fluids were topped up.

"No, it's not the car. That's perfect as always," she continues.

"Then what can I do for you?" I ask, completely confused as to why she is here and why she is so annoyed.

"You can start by telling me what you did to Addy," Mrs. Nichols says.

"To Addy?" I repeat. This conversation is getting stranger by the second.

"Yes, to Addy," she repeats.

"Mrs. Nichols, I'm sorry, but I haven't done anything to Addy," I tell her, but I don't mention the argument or the fact that I haven't seen him since Friday.

"Then why is he leaving town?" she demands.

"Leaving town?" I ask, not sure I heard her right.

"Are you a parrot today? Yes, leaving town. I heard it myself this morning," Mrs. Nichols tells me. "Straight from the horse's mouth, and I know you're involved."

"Mrs. Nichols, I have absolutely no idea what you're talking about," I tell her because it's the truth. Addy has always said that Madison Springs was his home and he never wanted to leave. So this is just as surprising to me as it is her.

"Beau Jackson," — Oh crap, if Mrs. Nichols is using my full name, I'm in trouble — "You sort this out now. Do you hear me?" she demands. "I have no idea what's going on with you two, but it stops today."

"Umm," I start, but before I say anything more, Mrs. Nichols shoots me a look, and I just nod my head in agreement.

"Good. Addy has had to deal with enough crap in his life; don't you add to it."

"Of course," I confirm.

"I've made sure to cancel the ladies' get-together tonight, so Addy will be home this evening," she adds before turning away from me, walking back to her car, and driving off.

Was that why Addy was coming to see me earlier? Was he coming to say that he was leaving town? But where did this come from? Surely it isn't linked to me...

Closing up the garage, I decide to walk back to the apartment. If I take my car, he'd know that I was there and might not come home, and I think we have to talk. In fact, after the run-in with Mrs. Nichols, we have a lot to talk about.

Walking in the front door, I look around the apartment and take in the sight and the unique smell of the place. It's a mixture of freshly ground coffee and a hint of spicy shower gel. The smell is grounding. This is home, and I've missed it. Checking the time, I see that Addy isn't going to be home for at least thirty minutes. So I have time to jump in the shower and freshen up before he gets back.

Showering in record time, I get dressed in some jeans and am just pulling a t-shirt over my head when I hear the key in the lock. Sitting down on my bed, I listen to Addy coming into the apartment, keeping my fingers crossed that he's alone. The door closes, and I hear the sound of his keys being thrown onto the side table. He still hasn't said anything, so he must be alone.

Getting up from my bed, I walk down the hall, lean against the doorway, and watch as Addy walks out of the kitchen, swigging from a bottle of beer.

"Is there another one of those open?" I ask and watch as surprise lights up Addy's face at seeing me standing there, but just as quick, the emotion is replaced with hurt.

"You know where the fridge is," Addy states, looking away from me and walking over to the couch. So this is going to be a much harder conversation than I thought.

Going into the kitchen, I grab a bottle of beer from the fridge and go back into the living room to join Addy, mentally hoping that he's still in there and hasn't run off to his room. But he's still sitting on the couch, staring at the black screen of the television while sipping his beer.

"How was work?" I ask, sitting down on the other end of the couch, twisting my body so that I'm facing Addy.

"It was work," Addy replies, still not looking at me. "The ladies canceled tonight for some reason."

"Yes, I know.," I tell him.

"How?" Addy asks before we both say, "Mrs. Nichols," causing us both to laugh, and it breaks the tension completely.

"She came to the garage and told me it was canceled," I say, and Addy just nods his head in agreement. "Can I ask you something?"

"Sure," Addy replies hesitantly.

"Was Mrs. Nichols telling me the truth? Are you leaving Madison Springs?" May as well start here and go from there.

"I'm thinking about it," Addy confirms, and I can't quite believe it.

"Why?" I ask.

"What's there to keep me here? You're moving out, and I think maybe it's time for a fresh start," Addy continues.

"What about Jamie? Isn't he worth staying for?" I wanted to add that surely, he would want to stay in town for his boyfriend.

"Jamie is a nice guy, but we're just friends and only ever going to be just friends," Addy says, finally looking over to me.

"But the kiss I saw?" I question.

"I told you on Friday that the kiss hadn't been repeated," Addy states, looking surprised.

"Oh," is all I can say because he had told me that, but I hadn't really believed it.

"Jamie took me by surprise with that kiss. In fact, we both agreed that we felt nothing. There was no spark."

Suddenly, hope fills me. Maybe, just maybe, I finally have a chance. When we kissed, there was definitely a spark, and I know that Addy felt it, too.

"You've been fixated on that kiss. Why?" Addy asks. "What was so different about that kiss?"

Looks like the time has finally come. It's time to tell Addy what's really been going on with me.

"I was jealous," I tell him truthfully.

"Jealous?" Addy repeats, his brows furrowed together in confusion. "I don't understand."

"Yeah, so" — and I take a deep breath — "whenever we've been in the clubs together and I've seen you with other guys, I always knew that it meant nothing. That you were just out having a good time. That the man you were kissing would never be seen again. But you were different with Jamie," I say, and Addy doesn't try to interrupt but lets me carry on talking. "I saw the smiles when you got a text. In all the years we've been friends, I've never seen you smile like that, and so I got jealous."

"But that's what I don't understand," Addy says. "Jealous of what?"

"Jealous that he was taking you away from me," I tell him and take a swig of my beer to dampen my suddenly dry mouth.

"Beau, no one would ever destroy our friendship. You know that." Addy says.

"Addy, it's not just that..." I start, but I'm not sure I can find the words to say, so I just take another swig of my beer and stare at Addy wondering what he's thinking.

"Then what?" Addy asks.

"It wasn't that I thought he was just coming between our friendship," I say but then realize I'm probably not making much sense, especially with the confusion that is still on Addy's face. "Can I ask you something?" deciding to go a different route.

"Um, yeah?" Addy answers, but I don't think he actually wants the question.

"Have you ever wondered why I never bring girls home?" I ask.

"I thought it was the same reason I don't bring boys home. To avoid that awkward greeting in the morning," Addy says.

"Okay," I start. "What about the fact I've never spoken to you about a girl I was interested in?"

"I just thought you wanted to keep your private life private," Addy says.

"From my best friend who I tell almost everything to?" I reply.

"Almost everything?" Addy asks, and I'd hoped that he'd pick up on those words when I said them.

"On Friday, you asked me what the hell is going on with me. Well, the thing is, I've been keeping a secret from you for a long time. A secret that, until Jamie came on the scene, I was able to keep under wraps."

"What type of secret?" Addy almost whispers to me.

"A big one," I reply, and I know that I should just come out to him, but I'm still so scared of how he's going to react.

"Beau, please!" and I can see the frustration on his face, "I'm getting sick and tired of all this bullshit. I really don't understand. Just tell me what's going on with you," Addy says in an impassioned plea.

"Before I do, please know that I've wanted to tell you so many times, but the longer the time passed, the harder it got," I say, hoping this will help lessen the blow that's about to come.

"Beau, you're killing me here. Will you just tell me already?" Addy virtually shouts at me.

"I'm gay." I finally say the words out loud, but they're barely above a whisper, "and I'm in love with you."

Chapter 27 — Addy

Gay.

Beau just told me that he's gay. I know that after our kiss, I shouldn't be surprised. I felt how hard he had gotten, but I thought he was probably bi. But he just said "gay," and not only that, but he's also in love with me. I have so many questions.

"How long have you known?" is the first one that pops out of my mouth. Is his sexuality a new realization? He said that he'd wanted to tell me for a while. I need to know how long that while was.

"Umm," Beau starts but then begins to fidget in his seat, an indication I'm not going to like his answer. "Not long after you."

And I was right. I don't like his answer. He's been gay all this time and never said anything? He kept a huge part of himself a secret, and I am trying my best not to get upset with him. To jump to my feet and storm out.

"I don't understand," I say, turning away from him to stare into my beer bottle.

"Don't understand what?" Beau asks, and I can feel him shifting in the seat next to me, moving closer to me. Jumping out of my seat, I place my beer bottle on the table. I need some space between us while we talk about this.

"How you couldn't tell me," I say to him and finally look at him. His face is etched with worry lines. The shine in his eyes diminished.

"At first, I wasn't a hundred percent sure, and then you came out. I knew I should have said something in that moment, told you how confused I was, but I couldn't. By the time I finally realized, I was too scared to tell you. I was frightened. Thought you would no longer want to be friends," Beau explains, and I can hear his voice shake as he talks. He really was worried about losing me.

"I can't believe it," I say, making my way back over to the couch.

"I am so sorry, Addy," Beau says as I sit back down next to him, and I watch as a tear runs down his cheek, and the sight breaks me.

Pulling him into a hug, I hold him as sobs wrack his body. I've never seen Beau in this state before, and it's breaking my heart. What on earth has he been dealing with all these years? To have to keep the biggest part of himself hidden....

"What about your parents?" I ask. "Do they know?"

A mixture of a chuckle and sob comes out of Beau on hearing the question. "I told them," he says, but the slight twinkle is back in his eye.

"When?" I ask, pushing him back so I can see his face.

"Yesterday," he says, and the corners of his lips turn up into a smile.

"Oh, Beau." And I can't help laughing at him. So not only did he keep this a massive secret from me but his parents, too. He had no one to turn to for help or advice.

"Well, they surprised me," Beau says.

"Don't tell me. They said they knew and thought we were going out," I joke.

"Yep," Beau says.

Looking over, I expect him to burst into laughter any second, letting me know that it was a joke, but Beau just continues to sit there stone faced.

"You're serious," I say, not quite believing that Josiah and Debra thought that me and Beau had been in a relationship all these... what, years? And never told them. "But..." I start, but I'm not sure what the rest of my sentence is.

"I couldn't believe it, either. They just presumed that we would tell them when we were ready and so never spoke about it," Beau continues.

"I'm literally lost for words." Because I genuinely am. Why on earth would they think we would keep something like that from them?

Both of us stop talking and just slowly sip our beers. Beau's secret is hanging in the air around us. But what does that mean for us? The kiss that we shared has so much more meaning now, but where do we go from here?

"Our kiss—" I finally start breaking the silence.

"Was amazing," Beau interrupts. "I swear I felt it in my toes." And he gives me the cutest smile that I've ever seen.

"That was a phenomenal kiss," I confirm.

"So, would you like another one?" Beau asks, and there is a slight blush on his cheeks. Is this his way of asking me if I like him?

My first instinct is to jump on his lap, but we have more things to discuss: namely, the fact that Beau said he was in love with me, and I think a part of me wants to make him squirm. Especially for keeping this hidden for so long.

"Well," I start and watch as Beau's smile gets bigger, "not right now." And I have to bite my tongue to stop from laughing when I see his whole body deflate.

"Oh," is all the response he gives me.

"Beau, I think I can understand why you didn't tell me you were gay at the start, but" — and I deliberately pause here and take a sip of my beer while Beau shifts in his seat, waiting for me to talk again — "why the hell didn't you tell me when your feelings for me changed?"

"Well," Beau starts, and he keeps shifting in his seat. He's never been this nervous in his life. I don't think I ever remember seeing him this bad even before a football game, and I have to admit that I'm enjoying watching him. "They happened at the same time."

"Hang on a minute." Did Beau just confess that he's been in love with me since we were in our teens? "When are we talking here? College? Or before?"

"Before," Beau whispers.

"How long before?" I ask.

"Last year of high school," he says sheepishly. "That's when I knew how much I cared about you."

"And yet you still couldn't tell me?" I ask again.

"Sorry," Beau says.

"Beau, I really do wish you had told me sooner," I say, "because I've been in love with you since I was sixteen. In fact, I think it was my feelings for you that confirmed that I was gay."

"Really?" Beau says, and I just nod my head. "So what happens now?" he asks.

Putting my beer on the table, I shift closer to Beau, removing the beer from his hand and placing it on the table along with mine.

"Well, we can start by trying another kiss. We need to make sure that it wasn't a fluke the first time around," I tell him.

I place my hand on the side of his face and can feel the rough stubble underneath my fingertips and can't resist running my thumb over it. Beau leans his head into my hand before slightly shifting to place a kiss in the center of my palm, and I honestly can't believe shocks of electricity that run up my arm and the goose bumps that raise up on my skin.

Beau turns to look at me, a smile on his face that's causing his eyes to shine, and I know I could get lost in them. Hell, what am I saying? I've been lost in them for as long as I can remember. Eyes that I hope look at me with love, and tonight I find out that they have been looking at me that way for years.

The couch isn't the easiest place to navigate a kiss, and considering we've both just declared how we feel about each other, I decide to make a brazen move. Pulling Beau closer to me, I shift us till we're in the middle of the couch and climb on top of him so that I'm straddling his lap.

"Now this is a better angle," I tell him.

"Hmm," Beau confirms.

Leaning forward, I place the briefest of kisses onto his lips before leaning back. "So, how does it feel to have finally told me that you love me?" I ask, hoping that he might be feeling as excited as me at this moment.

"Today wasn't the first time I've told you," Beau replies.

"What? When have you told me? Had I been drunk at the time?" I'm suddenly trying to remember every drunken night when I came home to Beau looking after me.

"No, you weren't drunk, and it was recently. Think," Beau says cryptically.

Recently? If Beau had told me that he loved me recently, that is definitely something that I would have remembered and even questioned. But my memory is coming up empty.

"Oh my god, seriously?" Beau chuckles. "Let me give you a clue." And he leans forward and firmly kisses me.

My clue is a kiss. That's when the memory of Friday night hits me. We'd been arguing about Jamie, and Beau had said that he hadn't wanted to hear about my kiss. He'd shouted, "I love you." Holy crap.

"Friday night," I tell him, and Beau just smiles and nods his head. "Oh God, and then I told you I loved you as a friend."

"Yep, that was a total kick in the gut," Beau says as he runs a hand through my hair, taking me by surprise. Such an intimate gesture. "There was me baring my secret to you, and you missed it completely."

"Beau, I am so sorry." But that doesn't seem to be right. At that time, I hadn't heard the actual emotion behind the words. Why, I don't know. "I love you" isn't something friends usually say to each other.

"Addy, it's okay. We were arguing. You weren't expecting me to say it, and I sure as hell didn't plan to tell you like that," Beau says.

"Oh, so there was a plan to tell me one day?" And because I'm close enough — and because I now can — I lean forward and plant another quick kiss on his lips.

"No, there was no plan. Just hoped that one day I would be brave enough to tell you. If it wasn't for Jamie coming onto the scene, I might never have even told you."

"Remind me to thank Jamie," I say, and before Beau can protest, I place both my hands on either side of his head and pull him forward. Beau instantly wraps his arms around me. Placing my lips on his, I gently run my tongue along the seam, asking him to open for me so I can deepen the kiss. Beau's mouth opens, and I slip my tongue inside. His lips are as soft and firm as they were Friday night, and just like on Friday, I can taste the beer we've been drinking.

Our tongues continue their duel as we explore each other's mouths. I can feel as Beau loosens his grip and slides his hands down my back until they're cupping my ass, and without breaking the kiss, he pulls me forward and all the blood in my body travels south. For a second, I feel quite dizzy, but then I can feel that he's as excited as I am, and my body takes over. I break the kiss, both of us breathing heavily, and slowly place kisses along his jawline and start going down his neck.

Making my way back up his neck, I connect my lips with his again, and he opens for me immediately. Our tongues continue the duel that only finished moments ago, and I start grinding my dick against his. I can feel his length, and I know it might be fast, but I need to feel him.

Running my hand down his chest, I pop the button on his jeans, pull down the zipper, and slip my hand inside, rubbing my palm over his length. I want to slip my hand inside his underwear, feel his skin against mine, but am I going too fast for Beau?

Leaning back, I break our kiss and stare at Beau. His lips are red, swollen and damp from our kiss and look amazing, but it's his eyes that catch my attention, radiating what I can only call pure happiness.

"Is this okay?" I ask as I run my hand over his dick again.

"Yes, that's more than okay," Beau replies.

"Just don't want to go too fast for you," I say.

"Addy," Beau says, giving me a kiss and grinding his dick into my hand himself, "do you think I'm a virgin?"

"Well," I start but then stop, feeling rather foolish thinking that, but I've never seen him with anyone. Yet when I thought he was straight, I automatically thought that he must have slept with someone at some point. I remove my hand from inside his pants.

"Addy," Beau says, "we've spent time apart."

"Yeah, I know, but.... Sorry, I wasn't thinking," I reply.

"Now if you don't mind, I was enjoying where your hand was," Beau says.

And I don't need to be told twice. I slip my hand back into his pants but take it a step further and slip my hand over the waistband of his underwear, and I finally get to feel him. He's long but not that thick and fits perfectly in my hand. The skin is soft but burning hot, and I gently start stroking him up and down. Beau arches his back off the couch, and a moan falls from his lips — it's the most glorious sound. To know that I am finally giving him pleasure...

Leaning forward, I capture his lips with mine again just as he moans out my name. Just hearing him say my name like that has me almost coming in my pants. I'd heard that sound a thousand times in my dreams, but the real-life version is something so much more. I continue to pump Beau's dick, drinking in every moan that falls from his lips, but I don't stop touching him.

"Addy," Beau suddenly shouts as he comes all over my hand.

Getting up from the couch, I rearrange myself so I'm able to walk to the bathroom. After washing off the evidence of Beau's enjoyment, I dampen a towel and grab another clean, dry one before walking back over to him. I hand him the damp towel to wipe himself down before giving him the dry one.

Once dried up, Beau zips and buttons up his jeans, and I just stand there, not sure what we're supposed to do now, so I decide to take the towels to the hamper in the bathroom. Going back into the living room, I spot Beau leaning back against the couch, eyes closed.

"I know you're there," Beau says, not opening his eyes, "and you're staring."

"You just look so peaceful," I tell him because he does.

Walking back to the couch, I sit down on the opposite end to Beau, still not sure what we're supposed to do now.

"What are you doing over there?" Beau asks, opening one eye. "Come here." And he opens his arms for me. Climbing into them, he wraps his arms around me, and I close my eyes. Before I can stop myself, I feel sleep take me.

Chapter 28 — Beau

An ache in my back and a heaviness on my chest has me opening my eyes. Disorientated for a second, I look at my surroundings. Why am I in the living room? But then memories of last night come flooding back. I finally told Addy everything, and he took it surprisingly well. When he jumped up from the couch, I thought he was going to bolt, but he listened to what I said, and by some miracle, he understood. Then we'd kissed. I thought that our first kiss had been amazing, but I was wrong. Oh, I was so very wrong.

When Addy had straddled my lap, my heart raced. I couldn't quite believe he was there. Then he kissed me, and the rollercoaster started. Having Addy touch me was everything I imagined and more. He made me come. No one had ever made me come by just touching me. But the mixture of kisses and Addy's scent pushed me over the edge.

When Addy climbed off me at the end, I instantly wanted to pull him back. I wanted him to stay in my lap forever. That was where he belonged, but he couldn't. I wasn't sure where he was going or if there was something I was supposed to do. What was the protocol when your best friend just gave you one of the best orgasms of your life? Well, the only answer I could come up with was to sit on the couch and await his return. Then when he came back with towels to wipe myself down, I wanted to tell him to leave them on the floor and just come join me on the couch, but was it appropriate to cuddle now?

Finally, Addy came back and sat at the far end of the couch, and that just felt wrong. What we had was so much more than friendship, and we both knew that now. So I opened my arms and invited him into them. The look of surprise followed by delight flashed in his eyes within seconds, but I caught them. Addy wanted this as much as me. After wrapping my arms around him, Addy laid his head against my shoulder, and minutes later, his breathing had changed as sleep had taken him. I followed soon after.

But falling asleep on the couch was a decision I am now regretting, even if it had only been a couple hours. I think the excitement of what had happened just drained us, so sleep took over, but neither of us had eaten. Shifting myself, I grab my cell off the table; I had the common sense to place it there earlier just before Addy straddled my lap.

Checking the time, I see that it's 8pm, so at least we haven't slept the entire night away, but Addy is still fast asleep, and we need to eat.

"Addy," I say, running my hands over his head and getting nothing.

"Addy," I try again but a little louder this time, and I get a grunt in response. I forgot how deep Addy can sleep sometimes.

"*Addy,*" I say sharply while giving him a shake at the same time. This does the trick as he slowly starts to sit up, rubbing his eyes, but then he looks at me with deer-in-the-headlight wide eyes.

"We kissed... again," Addy says. "Then you... oh my God. I thought I had dreamt it."

"No, you didn't," I say, and because I can — well I think I can — I lean over and give him a kiss.

"You're gay, too," Addy says.

"Should I be worried? You're going over everything that we've discussed and, I thought, resolved earlier," I state and can't help chuckling to myself.

"Sorry," Addy replies. "I think falling asleep just addled my brain."

"Yes, and you're probably hungry, too," I say to him. "I'm going to order us a pizza and then we need to talk. Without kissing." I quickly add, "About us."

"Yeah, we do," Addy says, giving me a smile.

I quickly order the pizza — no need to ask what he wants since we get the same one all the time — and get up from the couch, stretch out my back, pick up the discarded bottle from earlier, and head into the kitchen. I pour what's left in the bottles down the sink because warm beer is awful and get us two fresh ones from the fridge.

Back at the couch, I hand a bottle over to Addy and take a seat, making sure to sit a little more upright to help my back.

"So do you want to talk now or once the pizza is here?" I ask.

"Now," Addy replies.

"Okay." Now I just need to figure out where to start. "So, we now know we both like each other," I say, deciding to go with the obvious.

"No," Addy states, and I look over to him. *Did he just say no?* No, we don't like each other? That makes no sense. "We don't *like* each other. We *love* each other. This goes beyond like," Addy finishes, smiling, and I can't help but giggle.

"Touché," I reply because he's right, of course. We've both declared our love for each other, so *like* wasn't the right word. "But what happens next?"

"What do you mean next?" Addy asks.

"I mean with us. Should I move out and we date like an everyday couple?" I ask.

"Like hell you're moving out," Addy says quite vehemently before a somber expression takes over. "Since you've been acting strangely, I've been thinking about our relationship. I couldn't understand why your actions were hurting me so much, and that's when I realized something. We might not have known it or even felt it happen, but we've been in an actual relationship without the kissing and, um, other physical stuff."

"My actions were hurting you?" Through all of Addy's words, those were the ones that I heard the loudest. It was never my intention to hurt him; I was trying to do the opposite. I dive across the couch and pull Addy into a hug. "I'm so sorry, Addy," I say into the side of his head.

"Need to breathe," Addy mutters breathlessly, and I release him. I hadn't noticed how ferociously I'd held him.

Letting him go, Addy gently pushes me back so that he can see my face. "It hurt at the time because I didn't understand why. Why were you suddenly avoiding me? But it makes more sense now. Especially if you were trying to give me and Jamie time together. You were looking out for my happiness over your own."

"That's the only thing I've ever wanted," I tell him truthfully. "Of course, I always hoped that you would find that happiness with me." If we're going all out on the truth conversation, may as well lay it all out in front of us.

"Oh, Beau. We should have talked a long time ago," Addy says wistfully.

"Maybe, but then wasn't our time," I tell him, because it wasn't. I'd lost count of the number of times I could have told him the truth and didn't, and I think it was because I thought that he would always be there, always be kinda mine. It was only when I realized that this wasn't the case that I needed to act. If Jamie had never come on the scene, Addy and I could well have stayed in the rut we'd gotten ourselves into. "So, what do we do now?" I ask, finally making our way back to my original question.

But before Addy can answer, the buzzer of our intercom goes off. The food had arrived. I hadn't even realized we'd been talking that long, and now we have to pause at the most vital point in the conversation.

"Next time we have a heart to heart, let's order the food once we've finished talking," I say as I get up from the couch and go and collect our order.

Getting back into the apartment, I see Addy swigging from the bottle of beer I'd gotten earlier. I had completely forgotten I'd grabbed them.

"Is that still drinkable?" I ask.

"Just about," Addy confirms as he takes another drink.

I place the pizza box in front of us on the table and pick up my beer. Taking a gulp of it, I see Addy is right: it's just about drinkable. We both take a slice of the pizza and take a bite. Sitting at opposite ends of the couch, we alternate between eating and drinking in silence till the pizza and beers are gone. Neither of us wants to continue while the food is there, probably because we both know if we'd carried on, the pizza would have been getting cold in the box and our beer would be getting warmer.

"So, us," Addy says when we have both finished. "I think we should go back to how we were before."

And my stomach drops and I'm not sure if the pizza is going to make another appearance. I suddenly feel sick. After everything, Addy wants us to go back to how we were before all of this? I'm not sure that this is something I can do. Now that I have had a taste of Addy, I want more.

"But with a little something added," Addy says.

"I think you need to explain," I say, but I'm so fucking confused.

"Like I said before the pizza, we were in a relationship, and I want that. I want what we had, but I want to be able to kiss you, sleep with you, go out into the world and tell it you're my partner."

"Partner? Shouldn't you be saying boyfriend?" I ask, as I always thought that someone said partner when they'd been together for a long time.

"Beau, we passed the boyfriend stage a long time ago," Addy says.

"Maybe," I reply, "but we never talked about our feelings before, so that just sounds a little fast for me at the moment."

"Okay," Addy replies, and I can see that he's thinking over what I just said.

Thinking about everything Addy just said, I know it's true. We really were closer than just friends. The only thing we weren't doing was actually sleeping together. It's why my parents thought we were already seeing each other when we weren't. But does everyone in town think we were secretly dating?

"Do you think the whole town thinks we've been dating like my parents?" I ask Addy.

"No, but I think that the gossip tree ladies have a suspicion about you, and they may have seen through your acting skills," Addy says.

"Oh no. They aren't going to leave us alone, are they?" I say.

"I have an idea," Addy says.

"Which is?" I ask.

"You'll see." Addy replies.

Thinking about the ladies in the gossip tree and the other members of the town makes me think about the run-in that I had with Chase. Addy needs to know the whole truth about what I said to his brother.

"Talking about the people in this town, I need to tell you something," I start.

"Okay," Addy replies.

"You know the other day when I kicked Chase out of my garage?" I ask and watch as Addy nods his head in affirmation. "Well, I left out a little piece of information. I kinda told him I was gay."

"You *what*?" And here I thought Addy was going to be angry that I told his brother before him, but he looks more amused more than anything.

"Look, he was spouting all his normal shit about you and how homosexuality was a sin. Any other time I would have just told him to fuck off, but we were fighting, and I just lost it and told him. Chase was actually the first person I've ever told."

"The first person you told that you were gay was my brother?" Addy asks, and all I can do is nod my head and wait, but suddenly Addy bursts out laughing. This was not the reaction I was expecting, but it's better than the anger I thought I was going to get.

"Well, that explains it," Addy says between outbursts of laughter.

"Explains what?" I ask, needing to know what's making Addy laugh so hard.

"Something Chase said to me that I didn't understand. He said that I'd infected you and he was going to tell the church what I'd done. I think he was trying to say that the town was going to hate me."

"He thinks you turned me gay?" I join Addy in laughing.

"Yep," Addy confirms, and we both just start laughing harder. "I'm going to need to kiss you in front of him when someone has a camera pointing at his face. I need to see his reaction."

"Addy!" I exclaim, pretending to be mortified that he would even suggest something like that but loving the idea, too "But to be honest, I wish you could have seen his face that day in the garage. It really was priceless."

Suddenly, Addy rushes over to me and jumps into my lap, and I have to wrap my arms around him to stop him from falling off me.

"Thank you," he says, giving me a chaste kiss on the lips. "Thank you for always defending me against my family."

"Addy, that's not something you have to thank me for. Any decent human should stand up against hate like that, and you don't deserve that treatment," I tell him because it's the truth.

Staring at Addy, I go in to give him a kiss when he suddenly yawns.

"Tired?" I ask.

"Yeah," Addy replies seriously. "I haven't been sleeping great."

Standing up from the couch, Addy yelps in surprise before wrapping his arms around my neck and his legs around my waist.

"What are you doing?" Addy asks.

"Putting you to bed," I tell him and carry him to his room, putting him on the bed and placing a kiss on his forehead. Addy lets go of me as I get up and leave the room, saying goodnight over my shoulder.

Back in the living room, I throw away the empty pizza box and bottles of beer, making sure that the front door is locked and all the lights are off before heading towards my room. Checking Addy's room as I go past, I see he is still fully clothed and sitting in the position that I left him in.

"Beau," Addy calls out.

"Yeah, Addy?" I reply, walking back to his room and standing in the doorway.

"Umm, would you stay with me tonight?" Addy asks, and I'm not sure if it's me or the floor in front of him, but then Addy looks up at me, hope lighting his eyes. "We don't have to do anything if you…" Addy's words trailing off, not able to finish that sentence.

Striding into Addy's room, I close the door behind me, peel off my t-shirt, and watch as Addy's eyes widen as he takes in my bare chest.

"Addy, you've seen me bare chested," I tell him as he keeps staring at me and licks his lips, and I can't help but laugh at his reaction.

Chapter 29 —Addy

Being carried into my bedroom had to be one of the most romantic gestures I've ever experienced, especially Beau placing a kiss on my forehead. But then he left. Left me sitting on the bed just staring straight ahead. I didn't want to be on my own tonight. I wanted Beau in my bed. Wanted him to hold me.

I can hear him in the living room tidying up, the tell-tale sound of the lock on the front door and the click of the light switch. From the corner of my eye, I watch as Beau walks past my room, and then I'm calling out his name and asking him to stay with me. I'm mentally keeping my fingers crossed that he agrees, but then he's striding across my room while pulling his t-shirt off. His physique has always been impressive. When he'd been playing football, his muscles had become so defined it was hard to keep myself in check, and even though his body has changed over the years, moving heavy car parts has kept his muscle in a trim state. Muscles that I am now allowed to explore. Kiss. Hold. I am so transfixed at the thought of kissing them that I wet my lips, and it's only when I hear Beau laughing that I realize he said something to me.

"Sorry," I say, looking over to him, and he just laughs harder.

"Addy," he says between chuckles, "I said you've seen me bare chested before." And then he's walking over to me.

Standing up in front of him, I can't resist and run my hand over his pecs and down his abs. "Yes, I have. But now I get to do this," I tell him and place a kiss in the middle of his chest and inhale his scent. I can smell the spiciness of his shower gel, and yet underneath it all, there's a hint of engine oil. It is quintessentially Beau, and I love it.

"Oh," Beau replies, and I place another kiss on his chest. Deciding to be bolder, I travel across his chest, leaving a trail of kisses behind.

"Would you like me to stop?" I ask just in case this is all too much for him.

"God, no," Beau replies. "But you have an unfair advantage over me at the moment," Beau says as I move around his body still trailing kisses.

"What's that?" I ask as I place a kiss in the center of his back and make my way back around to his front.

"I can't see you," Beau says.

"Oh," I reply, suddenly nervous. I am not built like Beau. I am not muscular. My body is trim, but I don't have defined abs. What happens if my body is a disappointment to him? I've been so careful to not be naked around Beau. In fact, I'm not sure if he's ever seen me bare chested even though we have been living together all these years. But my insecurities start to take hold. What happens if he doesn't like what he sees? What type of guy does he normally go for? Am I even his type?

"But I think I can change that," Beau says as he starts pulling my shirt out of my pants and unbuttoning it, then pushing it off my shoulders. Beau drops the shirt on the floor, takes a step back, and just looks at me, not saying anything.

"Are you disappointed?" I ask when Beau just continues to stare at me.

"No," Beau answers vehemently, "But you're right."

"Right about what?" I ask, beginning to feel a little self-conscious.

"It's a whole different ball game when you know you can do this," Beau says, a smile lighting up his face as he steps forward again and places a kiss in the middle of my chest right before he's wrapping his arms around me and crushing me to him, chest to chest. I'm instantly wrapping my arms around him. I've been in this situation before, hugging a man bare chested, but something about being able to do this with Beau is special.

Beau starts to trail a finger down the middle of my back, causing goose bumps to rise over my skin. "You like that then," Beau whispers, and before I can answer, he's running his finger back up my spine. Beau takes a small step back so our chests are no longer touching, now running a finger down the center of my chest, stopping at the button of my pants.

"You got to feel me, so it's only fair I get to feel you," Beau states, popping the button and pulling down the zipper. But unlike when we were on the couch, Beau pushes my pants down so that they pool at my ankles. He runs a finger along the waistband of my underwear before slipping his hand inside, wrapping his fingers around my dick, and it feels amazing. He slowly begins to pump, his grip is firm, and I can feel his calloused fingers as they rub against my skin, adding to the sensation, and a moan falls from my lips. I'm going to need to watch myself; otherwise, I'll end up coming all over Beau's hand.

Beau lets go of my dick and begins to push me backwards, but with my pants still around my ankles, I almost fall over. He steadies me before whispering, "Sorry." He drops to his knees and taps my leg for me to lift it. Placing my hand on his shoulder to steady myself, I lift my leg. Beau slips off my shoe, sock, and then pulls my leg out of my pants before repeating the process with my other leg, tossing my pants to join my shirt. I'm left standing virtually naked with just my underwear left tented by my dick.

But before I can comprehend what's happening, Beau is sliding my underwear down my legs, and I automatically lift each leg. My underwear is tossed onto the pile of already discarded clothing, and I am now left completely naked, dick standing to attention, and Beau on his knees in front of me.

"My God, you're beautiful," Beau mumbles, and I am about to say, "So are you," when Beau engulfs my dick with his mouth in one go, and all thoughts leave my mind. His mouth is warm, and I feel his tongue as he runs it over my sensitive head, causing me to call out Beau's name. He draws back, and just when I think he's going to let me go, he slides back down.

He starts to run his hands up the back of my legs till he's cupping my ass and giving it a squeeze. My body clenches at the action, and I know that if I'm not careful, I'll be coming down his throat.

"Beau," I manage to get out. "Stop."

Beau looks up at me, and there's a flash of uncertainty in his eyes as he lets go of my dick with a pop.

"I don't want to come down your throat," I tell him, leaning down to give him a kiss and hoping he gets my meaning. Even though when I called him back in here I said we didn't have to do anything, I knew deep down that I wanted to feel Beau inside me, and I think he wants that, too. Beau gets up from his knees and just stands in front of me for a second before taking me in his arms and kissing me. His tongue licks at the seam of my mouth, So I open for him, his tongue invading my mouth and dueling with my own.

I can feel his hard dick through his jeans pressed up against my own, and I run a hand over it, getting the desired moan from Beau.

"Bed," Beau whispers, breaking the kiss, and I know I don't have to be told twice.

I climb on to my bed, resting my head on my pillows as I look over toward Beau. He pops the button of his jeans and pushes them down, taking his underwear with him in one movement. Then he's standing there, naked. I thought he was magnificent when he was just bare chested. I was wrong. He's a walking wet dream. His legs are just as toned as the rest of him, looking strong and powerful, and even though I had my hand around his dick a few hours ago, seeing it standing hard and proud is something else.

I want to taste him like he did me. Feel the weight of him against my own tongue. Tease him and bring him to the edge so that he's screaming out my name and coming down my throat. I shift to the edge of the bed to do just that, but Beau stops me and pushes me back up the mattress. Placing his hand on either side of my head to support his weight, he carefully lays on top of me and grinds his dick against my own.

"So, do you have supplies?" Beau asks, and he gently gives me a kiss.

Supplies? What on earth is Beau going on about? But then I realize... Shit, he means lube and condoms. I have lube but no condoms. Double shit. I've always used condoms with my one-night stands but have been regularly tested, anyway. But my last test was six months ago. It came back negative, and I haven't been with anyone since. Would Beau want to go bareback?

"Lube is in the top drawer," I say, looking over to the bedside tables. "No condoms, though," I add.

"No problem. I have some in my room," Beau states and is about to shift off me, so I wrap my legs around him to keep him in place and take a deep breath.

"Wait," I start before blurting out, "I'm negative," hoping that he'll get my meaning.

"Addy," Beau starts, his voice laced with surprise.

And that's when it dawns on me. I know that I'm negative, but what about Beau? He told me that he's been with other people. I know that he would be careful, he's always given me enough lectures about that when we were out. But what if this isn't something he wanted to do, and I suddenly feel very foolish.

"Sorry, Beau. Go get the condoms," I say.

"I think you misunderstood my surprise," Beau says as he leans down to give me a kiss. "I just wasn't expecting that. Are you sure? I am negative, too. I can get you my results."

"You're kidding, right? I've been waiting for this day since I was sixteen. To feel you bareback…" And I don't finish my sentence because the smile that spreads across his face is all the answer that I need.

Beau leans over to the bedside table and opens the drawer, pulling out the bottle of lube and placing it on the bed beside us.

"You're sure?" Beau asks again.

"One hundred percent," I confirm.

He leans in and kisses me briefly on the lips before placing a kiss on my cheek, then my jaw line, down the side of my neck, and he keeps going. I close my eyes, savoring every kiss and caress of my body. Beau then sucks a nipple, the shock sending waves of pleasure pulsating through my body, and I feel like I am on fire.

Beau lets go of my nipple and, using his own legs, spreads mine apart and moves so that he is kneeling between them.

"Pillow?" he asks, looking up at me. Grabbing the spare pillow, I pass it to him. "Up," he says. I know that he wants to put the pillow under my hips to raise me up slightly, so I do as I'm told. "If I'm going bareback," Beau whispers, kissing the side of my leg as he moves them so my feet are flat on the bed, "then I want to see you come," he states bluntly.

Picking up the lube he pops the cap and squirts some into the palm of his hand and rubs it over his fingers.

"Ready?" he asks gently, and I nod and then feel his finger at my entrance, where he slowly pushes his way in. Even though this is Beau and I have been dreaming of this happening, I clench around his finger.

Beau doesn't say anything, just slowly removes the finger before pushing it back in, and I relax around him. Pulling out completely, I watched as he picks up the lube bottle and squirts more into his hand. Then Beau is pushing two fingers inside me, and I feel myself stretching around him, and the feeling is amazing.

Beau picks up the lube bottle once more, and I know that I want him inside me now. "I want you now," I say, and he knows what I mean.

"Are you sure?" he asks, and I just nod my head.

Popping open the lube bottle, he squirts some in his hand and then slicks up his dick, and when it is well coated, he shuffles forward. I can feel the head of his dick at my hole, and then he's pushing in and a wave of pure, unadulterated happiness washes over me. Any pain I might have felt is gone. All I know is that Beau is inside me.

Beau takes his time, making sure I've adjusted to his size, and it's only when he's fully seated that he begins to move, sliding back out before pushing forward again. It's pure ecstasy, and I have to fist the bed sheets underneath me. A moan erupts from my throat as he begins to speed up, his dick sliding in and out of me.

Suddenly, Beau shifts his angle, pulls out, and slams back into me, pegging my prostate. Pleasure explodes within me, and I can't help my scream, and Beau does it again. Pulling out and slamming back into me, each time hitting the same spot, and my orgasm builds. Beau grabs hold of my dick and starts pumping it in time with his movements.

"Beau!" I scream his name and my back arches off the bed as my orgasm hits me like a freight train, and I'm coming, clenching and squeezing Beau as he hits my prostate one last time before he is coming with me, shouting, "Addy," as he lets go of my dick to place his hands on the bed to support himself.

Neither of us say anything, both breathing hard, both waiting for the chance to be able to move and talk again. Closing my eyes, I relish the orgasm I just had. The reality far surpassed my dreams. Then I feel the bed moving, and cracking one eye open, I watch Beau get up only to return a few minutes later with two towels, mirroring what I'd done earlier. He cleans us both up, but unlike me earlier, he discards the towels on the floor and climbs back up the bed and lays down next to me.

"Come here?" Beau asks as he opens his arms. Moving over to him, I lay on his chest and entwine my legs with his as he wraps his arms around me.

We don't say anything; we both know no words are needed. We both know how amazing that was. And as I lay there on Beau's chest, listening to his breathing change as sleep takes him, I know I've found my family. With a smile on my face, I hug Beau tighter for a second and let sleep take me.

Chapter 30 — Beau

I have no idea how long I've been awake, but I've been too afraid to move. Okay, so afraid might not be the right word; but waking up with the man you've been infatuated with for more than a decade lying on your chest sleeping is just, well, wonderful. I'd managed to stop myself from running my hands through his hair even though I wanted to feel the strands as they slipped through my fingers.

The sound of the alarm going off on Addy's cell has him stirring in my arms before rolling away to look for his phone. Grabbing his pants off the floor, he silences the alarm before rolling back and resting his head on my chest, and I'm not sure he opened his eyes once while doing that. I completely forgot that we both have to get up and go to work today. I could have sworn it was a Saturday, but it's not. It's a Tuesday, and we both have customers who need us.

Addy pulls me closer to him as I hear him say, "It wasn't a dream."

"What wasn't a dream?" I ask, but I think I know what he's about to say, and a smile tugs at the corner of my mouth.

"Last night," Addy replies, looking up at me. His eyes are still heavy with sleep.

"No, it wasn't," I confirm, leaning down and placing a kiss on Addy's forehead, which causes his eyes to widen and a smile lights up his face.

"Holy shit," he exclaims before chuckling to himself. He lifts his head off my chest and shifts positions so he's further up the bed. "Morning," he says before placing a kiss on my lips and going back to resting his head on my shoulder.

"We have to get up soon," I tell him, but neither of us make any attempt to move.

"Can't we just stay here all day?" Addy asks.

"I really want to say yes, but we both have customers waiting for us," I say.

"Can't we just stay closed?" Addy almost wines.

"No, we can't," I tell him. "But I can come meet you after work."

Addy actually groans at this statement. "I have to work late tonight. Mrs. Nichols canceled the ladies last night, but only if they could move it to tonight."

"That's okay, I can come help you set up and then come home when they arrive," I say.

"Wait," Addy suddenly says, shifting so that he's resting on his elbow and looking at me. "Are you ready to tell the town, well, the gossip trees ladies, anyway?"

"Addy, you know full well that the moment the ladies find out about us, then the whole town is going to find out," I tell him.

"Yeah, I know," Addy says, but I can't miss the hopeful look in his eyes at the thought of coming out as a couple.

"Could I at least tell my parents first?" I ask.

"Yes, of course," Addy agrees, but then grabs his bottom lip in his teeth, a tell-tale sign he's overthinking something.

"But?" I ask.

"But," he starts, "do you think you can tell them by tonight? The idea I have would be *perfect* for tonight."

"Are you going to tell me the plan?" I ask.

"No," he states, and I can't help but laugh.

"Okay, fine." I try to move positions, but Addy is still pinning me to the bed. "Pass me my cell. It's in my pants' pocket."

Addy rolls away from me and looks around on the floor before reaching out. Rolling back over, he hands me my cell and resumes his position of lying on my chest. Opening the contacts on my phone, I go to my favorites so I can dial my dad's number. He's one that would be awake at this time.

"Beau, everything okay?" Dad asks, panicking at my unusually early call.

"Everything is fine, Dad," I reassure him. "But can I come and talk to you and Mom at lunch?" I ask.

"Do you know how worrying that sounds, Beau?" Dad says back.

"Trust me, Dad, everything is fine." Looking over at Addy watching me, I add, "In fact, everything is more than fine."

"Well, that *is* interesting," Dad says, and I think he may have already guessed what I am going to tell him but doesn't say anything more.

"I'll be over about one if you can tell Mom," I add.

"Will do. See you later, son. Oh, and say hi to Arden for me." And I swear I can hear him chuckle before he hangs up the phone.

"My dad has worked out what I'm going to tell him," I say to Addy as the alarm on his cell goes off again. "Come on. Up."

I think that Addy is going to protest again, but he doesn't. Instead, he rolls away from me and sits up on the edge of the bed. "I'm going for a shower," Addy announces before standing up completely naked and walking out of the room.

Laying back down on the pillows, I listen as I hear the shower turn on and think about Addy standing under the hot stream of water, the droplets running down his body. And just the thought of Addy like that has me hard, but I know now that I'm able to see it with my own eyes.

Moving to the edge of the bed, I get up and make my way to the bathroom, mentally keeping my fingers crossed that he hasn't locked the bathroom door. Turning the handle, the door opens, and I'm hit with a cloud of steam but forge forward anyway. Addy is already standing under the stream of water, and I don't think that he's heard me come in.

Quietly getting in behind him, I wrap my arm around his waist, causing Addy to yelp in surprise.

"Want some company?" I ask as I kiss the back of his neck and run my hand up and down his chest.

Addy leans back into me as I continue to run my hands up and down, getting lower and lower each time. Addy's dick gets hard and stands at attention with my ministrations. Taking hold of his dick, I start to slowly pump, placing a kiss in the crook of Addy's neck, and I'm eventually rewarded with a moan.

I run my thumb over the head of his dick, rubbing and teasing him till he's standing on his tiptoes and leaning his full weight back into me. I wrap an arm around his waist to secure him to me to make sure we both don't fall. I nestle my own hard dick between the cheeks of his ass, moving slowly in time with my stroking of Addy's dick.

I feel Addy tense in my arms as he shouts my name, coming over my hands, his body shuddering in my embrace, and the water instantly washes away the evidence of his orgasm. I keep a firm grip on him as I continue to rub my own dick between his ass cheeks. Slowly, my own orgasm builds and then I'm coming, shooting my load over Addy's bare ass. Turning him around in my arms, I let the water wash the remainder of my come from his body.

Picking up my shower gel, I squirt some into my hands and soap up Addy's body before pushing him back under the stream of water.

"You're going to smell like me all day now," I whisper in his ear, and I'm certain that I hear Addy moan.

Moving us around so that I'm standing under the now lukewarm water, I finally let Addy go when I'm sure he is steady on his feet and wash my own body before turning off the water. Addy still hasn't said anything but just stares at me. Grabbing a towel off the towel rack, I rub down Addy's arms before wrapping it around his waist.

"Go get ready for work," I say, pushing him toward the bathroom door while patting his ass.

Addy leaves the bathroom, but he's definitely not as steady on his feet as he was when he left his bedroom. Carefully going over to the cabinet in the corner, I pull out a towel, run it over my own damp body before wrapping it around my waist, and head out of the bathroom to my own room.

Pulling out some clean underwear and a pair of my blue stone-washed jeans, I quickly put them on before getting a plain white t-shirt. Once dressed, I towel dry my hair and just run my fingers through it to style it and then make my way out to the kitchen. Addy is dressed in his classic black pants and a white shirt and is leaning against the counter sipping on some coffee as he hands me a mug. Taking a sip, I relish the taste and the bitter aftertaste that lingers in the back of my throat. We both just stand there sipping our coffee, not saying anything, but words are no longer needed.

"What do you want for breakfast?" Addy asks.

"I think I'll just get some toast. Mom will probably want me to feed me at lunch," I tell him.

"I'm going to have to grab something at the shop. I've been a little delayed this morning," Addy tells me, giving me a little smirk, then he looks at the clock on the kitchen wall. "And I have to get going."

Addy finishes his coffee, turns to the sink, and rinses the mug, placing it on the countertop and then walking past me, out of the kitchen. Placing a couple of slices of toast in the toaster, I move over to the doorway and lean on the door jam to watch as Addy comes back into the living room, walks over to the table by the front door, and picks up his keys.

"So, see you later?" Addy asks as he opens the front door.

"Stop," I call over to him, which he does and looks back over to me, confusion all over his face. "What do you think you're doing?" I ask.

"Umm, going to work," Addy replies.

"I think you might be forgetting something," I say as I push off the door jam and walk over to him.

"No," he says, looking around him.

"You forgot this," I say as I reach him and lean down, placing a kiss on his lips. "Have a good day." The look of surprise is comical.

"Shit, we can do that now," Addy whispers.

"Yep," I chuckle as I turn away from him and walk back toward the kitchen, saying, "See you later," over my shoulder.

I hear Addy chuckle to himself before I hear the front door open and close. Going back into the kitchen, I butter my toast and head back to my room. Opening my closet, I spot the place where my bag should be and remember that some of my stuff is still at the motel. *Shit.* I'm going to need to get it and check out. Checking the time on my watch, I have just about enough time to do it this morning, but I'll need to leave now.

The motel check out was quick, and thankfully it was the owner, who wondered why I was checking out earlier as I had the room booked for a few more days, but I explained that my plans had changed. They seemed happy with that, and so thirty minutes later, I'm pulling up outside the garage and onto the gravel drive, I groan when I spot Chase's car parked off to the side. *What the hell does he want?*

Getting out, I walk over to the door and try to ignore Chase, but I hear the car door open, then close, and the crunch of the gravel as he walks toward me. Turning on the spot, I look over to him.

"Chase, what do you want? I thought I made myself clear the last time you were here." I don't even wish him a good morning, which I know is rude, but I really don't want to talk to him. I know that whatever he's going to say, I'm not going to like.

"I want to talk to you," Chase starts, "I've been praying for you."

"I don't need you to pray for me," I tell him. "Is there anything else? I need to start work."

"I have something for you," he says and pulls what looks like a leaflet from his pocket. "I was talking to the church, and we thought this would help you," he says as he hands me the leaflet.

After looking at the tagline — *Pray the gay* ' — I'm not even sure why I even carry on reading, but I do. The leaflet goes on to talk about a camp where they pray away the sin of homosexuality.

"You're joking, right?" I snap at Chase, throwing the leaflet back in his face.

"No, we just need to get you away from my brother. We can heal you then. Save your soul. God will forgive your sins," Chase says.

"Leave," I tell him through gritted teeth.

"Beau, please listen to me. This isn't right. I don't know how my brother was able to corrupt you, but he did, and I know the church can save you," Chase adds, and it's the final straw.

Walking up to him so that I am just inches from him, I pull myself up to my full height and stare at him. "Your brother did not *infect* me. I've always been gay. I would've been gay without ever meeting your brother. You can't save my soul as my soul doesn't need saving. Now get off my property." Turning away from him, I try to take some breaths and unclench my fists.

"This isn't you, Beau; this is my brother talking. You're the star football player," Chase says after me.

Stopping, I turn to face him but don't move because if I get closer to him, I'm likely to punch him in the face, which really isn't a great idea.

"Chase, I'm going to say this one last time, and I need you to listen and listen good," I say. "Addy didn't infect me, didn't turn me gay. This is who I have always been, and it's who I will continue to be. Now, if you don't get off my property, I am going to call the sheriff."

Finally, Chase seems to get the message and turns to leave. "Actually, Chase," I say and watch as he turns, a smile on his face, "there is something else. Addy and I are together, and last night we made it official. And just so you know, I've had a few lovers in my time, but your brother rocked my world in ways you could never imagine." The look on Chase's face is priceless, and I can't resist adding, "And if you, your mom, or that church hurt him in any way, you'll regret it.

The smile drops from Chase's face, and he walks back over to his car and drives off so fast that gravel sprays behind from the back wheels. Turning back towards the garage, I can't help but smile and really can't wait to tell Addy.

Chapter 31—Addy

I can't believe the difference a few hours can make. This time yesterday I couldn't understand what was going on between me and Beau, and now suddenly we're a couple and it feels perfect. Last night was amazing and left me sore in the best possible way. There have been a few instances already where I've sat down, forgetting, and the soreness makes me jump up. But then I would remember why I was sore, would remember the look on Beau's face as he pushed himself into me.

When I woke up this morning, I'd initially thought it had all been a dream, one of my most vivid dreams, but then I felt skin underneath my cheek and the memories from last night had come flooding back. When I asked him to stay, it wasn't my intention to have sex with him... well maybe there was a small flicker of hope that we would. I thought it would take us a while before we reached the point of sleeping together. I was counting on fumbles on the couch, maybe the odd blowjob here and there, but we seemed to bypass that entirely and God it was worth it.

"Someone looks particularly happy this morning." The sound of Jamie's voice behind me has me turning to face him.

"Morning," I reply back and automatically start to make his usual coffee, but I can still feel the smile on my face.

"You had sex," Jamie whispers, leaning over the counter. There are no other customers in the shop, so I have no idea why he felt the need to whisper it.

"What th—" I start to deny it, but then realize I don't want to. "How the hell can you tell?" I ask instead.

"Because you haven't stopped smiling since the second I got in here. You also look like you are about to break out and dance, and your cheeks are fucking glowing," Jamie replies, but there are no hurt feelings, no annoyance in his voice. He actually sounds happy.

"Yeah, I did," I tell him, and Jamie actually makes a whoop noise.

"I knew it!" But then he looks more closely at me. "Holy shit. Not with Beau?"

And I just nod, and I can feel my cheeks burn as I blush.

"Come on, I need info." He looks around the shop at the empty seats. "You have no customers, and I can delay getting to work for ten minutes."

Making myself a coffee, I go over to Jamie and gingerly sit down opposite him but don't miss the smile when he catches me wince or the "lucky shit" he tries to whisper under his breath. I tell Jamie all about getting home last night and finding Beau, how we talked, that Beau told me that he was gay and admitted how long we'd liked each other. Jamie listened to every word sitting on the edge of his seat. He never interrupted, never asked me questions. Just listened.

"Well, I just want to say I told you so," Jamie says when I get to the end of my talk, and he leans back in his chair.

"Told me what?" I ask.

"That Beau liked you," Jamie replies. I open my mouth to argue with him but then change my mind because he's right. He told me that Beau had feelings for me, and I just couldn't see it.

"You did," I reluctantly say, and Jamie can hear the tone behind my words.

"You can make up for disbelieving by making me the best man at your wedding," Jamie says, and the damn smirk is back on his face.

"Woah. Wedding?" Not able to believe that he just said that, "We just got together last night. Marriage and a wedding are a long way off. I don't know if Beau even believes in it."

"Six months. I give it six months before you're telling us you're engaged," Jamie adds, still smiling.

"You're enjoying this," I tell him, and Jamie throws his head back and laughs.

"I am loving every single second, and I cannot wait to do the same with Beau," Jamie replies.

"No, please don't. He's not out to the town yet," I tell him.

"Addy, it's not going to take long for the town to find out, and I have a feeling they're going to be as happy as I am. You guys are great together."

"Thanks." But I have to admit that it's strange to hear Jamie say that considering maybe only a week ago we were discussing going out together. If we hadn't kissed when we did, would I now be sitting here discussing my evening with Beau, or would we be talking about my and Jamie's date? But... everything happens for a reason. Plus, Jamie and I are definitely better as friends than lovers.

"I better get going," Jamie says, finishing his coffee. "If I hear any rumors about you and Beau, I'll come and let you know."

"Thanks, Jamie," I say. "The three of us will need to go grab a beer this week."

"Yeah, that'd be great. It would be nice to get to know Beau better. Hopefully we can become friends," Jamie replies.

Jamie gets up from his seat and walks to the door, shouting, "Bye," and I just wave to him as I get up from my seat, pick up our empty coffee mugs, and go back behind the counter. I place the mugs off to the side, on a tray, ready to be taken into the kitchen for washing, and go about checking everything is set for the day ahead.

The rest of the day went by in a flash. Every time I looked at the clock thinking that maybe ten minutes had passed, I would be surprised to see that it had almost been an hour. A steady stream of customers came into the shop, but it was finally closing time. Walking over to the door, I flip the sign to *CLOSED* but don't lock up. Beau should be here any minute, so there is no point locking the door just to have to unlock it again.

Going behind the counter, I grab a tray and start clearing the tables. I've just cleared one and am back behind the counter after taking the mugs to the dishwasher when the front door opens and Beau walks in. *My* Beau, and I feel the smile spread across my face at the thought.

"Can you lock the door? I only left it open for you," I ask.

Beau dutifully turns around and closes the door before walking over to me, coming behind the counter, and pulling me into his arms, then leaning back and giving me a kiss before finally saying, "Hey."

"Hey," I reply, and because I now can, I give him another quick kiss. "Now go make yourself usual and clear some tables."

"I've been your boyfriend for five minutes and you're already barking orders." Beau giggles but turns away from me and starts clearing tables.

Boyfriend. It was the first time he had called me that, and I definitely prefer hearing that over partner right now. It shocks me for a second, and I can't help but stare at him as he clears the table. For so long I've wondered if it was something that could ever happen but hearing him say it is music to my ears.

"I was barking orders at you before you were my boyfriend," I say to him, wanting to say the word out loud myself, deliberately using boyfriend not partner after our conversation yesterday. I closely watch his reaction and am rewarded with a smile when he hears me say it. Guessing we're both happy then.

"How was lunch with your parents?" I ask as I start making a fresh filtered coffee for the ladies tonight.

"It was good. I was right. Dad had already guessed, and Mom was so happy, but I got told off for not bringing you, so I said that we'd go there over the weekend," Beau says, looking up at me.

"Oh, that's good to hear," I reply, "but they actually told you off for not bringing me?" I'm trying not to laugh.

"Yeah," Beau replies. "Hence why I said we'd go over on the weekend."

"If we go, does that mean they're going to tell me off, too?" I ask. I know what Beau's parents are like. They would have no issue giving me the third degree, too. Is it wrong that I'm kinda excited that they might? To be included in the family like that...

"But you should have heard my mom. She was saying how she always thought of you as a son and now legally you will be. I swear while I was sitting there, she was planning our wedding," Beau says while placing the mugs from a table onto the tray.

"Seriously? Her, too," I say out loud.

"Someone else said something?" Beau asks, looking up at me.

Shit. I never thought to check with Beau if we could tell people. I know we talked about his parents and the ladies tonight, but we never talked about telling other people. I really hope he's okay with this.

"Jamie came in this morning and, well, he guessed what we got up to last night. And then he kinda told me that he had to be the best man at our wedding," I tell him.

"Oh," is the only response that Beau gives me. He doesn't even look up from the mugs that he's clearing.

"Was it okay that I told him?" I'm getting worried about how quiet Beau has gone.

"Yeah, of course. Was he ..." And he goes quiet for a second and stops picking up the mugs in front of him. "Okay with us being together?"

"Beau, I think that I told you he knew how the pair of us felt about each other before we did. He was completely fine. I even suggested the three of us go out for a beer, and he seemed up for it," I tell him.

"Yeah, that would be nice. Would be cool to get to know him better," Beau replies, and I can't help but snort. "What?" he asks, finally carrying the tray of dirty mugs over to me.

"Jamie said the same thing," I tell him and am rewarded with a smile. "Now, get tidying. The ladies will be here soon."

"Are you going to tell me your plan?" Beau asks as he goes over to the final table.

"Nope," I tell him. It needs to look like it's spontaneous.

Ten minutes later, all the tables have been cleared and Beau has wiped them down. We'd just moved them together to make the large table that the ladies like, and Beau had gone into the back, leaving me to set out the mugs, when Mrs. Nichols is knocking on the door.

"Good evening, Mrs. Nichols," I say as I open the door.

"Are you staying?" Mrs. Nichols demands without missing a beat.

"Yes, Mrs. Nichols. I'm staying," I tell her.

"In that case, good evening," Mrs. Nichols replies, and at that moment, Beau comes out from the back.

"Beau!" Mrs. Nichols exclaims and looks between me and him.

"Mrs. Nichols, lovely to see you. How are you? How is Mr. Nichols?" Beau asks, being friendly as always.

"We're good, thank you. I'll tell Mr. Nichols you were asking after him," Mrs. Nichols replies, and then, making a big thing of pulling out a chair and turning her back to Beau, she whispers to me, "So, you made up? Anything else?" But she's not as quiet as she thinks, and I can hear Beau chuckle behind me.

"We talked," I confirm, "and we're friends again." I don't miss the flash of disappointment on her face, but it's all part of my plan.

"That's nice," Mrs. Nichols replies.

Walking to the counter, I pass behind Beau, and because I can, I grab his ass, which makes him yelp in surprise. Mrs. Nichols turns back and looks at him before turning around again.

"Thought you would have told her," Beau whispers over to me.

"Soon," I reply as I pick up the coffee pot and go over to Mrs. Nichols. "Coffee?" I ask, and she nods. "Who's joining us tonight?" I'm wondering what audience we'll have.

"I think all the ladies will be here tonight," Mrs. Nichols confirms, "but some will be arriving a little later. Mrs. Philips and Gladys should be here shortly."

Not quite the audience I wanted, but these three ladies are the gossip queens, so they're probably the best ones to come out to. Mrs. Nichols was right, and within minutes, Mrs. Philips and Gladys have arrived and are pulling out their chairs to sit down. They wished me a good evening, but I think they were staring at Beau while they did since he's behind the counter and leaning on the back workbench. It's time for my plan of action to start. I just need to wait and hope one of the ladies asks if Beau is staying to help, and as if on cue, I hear a voice.

"So have we got two helpers this evening?" Gladys asks, looking to me, then Beau.

"Not tonight. Beau came over to help me set up. It was quite a busy day," I reply, and looking over to Beau, he shoots up an eyebrow in a *what the?* expression. Making sure the ladies can't see me, I give him a wink. It's my way of letting him know to go along with what I am saying.

"Oh, that is a shame," Gladys replies. "It's always so nice to have two handsome men look after you."

"I'm sorry, Gladys," Beau says, coming from behind the counter. "But as you lovely ladies are here, I think it's time for me to get going," he finishes, and I can't believe my luck. I thought I was going to have to whisper to him to leave.

"Thanks, Beau," I say. "See you back at the apartment later." Beau hesitates for a second, and I know that he wants to give me a kiss goodbye, and that would work, but I have my plan working out differently.

"Yeah, see you later." Beau walks around me and takes a few steps away and is almost by the door when I call out, "Wait, Beau. You forgot something." I try to repeat the words that he said to me this morning, and Beau catches on instantly. Going up to Beau, I pull him into an embrace and kiss him hard and then let him go. This doesn't need to be a full-on kiss with tongue but a kiss that conveys our relationship. Beau smiles at me and turns to open the door when we hear a voice behind us.

"*Not* so fast, Beau Jackson," Mrs. Nichols exclaims, and Beau stops in his tracks and turns around to face the ladies. "And you, Mr. Miller, can come here, too."

The pair of us turn to the ladies, and I take hold of Beau's hand as we walk over to them.

"Yes, Mrs. Nichols," I say.

"Do not just stand there all sweetness and light and say 'yes, Mrs. Nichols' like we didn't just witness that." Mrs. Nichols says, and I can tell she is trying to pretend to be annoyed but there is a smile playing on her lips.

"I was just saying goodbye to my boyfriend," I add, and I didn't know that Gladys was able to move so fast as she jumps out of her chair and rushes over to me and pulls me into a hug.

"It's about damn time," Gladys says, looking from me to Beau, and I can't help but burst out laughing.

Chapter 32 — Beau

I had been thinking about what plan Addy had to tell the ladies all day, and I was still confused up to the point where I'd almost made it to the door and Addy had said that I'd forgotten something. Those were the same words that I'd said to him this morning, and I knew that he was going to kiss me in front of them. It really *was* perfect, but...

"Gladys, did you just say it was about time?" I ask, because even though she just said damn, I couldn't use the same word back to her as she lets go of Addy and sits back down in her seat.

"Yes," Gladys confirms, as if this will give me all the answers that I need.

"Excuse me," I start, looking over to Gladys, "but what was about time?"

"You and Addy, of course." But it's Mrs. Nichols who answers.

"What?" I ask, not quite believing what the ladies are saying.

"Beau," Mrs. Nichols says, "we've known that you batted for the same team as Addy, well, probably before you did."

What!=? I open my mouth to say something, but there are no words. What do you say to that? For all these years, I thought that I'd kept my secret safe, and yet these wonderful ladies knew all along.

"Does the whole world know?" I wonder out loud.

"Oh God, no. Just the gossip tree," Mrs. Nichols adds, shooting a look over to Addy. "And yes, we know you call us that, too, Addy."

I think that Addy is going to be embarrassed, but instead, he just bursts out laughing.

"Apologies, Mrs. Nichols," Addy says, but he's smiling at her.

"Oh, shush. We all think it's funny," Mrs. Nichols states. "So, we need details, please."

"Details?" Addy asks.

"Yes! When did you get together? Have you slept together?" Mrs. Nichols asks.

"Who topped?" Gladys interrupts.

"*Gladys!*" And this time it's Mrs. Philips who shouts at Gladys. "You can't ask them that."

"Why not?" Gladys replies.

"Because you can't. That's very personal," Mrs. Philips says.

"But I looked it up," Gladys states, "because I wanted to make sure I had all the information for when these two finally got their heads out of their asses and got together."

"Gladys," Mrs. Nichols says while giving her friend an exasperated look. "you look up how to be supportive. You don't look up sexual stuff."

"Well, what if either of them needed advice?" Gladys points out. "I would be able to recommend websites."

And that's the final straw. Both Addy and I burst out laughing. These women are the most precious people on the planet. I watch as Addy walks around the table and hugs Gladys and whispers something in her ear that none of us can hear.

"Oh my," Gladys responds and looks over to me before looking back to Addy. "You lucky thing."

"I know," Addy replies and comes back to stand next to me.

"Ladies" — all three of them turn to look at me — "how long have you known about my feelings for Addy?"

The three ladies look at each other, and it's like they're telepathically talking to one another, and with a nod, they agree on whatever they're going to say. "Since you were eighteen. Maybe just before you went to college."

"Eighteen," I say. "I don't even think *I* was sure then."

"Don't lie, Beau. You knew, but you weren't ready to admit it to yourself," Mrs. Philips says gently. "I remember watching you at a game once. You'd scored a touchdown, the whole stadium erupted, but you were just scanning the crowd. The moment you found Addy and saw him cheering, your whole face lit up. That's when I knew."

"Oh," I say because I remember that moment. I remember thinking that I wish I could run into the stands to celebrate with Addy. It had been a great football game, and that touchdown had been amazing. I'd received the ball at the fifty-yard line and gone on a full sprint, weaving and dodging. I even think I might have jumped over one of the players and scored. The euphoria had been instant, and I only wanted to share that with one person.

"But I told everyone I was straight," I mumble, thinking about the game and remembering the random cheerleader I hugged.

"And you were a good actor," Mrs. Philips says. "But we watched you grow up. The rest of the town believed it, but we knew better."

"It was how he behaved when Addy lost his dad that confirmed it for me," Mrs. Nichols states, and it's like they are talking amongst themselves and not about my life.

"Oh, yes," Mrs. Philips confirms.

"Sorry, ladies, but what?" I ask. They're talking about pivotal parts of my life like I'm not standing there.

"Beau, you have to realize that you went above and beyond what a normal friend would do. You dropped everything. You supported Addy through every step," Mrs. Philips says.

"I was his best friend," I say, trying to defend myself. "And what about Addy? When did you know he loved me?" I ask, hoping to take some of the attention off me.

"Yesterday," Mrs. Nichols states.

"*What?*" I exclaim. Surely if they'd known how I have felt they must have figured out Addy, as well. "If you knew about me, you must have known about him."

"Well," Mrs. Nichols starts, "I wasn't a hundred percent like you."

"I knew," Gladys pipes up, and I think that she's wanting to get one up on the ladies around her. "When Beau had his accident, Addy dropped everything. He was there at every hospital appointment. I remember seeing him."

Gladys had worked in the local hospital until she retired, and I remember seeing her there. She would always wave and say hello, so of course she would have seen Addy with me.

"Someone would only worry like that if they loved that person deeply," Gladys continues and gives Addy a very sweet smile.

"Now, stop avoiding. We want the details," Mrs. Nichols blurts out.

"Beau," Addy says, looking over to me, "give the ladies the details." Oh, the little shit.

"Mrs. Nichols, Mrs. Philips, Gladys," I begin, looking at them all in turn, "we talked last night, and thank you, Mrs. Nichols, for coming to see me at the garage. So" — and I make a big thing of looking at the clock in the corner — "we've been together for about twenty-four hours," I tell them.

"Oh, that's wonderful!" Mrs. Nichols states and then looks over to the ladies. "I'll have to get a new hat for the wedding."

"Mrs. Nichols... wedding?" I ask.

And without missing a beat, she says, "Yours and Addy's."

Oh, seriously? And Addy bursts out laughing. In fact, he's laughing so hard that he excuses himself and walks behind the counter to compose himself.

"Mrs. Nichols, did you hear me? We've been together for one day. Wedding bells are a long way off," I tell her, but it seems that half the town is ready for us to get married.

"Oh, pish posh," Mrs. Nichols says. "You and Addy have been together for years. You just kiss now and have sex."

And for the first time ever, I'm lost for words. What on *earth* do I say to that? Mrs. Nichols is not a woman to be argued with. So I just stay silent and look over to Addy, who's still trying to stop laughing and is wiping away tears. He's enjoying this interaction way too much.

"And on that note, I think I'm going to leave you ladies to it," I say, wanting to get out of this meeting. I have way too much information to deal with tonight. Going over to Addy, I give him a kiss and can hear the ladies behind us go, "Awe."

Just as I have opened the door to leave, I hear Mrs. Nichols ask Addy if he's told his family, and it stops me dead in my tracks. Part of me wants to go home and have this conversation about my interaction with Chase in private, but I'm sick and tired of standing back and letting Chase talk to Addy like he's nothing.

"I haven't told them yet," I hear Addy reply.

"You don't have to," I say, turning around and walking over to Addy.

"What?" Addy questions as he looks up at me.

"Chase came to the garage this morning," I say, and I actually wish I had the leaflet that Chase gave me. It would be evidence to confirm that everything I'm about to say is the truth.

"And?" Addy asks, and I can hear the trepidation behind his voice.

"I told you about what I'd said to him the other day," I say to Addy, but then kinda wish I hadn't because these ladies have better hearing than most bats.

"What did you tell him?" Mrs. Nichols asks, and I really don't want to explain the whole interaction again, and so tell her the most condensed version I can think of.

"Chase came to the garage spouting crap about Addy again. I lost it, told him I was gay, and he went and told Addy that he infected me." I think that about sums it up in one sentence.

"Infected him with what?" Mrs. Nichols asks.

"Homosexuality," Addy replies for me before looking back over to me. "Beau, why was he there?"

"He came over to talk to tell me about a camp he wanted me to go to," I start. "A camp that would save my soul and cleanse me of my infection."

"Holy shit," Addy exclaims, and considering he just swore in front of the ladies, something he would usually *never* do, it's a good indication of how shocked he is. "He wanted you to go to a conversion therapy camp?"

"Yes," I confirm.

Addy goes over to the table, pulls out a chair, and sits down. I instantly go over and pull out the one next to him and take hold of his hand.

"Sorry, but a conversion camp?" Mrs. Nichols asks.

"It's a place where people are sent to change their sexual orientation," Gladys pipes up. She really must have done her research, bless her.

"But you can't change that. It's the way you're born. Like I had blonde hair," Mrs. Nichols states, but I'm not fully listening to her. I'm watching Addy. He's gone as white as a sheet and isn't saying anything.

"Addy?" I say his name gently, and when he turns his head to look at me, the look of hurt and pain in his eyes kills me.

"I am *so* sorry," Addy mumbles. "I am so sorry Chase did that."

"Addy, this isn't your fault. We both know what your family is like," I tell him. "But I have to say that I didn't take too kindly to it."

"I bet," one of the ladies says, though I'm not sure which one. At that moment, the only person getting my attention is Addy.

"I told Chase that we're together, but I couldn't leave it at that. I might have also told him that I had a few lovers in my time but that you rocked my world in ways he couldn't imagine," I tell him and wait for his reaction, hoping this will break the melancholy that has taken hold. And when I see the twitch of a smile on Addy's lips, I know I have.

"You didn't," Addy says, looking up at me again, but the pain that was in his eyes just moments ago is gone.

The ladies must have been waiting for his reaction, too, because the moment they see Addy smile, I hear them giggling and someone say, "Good for you."

"I did," I confirm for Addy.

"Thank you." Addy says.

"Addy," I say and squeeze his hand, "I would never normally say this, but you need to stay away from your family. They're toxic."

Addy looks up at me but doesn't say anything, just keeps looking at me.

"From the moment that you came out, they've been nothing but mean to you, and you don't deserve that," I say to him.

"Addy," one of the ladies says, and I look up to see it's Mrs. Philips speaking, "Beau is right. When you came out, no one in this town cared. In fact, we embraced it. We didn't care. You were just Addy. The only people who objected were your own mother and brother. The two people in this world who should love you unconditionally."

In that moment, I could hug Mrs. Philips, because I can see Addy is listening to every word that she's saying, and I know he's taking it in.

"But she's my mom," Addy mumbles.

"Yes, she is, and she should know better. You don't love your children with conditions. You just love them," Mrs. Philips repeats.

"Addy," Gladys pipes up, "If you're worried about not having a mom or someone to talk to, then I'll tell you that there are three ladies sitting around this table who would adopt you in a second. Each one of us will be there to support your triumphs and be there to pick you up when things are tough. Plus, you have Beau now, and I know Josiah and Debra think the world of you."

I'm not sure how the ladies can go from asking inappropriate questions that make me want to leave to saying something so profound that I feel lucky to live in this town and know these women. I think there are people all over the world that could learn some valuable life lessons from these ladies, and I hope that Addy is one of them.

During this entire interaction, I haven't let go of Addy's hand, and I give it another squeeze now, and he looks up at me.

"Addy, I would never tell you what to do, but I love you and am finally able to tell the world that. If you decide to keep your family in your life, I will keep on loving you, but I think it's time you walked away."

"Addy, sweetheart," Mrs. Nichols says, and I think that this is the first time I have ever heard her use a term of endearment. If Addy ever needed proof of how much these ladies think of him, that right there is it. "Listen to Beau. What he's saying is true. Don't let them win. Show them how much better you are than them."

Addy looks around at all of us, and I can see the tears on his water line waiting to be shed, but he's also smiling. "Thank you," he says as he's looking over to the ladies. "I needed to hear that. I know what I need to do now."

Chapter 33 — Addy

My plan had worked like a charm. Without prompting him, Beau had voiced his intention to leave, and I had outed our relationship to the ladies. But what I *hadn't* expected was their reaction; I now love them all the more for it. From the second I kissed Beau and called him my boyfriend, the ladies had smiles on their faces. But some of the questions they asked...

It was only when Gladys had questioned about which one of us topped and bottomed and then added on about the websites she had visited that both me and Beau lost it. It was just, well, Gladys, but I would have loved to ask her which sites she had gone to. Her search engine history would be such an eye opener, but I was also so incredibly touched that she would do that that I went over to her and gave her the biggest hug I could while whispering, "Bottomed. Amazing. Will feel it for days." The 'oh my' and the blush that tainted her cheeks had been worth it. Beau will probably kill me when I tell him, but I couldn't resist saying something.

Finally, Beau and I had satisfied all their questions, and Beau was leaving. I had been looking forward to spending the next few hours with the ladies, since I was sure there would be more questions, but then Mrs. Nichols had brought up my family, and suddenly the mood changed.

When Beau had turned around to come back in, my stomach dropped. Something in the pit of my stomach told me I was not going to like this conversation, and I'd been right. Chase had gone to Beau with what? A treatment plan to cure him? I couldn't believe it. The audacity of my brother, and yet there was this pang of something else that I hate to admit may have been jealousy. In all the years that Chase has been harassing me, he never once mentioned a conversion therapy camp, only that I was to leave town. What was the difference between me and Beau? Why was Beau deemed worthy of therapy but not me?

Then Beau had told me that I needed to cut my family out of my life, had even called them toxic. I thought that the ladies were going to disagree with Beau, but they didn't. They'd agreed with him. I had wanted to defend my family because they're my family, but the ladies and Beau were right: they hadn't been my family from the moment I came out. These ladies, Beau, Josiah, and Debra, they were my family, and I knew what I needed to do.

When all the discussion on my family had finished, Beau had finally been able to leave, and when I kissed him goodbye, we had another chorus of "awes" from the ladies, one of them saying, "I'm never going to get sick of seeing that."

Soon after, more ladies arrived for the class, and before I knew it the two tables were full and there was the constant noise of their chatter. At the start, there was the odd gasp and one of them saying, "Really?" a lot louder than intended, followed quickly by "About time" or "I knew it." I guess Gladys, Mrs. Nichols, and Mrs. Phillip were getting the ladies up to speed on me and Beau. I decided to move back behind the counter and give them some peace to talk, and I only went over a few times to refill coffee mugs.

I don't think my family or the conversion therapy camp were mentioned, and I'm grateful that they weren't. I wasn't ready for that news to travel around the town yet, plus I knew it would get out soon enough.

Not long after all the ladies leave, I'm all alone in the shop with nothing but my thoughts to keep me company. I need to go and talk to my mom and Chase, and I need to do it sooner rather than later. Looking at the clock in the corner, I see that it's just after seven. Mom and Chase will both be home now. They always have a church meeting on Tuesday and go straight home afterward. What I need to do has to be done tonight. It's the only way I can finally be free.

Clearing up the dirty mugs, I place them in the dishwasher, ready for it to be run in the morning. Normally I would've moved the tables back, but I'll come in early in the morning to do that. I have to get going, but I also know that I need Beau with me. Closing the shop, I dash back to the apartment.

Opening the front door, I walk in to see Beau sitting on the couch and twisting in his spot to look at me.

"Evening. How were the ladies after I left?" Beau asks.

"Loud," I tell him.

"You're home earlier than I was expecting," Beau says, getting up from his spot and coming over to me, pulling me into a hug and kissing me. A thrill travels through my body that we are finally able to do this, and just like the ladies, I'm never going to be sick of doing that.

"I want to go and visit Mom and Chase," I say.

"Okay," Beau says, looking at me. "When?" he asks.

"Tonight," I state.

"Okay," Beau answers., "Give me two minutes to go grab some shoes." He turns around and rushes down to his room. Coming back, he picks up my car keys from the bowl on the side table. "Let's get going," he says and grabs hold of my hand and leads me out of the apartment.

Getting to the car, Beau heads straight to the driver's seat. I know that I should tell him that I can drive, but it's probably better that he does. My brain is going a mile a minute, and trying to concentrate on the road in front of me is probably not going to be the easiest.

Pulling out onto the road, Beau reaches over and grabs my hand and brings it up to his lips, placing a gentle kiss on my knuckles.

"How are you doing?" Beau asks, giving me a quick look.

"I'm okay," I tell him, giving him a slight smile.

"You sure?" Beau asks, but this time, he keeps his eyes on the road.

"Yeah. I needed to hear what you and the ladies said," I reply because it's the truth. I may not have wanted to hear it, but they had been right.

For the rest of the drive, we remain silent, neither of us wanting or needing to talk. Beau just keeps hold of my hand and gives it the occasional squeeze. Both of us know that this is going to be a tough conversation.

Pulling into my mom's driveway, I look at the house that I grew up in but hasn't felt like home in a very long time. I take some deep breaths and open the car door. Beau takes my hand again once we're on the porch and stands beside me as I knock on the front door and wait for it to be answered.

The door slowly opens, and it's Chase standing there. At first, he has a smile on his face, but when he sees me standing there, the smile drops instantly. Then he clocks Beau holding my hand and what I can only call a grimace appears on his face.

"What do *you* want?" Chase asks, looking from me to Beau.

"I want to talk to you and Mom," I tell him but don't say anything more as to what I want to talk to them about.

"About?" Chase demands.

"I think you know what it's about," I snap back at him.

"Addy, I really have no idea what you're talking about," Chase replies.

"Bullshit," I say through gritted teeth.

"Chase, who's at the door?" And then my mom appears, and just like Chase, she walks up with a smile on her face that vanishes when she sees me.

"Hi, Mom," I start, trying to keep myself calm. "Can we come in?" I make a point to try and emphasize 'we.' "I want to talk to you and Chase."

Mom doesn't say anything, but I see her look at Beau's hand in mine, and just when I think she's going to throw us onto the street, she surprises me by saying, "Come in." The look of disgust on Chase's face is priceless, but he doesn't argue with Mom, just opens the door wider and lets me and Beau through.

Following Mom and Chase, we go into the dining room, the scene of so many previous conversations. It seems fitting somehow. Chase pulls out the chair for Mom before sitting down himself, and Beau and I follow suit. I'm sitting opposite Chase, and Beau is opposite Mom, and that's when we finally let go of each other's hands.

"Arden, you wanted to talk," Mom states, looking over to me.

"Chase, did you visit my boyfriend?" I don't miss the gasp from my mom as I say this. "Mom," I say looking over to her, "don't pretend to be shocked. I know that Chase would have told you we are together." Mom purses her lips but doesn't respond, so I turn back to Chase. "As I was saying, did you visit my boyfriend with a leaflet on a conversation therapy camp?"

"Yes, I came with a leaflet for Beau to save his soul. To rid him of the infection *you* gave him," Chase states, leaning forward and placing his hands on the table.

"Homosexuality isn't a disease you can catch," Beau snaps at Chase. "I wasn't infected by Addy. I was born this way."

"Homosexuality is a sin in the eyes of God," Chase counters, "and that camp would cleanse you of that sin and save your soul."

Beau goes to say something more, but I reach over and grab his hand, squeeze it, and he looks over to me. I shake my head, my way of silently telling him to drop it.

"Is the camp new?" I ask Chase.

"It's been going for a few years with an excellent success rate," Chase confirms, but when he says the last part, he looks over to Beau, as if this statement is going to make Beau realize he needs to attend the camp.

"Yet you have never mentioned the camp to me," I state.

"Some souls are worth salvation," Chase says, "and some… aren't." He adds the last part while looking straight at me. Beau squeezes my hand so tightly at this comment that I almost yelp. He knows as well as I do what Chase meant by that statement.

"So, you deemed that my soul not worth saving?" I ask.

Chase doesn't answer me, but his silence is all the answer I need. Between Beau and I, Chase had decided that Beau needed to be saved. There was the proof of who he preferred.

"And you agree with this?" I ask, looking over to my mom.

"Yes," she answers without hesitation. "Beau was such a good boy until he became friends with you. You corrupted his soul over the years and damned him to hell. That camp will save him."

"But it wouldn't save me?" I say again, not sure why I'm asking the same version of question. I think it's because I can't quite believe what I'm hearing and am hoping that I'll get a different answer.

"Your soul is too corrupt to be saved. Your damnation was sealed a long time ago," my mom says. "Your father would be so disappointed to see the man you've become."

Out of all the words Chase and Mom have said this evening, these final ones from my mother are the ones that cut the deepest. She might be right. Dad would never have accepted my sexuality, but I would have hoped we could have at least talked, and maybe I could have changed his mind.

"If this is the way that you feel, why have you continued to be present in my life?" I ask.

"A question Chase and I have asked ourselves on many occasions. We hoped that you would listen to our advice and leave this town and never tell anyone we are related," Mom answers.

"Well, I would like to tell you that I am not planning on going anywhere. Madison Springs is my home," I tell them, keeping my voice as even as possible even if my insides are boiling with rage.

"You and Beau will never be accepted here. When the town finds out what you did to the town hero, you will be kicked out. As you should be," Chase spits, and there is no mistaking the venom behind those words.

"Well, Chase, Mom, that's where you are very wrong. The town knows about me and Beau, and they've accepted us. In fact, some of the residents have been waiting for us to announce our relationship for years. The only people who are going to be despised in the end are you and your church."

I look over to Beau, and a sense of relief washes over me. Relief that I'm no longer going to have to deal with Mom and Chase's bullshit. That after tonight, they will no longer have that strangle hold over me.

"I learned something tonight," I say, looking over to my mom. "That a family should love a person unconditionally. Regardless of their faith or sexuality; that's what I get from this town, and I'm not planning to move anymore. The only place I'm not accepted is in this household. A place where love should be given without restrictions. Well, Mom, from tonight and going forward, you will only have one son." If I hoped to get some reaction from her, it didn't happen. She just keeps looking at me, but when

I look over to Chase, the smile on his face tells me how happy he is to hear this news.

Getting up from the chair, I hold out my hand to Beau, who takes it and rises from his chair. I stand in the dining room and look around for one last time. This is the last time that I will ever stand here, so I say my silent goodbye. Walking out of the room, I don't say goodbye to my mom or Chase; they don't deserve it. Opening the front door, we both step out, and I slam the door behind me for a sense of finality.

"You okay?" Beau asks, pulling me into a bear hug. "I can't believe some of the shit they just said."

"I'm good," I tell Beau, because I really am. "I should have done that a long time ago."

"Yeah, probably should've, but everything happens when the time is right," Beau says before leaning down to give me a kiss. "Now, let's go home. We need to celebrate," Beau adds.

Home. I once thought this house was home. I was wrong. Home is so much more than walls and a roof. A home is a place where you can be yourself. Be free. That's what Beau gives me. He gives me his unconditional love. It may have taken us a long time to get here, but Beau has given me everything I ever wanted. Beau gave me a home, a family, but more importantly, he gave me his heart.

Epilogue—Beau

Six Months Later

A week. That's how long we lasted before I moved all my stuff into Addy's room, but I'd never actually slept in my bed again after we shared that first night together. Six months later, I wake up and sometimes can't believe that Addy and I are together. For those few brief moments between being awake and asleep, I think it's a dream, but then I'll feel Addy's body next to me, his arm across my chest, holding on to me like he thinks I'm going to float away. Yet the thrill of knowing he's there hasn't diminished.

Just like the ladies had said, the town had accepted our relationship. There were quite a few residents who had been surprised, but it was because they thought we were already in a relationship and had been afraid to come out. It seems like everyone thought we were dating except us. It makes us laugh now when we talk about it.

Talk of the conversion therapy camp that Chase had tried to get Beau to attend hadn't gone over very well. They still all saw me as this hero football player, and at one point, some of the businesses were going to refuse service to anyone from the church, but both Addy and I had managed to get them to change their minds. But the hostility remained, and no matter what we said, we were told they wouldn't forgive them for trying to change me, that I was perfect the way I was. Those days I was proud to live in such a forward-thinking town.

Yet on other days, I would be rolling my eyes, because once the dust had settled, the questions started on when Addy and I were going to get married. No one seemed to notice when we said we'd only been together a week or a month. They would argue that we'd been together for years, even if we hadn't known it. But Addy and I had never talked about marriage. I wasn't even sure it was something he believed in.

We'd been officially dating for about two months when Addy came home from the shop one day to tell me that at least five customers had asked him when we were getting married. He'd laughed, but I'd finally asked him if that was something he believed in. The relief I felt had been instant when he said that he did, and that was when the planning started.

I waited for the town to get sick of asking us and us telling them that we would when we were ready to the point that we were hardly asked any more. I wanted the town to be surprised, which is why four months later, I'm standing on the ten-yard line on the high school football field waiting for Addy.

I'd sent him a text at lunch time asking him to meet me here after work. School was on a break, so there would be no one about but us. Nerves were wreaking havoc, my hands were shaking and sweating, and I had to keep wiping them on my pants. Pulling out my cell, I check the time, and when I look back up, I see him strolling across the field, still dressed in his black pants and shirt from work.

"What's with the cryptic text to meet you here?" Addy asks as he reaches me, giving me a kiss, and I just start right up with my speech.

"I was standing here, at this exact spot, when I first realized I loved you. I had scored a touchdown, and you were the first person I wanted to find in the stands. The only person I wanted to celebrate with. Over the years, that love has never faded but instead, grew stronger." I pause for a moment and take a deep breath. "I was lucky; I fell in love with my best friend, the person who knew me best in the world."

Getting down on one knee, I love the gasp from Addy as he realizes what I'm going to do. I pull out a ring box and flip it open. There, nestled in the middle, is the ring I had commissioned. I found a specialty ring company who added sand to silver rings — they carve a groove in the middle and add the sand, then seal it with resin. I called them and asked if they could do the same with coffee grounds, and they did. So the ring staring back at Addy is a simple silver band with a band of brown through the middle. But the resin used had flakes of gold in it that sparkled when they caught the light.

"Addy. Will you marry me?" I ask, wanting to keep this simple.

"Yes!" Addy says. "But your knee," he points out, pulling me to my feet. As usual, he's always thinking of me.

Taking the ring out of the box, I slip it on Addy's finger. He pulls me into a hug and whispers in my ear, "Best friends forever."

Acknowledgments

I want to thank the real Beau and Addy for being wonderful dear friends and the inspiration for these characters. Without your friendship this story would never have been born.

To Becca, thank you for being the best PA. Being there when I need to vent and creating beautiful graphics, sometimes very last minute.

To my beta's thank you for taking the time to read my words - I adore you so much.

Finally, I want to thank every reader who has taken the time to read my stories and love my characters as much as I do. Without you I wouldn't be here, wouldn't be continuing to write. I appreciate each and every one of you.

About Author

Kelsey Hodge has always loved reading; it is something she has been doing since she was a child. Loving the escape the imagination can bring. The desire to write stories of my own was a dream, that Kelsey never thought would become a reality, but after encouragement from a wonderful partner, the words started, and they haven't stopped. Writing has become a passion, the characters in her books, her friends and Kelsey cannot wait to bring you along on the adventure ahead.

Also By Kelsey Hodge

For the Love of Flowers
or the Love of Teaching
For the Love of the Best Man
Legend of the Easter Dragon
Mistletoe and Dragons
Resurrection of the Easter Dragon
Return of the Christmas Dragon
Christmas Tree Wishes
Racing Hearts

Printed in Great Britain
by Amazon